just friends

just friends

just friends

New York Times Bestselling Author

MONICA MURPHY

Interior design and formatting by:

E.M.
TIPPETTS
BOOK DESIGNS
www.emtippettsbookdesigns.com

chapter one

I miss you so much!

       I miss you too.
       I have a surprise for you.☺

What is it?

     When you come home you'll find out.

But that's not until next week! ☹

        It's worth the wait. Trust me.

Does Dustin know the surprise?

         Yes but he won't tell you.

How do you know?

      Cuz he knows I'll kick his ass.☺

I stare at my phone screen, frustrated at my friend Emily's secrecy. She knows I hate surprises. I always have. Surprises usually bring bad news, at least for me.

Surprise! Pop quiz.

Surprise! You're failing Chemistry.

Surprise! He likes someone else.

Surprise! You're getting a baby brother.

Surprise! You're getting a baby sister.

Surprise! Your dad and I are getting a divorce.

Not necessarily in that order, but you get the gist.

Deciding to change tactics, I start texting Dustin.

What's up?

> **The usual. What's up wit u?**

Bored. Lonely.

> **If you were here with me…**

What?

> **I'd make sure you weren't bored.**

> **Or lonely.** ☺

I smile, trying to fight the butterflies that flutter in my stomach when he talks like that. Dustin and I have been close since we were young. He's one of my best friends. I've told him everything. Confessed who I liked, who I'm mad at, how far I've gone with guys—which isn't very far—and he's admitted all his secrets too. He's the first person I got drunk with. The first person I got high with.

He's also the first boy I tongue-kissed. When we were thirteen and feeling like losers who'd never done anything, we at least had each other.

But it was forgotten. Kid stuff. Until last spring when we were at a party, got drunk together and started making out. Next thing I knew we were slipping our hands down each other's jeans, getting each other off. It happened again—and then again, right before I left for my dad's.

I had to push him off of me before we took it too far.

I can still remember the pained expression on his face, and the memory of that night hurts my heart.

The memory also makes my heart flutter with excitement. Even though he's my best friend and I don't want to ruin our friendship, I can't help but wonder what would happen if we really were together. I trust Dustin. We're close without being in a relationship-close. I can also admit—only to myself—that Dustin is a good kisser. And he knows what to do with his fingers.

My cheeks are hot just remembering.

Where are you?

In bed. Naked. ☺

Dustin…

I know. Sorry.

I chew on my lip, mad at myself for looking like a prude via text. The problem with messing around with your best friend who happens to be a boy is that they form certain expectations. We've crossed the line. In his eyes, there's no going back. He wants more. He wants it—me—all the time. I think I want that too, but I'm not sure.

What's Emily's surprise?

I can't tell you.

Why not?

I was sworn to secrecy.

Come on D. ☹

He doesn't answer and I don't push. But I'm frustrated. Being stuck at my dad's for the summer is the worst. Mom and Dad split when I was eleven and at first, being divided between two homes was awesome. I went to Dad's on the weekends and it was like one big party. We went out to eat, he bought me whatever I wanted, took me on trips. Summertime was even better. We'd go on vacations to the beach, or Disneyland, wherever I wanted to go. Birthdays I got twice as many gifts and the same with Christmas.

Mom's house, where I'm at most of the time, is the drag. Homework. Clean my room. Help out since she works and isn't always home to cook a decent meal. It's like a cycle set on repeat. *Do your homework, clean your room, do your laundry, help me, help me, help me.*

Dad's house was my escape. Until it wasn't.

He moved from California to Oregon for a new job and met and married Christine, who's much younger than my dad. Christine convinced him they should try for their own family. Now I have a little brother and sister named Dakota and Sierra—I know, I know, they sound like national parks—and trust me, they are a pain in my ass. Always getting into my stuff, always extra loud way too early in the morning.

No more epic summer vacations. I'm stuck in Oregon from mid-June to early August, where Dad works all day and Christine is at home, staring at me with obvious disappointment every time she spots me. So I hide away in my room, counting down the days until I can go back to Mom's.

At least at home, Mom doesn't really care what I do. As long as my room is clean, I help with chores, the homework is done and I come home by curfew, I can do pretty much whatever I want. She's rarely home anyway. Between her job as a nurse and her new boyfriend, she's busy. We talk on the phone once a week while I'm at Dad's and we occasionally text, but it's not the same.

I miss her when I'm not there and she drives me crazy when I'm home. But at least she's around more than Dad. He can't give me any time. He's too busy working or with Christine and his new kids, the better kids, the ones he wants to stick around for. Playing family man like it's some sort of show he's putting on for whoever's watching. I don't even know why I come here anymore, but Mom put a guilt trip on me, claiming this would be my last summer visiting Dad before I graduate high school.

She's right. So I'm suffering through one more summer before I can end this charade once and for all.

My phone buzzes and I grab it, reading the text from Dustin.

Check out E's IG.

I do as he says, scrolling through my feed. I've ignored Instagram pretty much the entire summer because looking at it makes me sad. Pics of my friends having fun back home while I'm stuck here with no social life? No thanks. I don't need to rub salt in the open wound.

But maybe Dustin's right and his request is a clue. Maybe Emily's account will show me the surprise.

I scroll and scroll, finally finding a photo of Emily with Dustin and another guy. A guy I don't recognize. Emily's standing in between them in a tiny lime green bikini, her skin red from the sun, chin-length dark brown hair tucked behind her ears and her lids lowered over her eyes at half mast, like she just took a hit or maybe she's drunk, the sloppy grin on her face confirming it. Probably both. She has a cup in her hand and the guy I don't know is looking at her like she's the best thing he's ever seen.

Huh. More like *he's* the best thing I've ever seen.

The caption below the photo says:

Summer daze make me feel good. #justfriends #friendzone #zoned #owned
#relationship #lies #heartbreak #friends #bullshit

I stare at the photo for a long time, then click on Emily's user name—crazysexycool4uuuu—so I can check out her other photos.

And there are a ton of them. The ones from late June show her in various swimsuits. Considering her parents are rich and she has her own credit card with a huge limit, she buys what she wants and damn the consequences. She looks good. Em's not curvy, but she's fit. In the eighth grade she played volleyball and softball. Gave that up once we got into high school because, and I quote, "I don't want anyone to think I'm some lezbo jock."

Politically correct and sensitive, that's my Em.

Early July photos show Em and her family visiting her grandparents, waving American flags and Em in a short video spelling her name out with a sparkler in her hand. Mid-July is Emily back at home, hanging with Dustin. Lots of photos of her and Dustin, always with their arms around each other, Dustin shirtless, Emily in a sexy bikini, their bodies pressed close.

Huh.

Frowning, I keep scrolling upward, since I went straight to June, wanting the surprise to ease up on me. Slow build, like the best kind of anticipation. But I'm starting to think there's no surprise at all. Unless she considers that guy in the photos the surprise.

Talk about lame.

Around July 19th is when I start to see the guy in her photos regularly. He's cute. Gorgeous really. Medium brown hair streaked with gold, sparkling light eyes—I can't tell if they're brown or green, or maybe they're hazel. Definitely not blue. Nice body, which I'm seeing a lot of since he appears shirtless in pretty much every photo. Most are taken by Em's pool and there are so many people there.

When did Em get so popular without me?

I close out Instagram and text Dustin.

Please don't tell me my surprise is the guy.

                                        More like he's E's surprise.

What do you mean by that?

                        They're hooking up. But he's a douche.

I lean back against my pillows, stunned. I can hear my little brother and sister squealing downstairs. I hear a bird chirping just outside my window and the next-door neighbor is playing his radio outside as he gardens, some easy listening station that makes me want to stab pencils in my ears.

They're hooking up.

I'm a little…jealous? That guy is hot. And I'm also jealous over the photos with Em and Dustin. I miss them. I miss being a part of that friendship. The three of us against the world, it's always been like that. And it always hurts when one of us is missing.

Most of the time I'm the one missing.

You don't like him?

I sink my head farther into the pillows and close my eyes, waiting for Dustin's reply. Everything's changed this year. Last summer I was miserable and texting Em and Dustin every single day. And if we weren't texting we were calling each other, though that was rare. What we loved to do most was FaceTime each other and watch movies together. Simple stuff.

Innocent stuff.

Now I've seen Dustin's junk and he's seen my boobs and we've swapped spit. It's just all so…weird. Yet exciting. I sort of want to pursue more, but how do I tell him? How do we make this work without ruining everything? I don't want Em to feel left out either…

I hear my phone and I open my eyes, grabbing it.

He's okay. I guess Em needs the distraction.

What do you mean by that?

He doesn't reply for a while and I start to get nervous, nibbling on my thumbnail, feeling like an idiot for even asking.

I'll tell you when you come home. Hurry up. I miss you. ☺

Aw. I miss him, too. A lot. We've known each other forever but grew extra close in fifth grade. I've been friends with Emily since middle school, when she first moved into the neighborhood. I love making friends with the new kids. It's like a hobby of mine, one that Dustin used to make fun of.

"You take in all the strays," he once teased me and I didn't protest because he was right.

Looks like Em took over my hobby this summer and made friends with the new boy.

My phone dings again and I look at the screen.

When are you coming home? Em wants to throw you a party.

I wrinkle my nose. I don't want a party.

Why? I don't need that sort of thing.

That's her surprise. She's hanging with the popular crowd.

Really?

Yeah. They swim in her pool when her parents are at work.

Huh. They're using her for her pool? That's lame. I'm surprised she'd let them. Most of the popular crowd at our high school can be rude. Snobbish. I'm on the yearbook staff so I have to deal with them a lot. Some are nice. I can't lump them all together as egotistical jerks, but a lot of them are. Em always agreed with me, saying she wanted real friends, not phony friends who only use each other.

Wonder when she changed?

chapter two

"You look tan."

I glance down at my legs. They're not my usual shade of pale, so I guess I could consider my skin tone tan. "There's not much to do there but lay outside in the sun."

"Doesn't it rain all the time in Oregon?" Mom flicks on the blinker and taps the brake, slowing so she can turn right onto our street. "And doesn't *anyone* in your father's house believe in sunscreen?"

The *anyone* comment is directed right at Christine, my stepmom. Mom hates her. Mom hates Dad too. Makes for awkward conversations when I come home from his place.

"It doesn't rain much where Dad lives," I say with a shrug.

She holds back a sigh and pulls into our driveway. The minute she puts the car in park I reach for the door handle, desperate to make my escape, but she grabs hold of my arm, stopping me. I glance over my shoulder, frowning at her. "What?"

"I was hoping you'd have dinner with me tonight. With me and...
Fitch."

Grimacing, I slump back into my seat, crossing my arms in front of
my chest. "Em asked me to come over as soon as I got home."

She did. I'd been so thrilled to finally hear from her a few days ago,
and we'd kept up the conversation, even though I was sort of hurt it
took her this long to reach out. She flat out ignored me pretty much all
summer. But I never brought that up and neither did she, though she
did send me a series of photos through Snapchat these last few days,
of various near-naked torsos. The lime green bikini almost sliding off
her chest and a big, male hand covering one boob. A boy's very pale,
very firm ass in shadow, his swim trunks pulled down, most likely by
her. And then the photos went poof because Snapchat saves nothing.

Yeah. Em has *definitely* had an interesting summer. Much more
interesting than mine.

The sigh Mom had been holding back finally escapes, a slow hiss
like she's a tire leaking air. "You can go over to Emily's house for a little
while, but be home by dinner."

I glance at the time on my phone. It's already almost five. Mom
likes to eat early. "What time is that?"

"Six thirty."

"Mom!"

Another sigh, though it's more a hiss. Like she's a snake. "Fine.
Seven. But no later than that, okay?"

"Okay." I push out of the car and slam the door, going to the trunk
to get my suitcase. I grab it and haul ass into the house, dumping the
heavy suitcase onto my bed before I dart into the very small walk-in
closet and check out my reflection in the full-length mirror that hangs
on the wall.

I don't look bad, but I don't look my best either. I tuck my reddish brown hair behind my ears and stand up straight, leaning in close to run a finger beneath each eye to get rid of mascara smudge.

Screw it. This is as good as it gets. It's just Em after all. No biggie.

"OH MY GOD!" I squeal as the door swings open. I'm smiling so hard my cheeks hurt and the matching smile on Em's face tells me she's feeling much the same.

"Looking good, *chica*!" Em pulls me into her embrace and hugs me tight, her thin arms clamped around me, her mouth at my cheek as she gives me a sloppy kiss. "I missed you," she murmurs against my skin.

Oh, wow. She's high. I can smell it on her and I disentangle myself from her embrace, offering her a weak smile. If I go back home reeking of weed, Mom will kill me. Or ground me forever.

Both equal punishments in my eyes.

Em giggles and stumbles a little bit. "I'm so glad you're finally back!"

"Me too," I tell her as I close the front door. "Did you miss me?"

"Always," Em says without hesitation. She's giving me a sleepy look, one that tells me she's sort of trashed and I wonder if she's drunk too.

Is this how she's spent her summer? Drinking and getting high with her so-called new friends?

"I've lost weight." Em does a little twirl, clad in the same lime green bikini I saw her wearing in that one photo on Instagram. "It's my new diet of weed and vodka. Keeps me skinny." She bursts out laughing and rests her hand on her hip. I can actually see her hipbone jutting out, the bikini bottom rides so low, and she's so thin. "Come out back. There's people I want you to meet."

"Where are your mom and dad?" I ask as she takes my hand and drags me through the giant, airy house. We may live in the same neighborhood, but her house is huge and ours is…normal. And boring.

I practically trip over my flip-flops as I follow after her. I can hear music playing outside, one of those annoying songs that was on constant rotation all summer. And I hear water splashing too, like someone's in the pool. Lots of someones, maybe. Is she having a party? Oh God…is Dustin here?

My heart starts to pound and I swallow hard, wishing I would've at least changed my clothes before I came over. Slipped on a bikini. Anything to look cute, to look good for…who? Dustin?

Yeah. Definitely Dustin.

I can't believe I'm thinking like this.

Em stops in front of the French doors that lead outside and turns to face me, jerking on my hand so I'm standing close to her. So close my nose wrinkles as the pungent scent of marijuana washes over me. I can only hope it doesn't cling to my clothes. And if it does, that Mom won't notice when I get back home.

"I want you to meet Ryan," Em says, her voice low and smoky. She sounds completely different, like we're co-conspirators sharing a major secret. Something we've done a time or twenty during our friendship. But this one feels…bigger than the rest. "He just moved in down the street and he's, well…we've been…"

I raise a brow. "Hooking up?"

"Livvy!" She smacks my arm, making me wince. "Shut your mouth. I was going to say we've been spending a lot of *time* together."

Is that code for hooking up? "Dustin already told me."

"Oh." The irritation flitting across her face is clear. "He has such a big mouth. I told him to be quiet. I wanted to be the one who told you."

Unease creeps over me. Was she purposely keeping Ryan a secret? How weird. "I saw him in your pics on Instagram and Snapchat."

She waves a hand, dismissing my words. "The Snapchat thing…
that was for fun. And I was just showing off on Instagram. Everyone
shows off there."

True. "So you're not hooking up with Ryan?"

The smile curving her lips is coy. Secretive. "Maybe. Maybe not."

Right. She so is. "You spent a lot of time with Dustin too," I point
out, sounding like a jealous bitch, but I can't help it.

"*Ew*, no. He only has eyes for you." With that startling remark, she
throws open the doors and grabs my hand, dragging me out toward the
pool. "Look who I found!" she calls "It's Liv! She's finally home!"

They really don't care. Barely anyone looks in our direction. There
are a few kids I recognize from school swimming in the pool, groups
of girls hanging out on the lounge chairs wearing the skimpiest bikinis
I've ever seen. Girls I barely know, have said hi to in the halls maybe a
handful of times.

What is Em doing, inviting them here? Not like she's friends with
any of them…

I spot Dustin on the diving board, a giant grin on his familiar face
when he sees me. I smile back like I can't help myself, taking in his
classically handsome features, the way his warm brown eyes sparkle.
He throws one hand up in the air in a wave before he hurls his long
body into the water in a perfect flip.

Such a show off.

"So you're the infamous Liv. You really *do* exist."

The deep, even voice coming from behind me makes me whirl
around, my lips parted like I'm ready to speak. But the second I catch
a glimpse, it's like all those words dried up in my throat. It's him. The
boy from the photos. And he's even better looking in person, which is
saying a lot.

My brain scrambles as I try to come up with the right thing to say.

He just stands there, clad in blue swim trunks that hang dangerously low on his hips, acres of golden skin on display. Droplets of water cling to his arms and chest and I watch one wind a path down his flat stomach, disappearing beneath the waistband of his trunks.

The words finally fall from my lips like I have no control over them. "And here I thought you were an actor Em rented for the summer to pretend to be her boyfriend."

His smile is slow. And wow, it ends up a powerful, knock me on my ass grin. Thrusting his hand out toward me, he says, "I'm Ryan."

"So formal." I take his hand and shake it, trying to ignore the buzz of electricity that flows from my palm to his. "Olivia."

"Nice to meet you," he says with a slight bow, his amused tone making me laugh. He holds onto my hand for a moment too long and I snatch it away from him, rubbing my fingers against my palm, trying to get rid of the sparks that still remain on my skin.

Ryan continues to stand in front of me, his smile still firmly in place, damp golden brown hair waving around his face. He's pushed sunglasses up onto his head and that allows me to finally discover his eye color.

Green. Rich, deep green like a mysterious forest.

I can't stop staring at him and he can't seem to stop looking at me either. I drop my gaze from his, but that feels like a mistake. His chest is like a work of art. Tanned, smooth skin stretched over lean muscle. It's obvious I'm checking him out, but I don't even care.

He doesn't call me out on it either. I think he likes that my gaze is roaming over every inch of him. And I have a feeling he's doing the same to me, despite my being the most overdressed girl here.

Okay, this is totally weird. I need to get away from him before the situation gets super awkward.

"Livvy!" Strong arms wrap around me from behind and a wet,

warm body presses up against me. I recognize the body, the voice, his scent immediately.

Dustin.

He presses his cheek against mine for a quick second before he dips his head and kisses my neck, his lips cold against my skin. A shiver moves through me and I playfully shove him off of me, rubbing my cheek against my shoulder, my now-wet clothes clingy and most likely unflattering. "You made me wet," I grumble.

"That's what she said," Ryan adds, and both boys laugh.

My cheeks are on fire and I look around for Em, who's nowhere to be found. Oh, there she is, over by the diving board, taking a swig out of someone's beer bottle before handing it back to him. He's big, tall and broad with blond hair and I recognize him as one of the football players from school. She's bouncing on the balls of her feet, laughing extra loud when he says something to her.

I frown. I've never seen her like this before.

Dustin takes a step closer to me, his arm nudging mine, and I glance up at him.

"Where are Lou and Cindy?" I ask, referring to Em's parents.

He shrugs, shakes his head and scatters water droplets like a dog, some of them hitting me. "They went on vacation a few days ago."

"Without Emily?" I'm shocked. They always go on a couple of family vacations every year. It used to be the highlight of her summer.

"She didn't want to go on this particular one since they're visiting her sister in Virginia, so they let her stay alone." Em has never liked her older sister. There's a ten-year difference between them and they have zero in common. "They won't be home for another three days. It's full blown party time."

The smile Dustin sends my way makes my knees melt. He's such a good-looking guy, what with his dark hair and equally dark eyes. He has a good body too, though his isn't as developed as Ryan's. Dustin's taller, though, well over six feet and he's on the basketball team at school.

And when he looks at me like this, I can feel that crackling chemistry between us. It draws me to him, makes me want more despite my fears. But what I have with Dustin is also warm and comfortable. I trust him. There's definitely an attraction between us, but I'm also afraid if we jumped into a relationship, we'd ruin our friendship in the process.

There would be no going back.

I shouldn't even worry about boys right now. My next goal is to graduate high school and get into a good college. Preferably one out of state and far away from here. And when I say out of state, I don't necessarily mean Oregon. Dad is dying for me to become a University of Oregon Duck.

If I can get down to southern California, I'd be happy. I want to get out of this valley, out of this hot city that will lead me nowhere. Growing up in central California, I've always felt like there's nothing here. We live in the suburbs, we go to the best high school in the school district and my neighborhood is pretty upscale, but yeah.

I'm desperate to get out of here.

"You met Ryan already." Dustin pauses. "What do you think?"

"He seems nice."

The disgusted look that crosses Dustin's face takes me by surprise. "Seriously?"

"What? Do you not like him?" Dustin pretty much likes everyone, or so I thought.

"Who does Dustin not like?" Ryan magically appears, moving closer so he's standing with us, on the other side of me.

I wave a hand, hoping he didn't hear what we said. "No one. Don't worry about it."

"Well, it certainly can't be you," Ryan says, his voice warm. "I think Dustin's ready to stake his claim with you."

Oh boy. This is strange. "No one can stake a claim. I'm not claimable." Is that even a word?

"Well, if he's not going to claim you, I'd like to try." Ryan flashes me a devastating grin. "You're everything Em described."

My stomach fizzes with nerves at the way Ryan watches me. "And how did Em describe me?"

"Redhead." He steps closer and gently tugs on a strand of my hair. "Freckles." He taps the tip of my nose with his index finger. "Pretty."

My cheeks are warm all over again. He shouldn't flirt with me. Even if he's just hooking up with her, he clearly belongs to Em.

"Livvy's gorgeous." Dustin slings his arm around my shoulders and wraps it around my neck, tugging me close to him. I have no choice but to go, wondering at the possessive way he's acting. Like he wants to prove something to Ryan. "She just doesn't realize it yet."

"Stop. I'm standing right here." I lightly jab Dustin in the stomach with my elbow, making him grunt, his arm loosening around my neck. I step out of his hold and Ryan laughs, shaking his head.

The glare Dustin sends him is murderous, the tension between them palpable.

Something's going on between these two. And I don't like it.

chapter three

You should come over and spend the night.

The text came from Em about thirty minutes ago and I still haven't responded. I know for a fact Mom won't let me go over there tonight and I also know Em will be persistent in trying to convince me to come over.

I can't win.

I was eating dinner when I received her text. I went to check it, but Mom cleared her throat, her gaze sharp as she watched me. I shoved my phone into the pocket of my denim shorts and smiled politely at her new boyfriend, Fitch.

His name sounds like it belongs to a pet, not a man, but whatever. He makes loving eyes at my mother and praises her cooking—which is just mediocre if you ask me—and earlier I saw him grab her ass in the kitchen. She swatted his hand away with a potholder and he just laughed, pulled her in close before laying one on her.

I looked away and made myself scarce. It felt like I was prying in on a private moment.

The dinner conversation had been strained between all three of us. I tried my best and kept saying I was tired when Mom asked me what was wrong. It was a better excuse than telling Mom her new boyfriend was sort of boring. That would only hurt her feelings.

I'm cleaning the kitchen when I finally decide to pause and answer Em.

Can't come over. Mom wants me to stay home tonight.

I send off the text, but mere seconds later Em's responding.

Forget your mother! I need you!

Lots of crying emojis follow this proclamation.

Sighing, I shove my phone back into my pocket and resume wiping down the granite countertops, careful to not leave any streaks. After the divorce, Mom had the kitchen remodeled, the entire house repainted, and she replaced her bedroom furniture too. Every last scrap of it right down to getting rid of the mattress, and it hadn't been that old to begin with.

"I'm purging," she'd told me with a gentle smile and a hostile gleam in her eye. "Getting rid of all that bad juju."

She'd never talked of bad juju before so I knew she was full of it, even when I was eleven. Adults don't think we're paying attention, but we so are. They also believe we don't understand what's going on, but that's a lie they tell themselves to feel better about their decisions.

I knew Dad had cheated on her, had overheard one of their raging fights late at night, long after they thought I'd gone to bed. Tears streaking down my cheeks as I clutched one of my stuffed animals close, listening to them scream accusations at each other.

Dad called her a cold, unfeeling bitch who withheld sex on purpose. Mom called him a cheating bastard who couldn't keep his dick in his pants.

I'm pretty sure they were both fairly close in their assessments of each other back then, now that I look at things, see the past through my seventeen-year-old clear-as-can-be eyes versus my younger self's rose-colored glasses. Mom loves to reference those stupid rose-colored glasses, especially when talking about Dad.

"After I took those rose-colored glasses off, I finally saw the reality of my situation. And at that one particular moment, Olivia, my life was a world of shit," she's told me more than once.

Did I mention Mom is a bit of a drama queen sometimes?

My butt buzzes and I pull my phone out, reading the new text from Em.

Don't ignore me bitch. Dustin wants you here. He's DYING to see you.

It's like she's trying to tempt me, though she doesn't know about Dustin and me. That's another thing I'm afraid of—Em's disapproval if Dustin and I really got together. I think she'd be jealous. I think she'd be upset and accuse us of leaving her out, which would never be my intention.

It's best I avoid them tonight, even though I'd love to see Dustin. I'm tired and afraid I might do or say something stupid.

But I also need to respond to Em's insistent texts.

I can't come over. Maybe tomorrow?

The phone rings in my hand, startling me. Emily's name flashes across the screen, the vibrating phone making my skin tingle. I slide the green button and slowly bring the phone to my ear, offering a tentative, "Are you sick? Why are you calling me?"

"I am sick. Sick of being without my Livvy!" I pull the phone away from my ear when she screams into it. "Come on, your mom will let you come over. It's me! I'm harmless."

Right now she's as harmless as a rattlesnake ready to strike. I'm pretty sure the girl is drunk and stoned and it might not be safe that she's staying home alone. Though from the background noise, I can only assume people are there. She said Dustin is.

"You're not harmless," I finally tell her as I turn on the water at the sink and rinse the rag I'd been using. "You're crazed right now."

She giggles. "Isn't it great? I almost did a strip tease for Ryan earlier in the pool house."

I go still. "Haven't you already done that?"

Her giggles fade. "Oh, we've messed around for a little bit, but nothing serious. He hasn't seen me naked or anything."

Why does this make me feel better? "Really?"

"Really. We're just friends." Her voice drops. "Though I guess I'm the sort of friend who gives blowjobs. Who knew?"

Her laughter is incredibly loud and I wince. "You actually gave him a BJ?"

"Don't be such a priss. I can't help it if you've never *done* anything."

I clamp my lips shut. I won't tell her about Dustin. Not over the phone. I should tell her in person, but I don't even want to admit it to... anyone. Not yet. It feels too soon.

Sighing, I'm determined to not give in. "I'll come over tomorrow afternoon. Okay?"

"Livvy..."

"Tomorrow," I say again firmly. "Bye, Em."

I hang up before she can say anything more.

chapter four

I don't make it over to Em's house until midafternoon the next day and I figure she's mad at me. I texted that I was coming over a while ago and she never replied, though the message said *read* beneath it.

Meaning she's not answering me on purpose.

So I let her be pissed, figuring she'll get over it soon enough. When I show up at her house, no one answers the door, though it was unlocked. I enter the house and look around, figuring that everybody is out by the pool once again. The place is a mess, especially the giant kitchen. There's half eaten food covering the marble countertops, empty liquor bottles stacked in the farmhouse sink, along with beer bottles and cans. Two liters without the caps on them—so the soda was probably already flat—sat near the giant stainless steel fridge and there are open bags of chips everywhere.

Shaking my head, I survey all the damage. I know I'm going to be stuck helping her clean up. It's what I do. Dustin and me, we're always bailing Em out of some sort of mess.

Frustrated, I head upstairs to drop off my bag in her room before I go outside. The door is partially closed, but I think nothing of it.

Imagine my surprise when I push the door open to find Em and Ryan sitting on the edge of the bed, their mouths fused, her arms wound around his neck and his hand on her boob.

"Ohmigod, sorry!" I squeak, dropping my bag on the floor with a loud thud before I start to hightail it out of there. Ryan's hand falls from her chest and Em shoves him away, leaping to her feet to come toward me.

"Liv! Finally you're here." She curls her arm around my shoulders and forces me to face Ryan, who's still sitting on the edge of the bed with his legs spread in that way boys sit, wearing only swim trunks again. Does the guy ever wear actual clothes? "We've been waiting for you. Tell Ryan hello."

"Hello," I say in a monotone, incredibly uncomfortable from interrupting what was surely a private hookup moment.

He smiles and rises to his feet, smoothing a hand over his rumpled hair, his biceps bulging with the movement. Hair Em was probably responsible for rumpling. "Hey, Livvy."

Tingles race over my skin and I force myself to ignore the signs. The signs that I might be attracted to this boy who just had his tongue in my best friend's mouth. I don't even know him. It's purely a physical thing, as in every single thing that makes him up physically, I find attractive.

And I shouldn't. He doesn't belong to me. He belongs to Em. I should be thinking about Dustin.

Not Ryan.

"I'm so glad you're finally here." Em turns toward me, and envelopes me in a warm hug, her mouth on my neck as she starts to speak again. "I've missed you."

I hug her back, my gaze meeting Ryan's as I say, "I've missed you too."

He sends me a playful, rolling eyes look that I ignore.

Em kisses my neck and pulls away, her blue eyes bright, her cheeks flushed. She's wearing a white lacy cover up over a black string bikini and her chin-length, gold-streaked bob is tucked behind her ears. She's effortlessly gorgeous, all rosy from kissing a cute boy for who knows how long. "Now that you're here the party can start."

I laugh and shake my head. "Looks like it's already been going for the last few days."

Em rolls her eyes and lets go of me, heading for her dresser. "I was just biding my time until you showed up."

"So I bring the party?" I tease, meeting Ryan's gaze once more.

"You definitely bring something," "he tells me before pulling me into a tight hug. My chest presses against his, my arms going around his waist for the briefest moment before I release him and back far away.

He makes me nervous.

"Aw, I love that you guys are already hugging!" Em cries as she watches us.

Guilt swamps me but Ryan just smiles. "I'll leave you girls alone." He looks at me. "See you at the pool."

And then he's gone.

The air seems to cool the moment he's left the room and I go to stand next to Em, watching as she digs through the top drawer of her dresser. It's an elaborate piece of furniture, cream-colored with an endless number of drawers, every one of them stuffed full of clothes. The one she's digging through now is overflowing with lacy scraps of fabric. There are panties in every style and color, boy shorts and thongs and bikinis, some of it standard, most of it sexy.

Her underwear drawer is like Em in a nutshell.

"So how's your summer been? Besides the partying and hanging out with the popular crowd? Have you done anything else?" I'm trying to make conversation but she's hardly paying attention to me.

"It's been so boring without you here," she says, her head practically buried in that drawer.

I think she's saying that to make me feel better. Not that she needs to. I'm a big girl. She's allowed to have fun when I'm not around.

"What are you looking for?" I ask.

"A black lacy thong I bought last week." She lifts her head and smiles at me. "I want to wear it tonight."

"But aren't we going swimming?"

Em blows out a frustrated breath. "Yeah, but I don't want to forget. I want to wear it for…" Her voice drifts and she purses her lips.

"Ryan?"

She sighs and slams the drawer shut, turning to look at me. "Well, yeah. But it's no big deal. We're just friends."

I raise a brow. "Is that what you call it? Because I hate to break it to you, but you were kissing him just a few minutes ago, and he had his hand on your boob."

"So crude." She nudges my shoulder with hers. "Voyeur."

"Just stating facts. Facts I saw with my own eyes." I pause, but she doesn't say anything. "I don't get why you can't say that you like him and he likes you. What's the big deal?"

"Because he refuses to make this a big deal so I can't, okay? He told me straight up that we're going to be just friends and that's it."

"Friends who kiss and offer up blowjobs?" I add helpfully.

She scowls. "Right. Look, I know the score. I can't pretend this is something more. He told me from the start his expectations."

"What about *your* expectations?" I'm kind of offended on her behalf, not that she notices.

"They're the same as his!" Em throws her hands up in the air. I'm irritating her, but I don't care. This isn't like Em. She doesn't hook up, not really. Not on a constant basis, though I've heard rumors in the recent past. Rumors I'd always brushed off. But now, it sounds like Ryan's only...using her.

Not that I'd say that. Not right now. She's mad enough.

I try reverse psychology on her. "So you're just using him."

"Right. Yes. That exactly." She points at me. "So I want to mess around, so what? He's the perfect guy to mess around with. First, he's gorgeous. And he's...experienced. No judgment. He's discreet. Crap, he really doesn't know anybody here and I love that about him. He doesn't really know *me*. I can be whoever I want with Ryan."

"And who exactly are you with Ryan?" I'm envious of that wistful tone in her voice. The fact that she's having so much fun with Ryan and doesn't care what anyone thinks must be so freeing.

Sometimes, I wish I were more like her.

"Free. Wild." She smiles wickedly. "So. Freaking. Wild. You wouldn't believe what we did last night."

Panic takes hold and I grab her arm, gripping her wrist with my fingers. "Did you..."

"No, we haven't had *sex* yet." She shakes off my hand and heads for her closet. "But we've done other things."

I nearly sag to the floor I'm so relieved. I don't want to be the last virgin. But I don't really want her to be the last virgin either and one of us is going to have to be eventually. This isn't a race.

Though it feels like one.

"I have a bikini for you," she calls from within her closet. "Wait until you see it!"

"I'm already wearing one." Dad had bought me a couple, though I really only wore one of them. It's not that warm where he lives and besides, all I ever did was hang out with Christine, Dakota and Sierra all day. That sucked.

"You don't have one like this, though." She emerges from her closet brandishing what looks like a sliver of turquoise fabric and a bunch of strings. "You are going to look so incredibly hot."

I take it from her and hold the two-piece out in front of me. The top is made up of two triangles and strings. That's it. The bottom is skimpy. It looks like it would barely cover my ass. "Em, come on. Everything will be hanging out."

"Exactly. And all the boys will die." She laughs and snags the bikini out of my hands before she flings it back at me. It hits me in the chest and I grab it. "Go put it on, hooker. You know you want to!"

I head for her giant , private bathroom, the bathroom I've envied for years because it connects to her room. It has a giant tub with jets and a big glass shower. A huge countertop with two sinks and all her makeup and hair stuff spread out all over it. What I would give for this much space, and all the privacy she could ever want...

"Can't undress in front of me? When did you get so modest?" she asks.

"I'm on my period," I tell her as I shut the door. A lie. I don't feel like stripping in front of her. I know she doesn't have a problem with stripping naked in front of me, but she's right. I've always been shy about that stuff.

"Gross!" She laughs. "That's going to ruin any prospects you might have tonight."

"I'm not looking to hook up," I tell her through the door as I tug the sundress I wore over to her house up and over my head, leaving it in a heap on the floor.

"Please. We all are." She hesitates for the barest moment. "Dustin's out there. He's been asking about you."

I pause in my stripping, my heart tripping over itself. "What is he saying?"

"How much he's missed you. I think he has a total crush on you, Liv."

Here's my chance to be honest. Taking a deep breath, I lean against the door, my forehead pressed against the cool wood. "We've sort of had a thing for each other."

Silence greets me from the other side for a moment. "What are you talking about?"

I slowly crack open the door to find her face almost directly in mine. "Dustin and I…we've messed around a few times."

Her mouth drops open. "Really?"

I nod, reaching out to touch her arm but she jerks away from my touch. "It was crazy. I don't know…I think I like him, too."

Em's expression is completely flat, her blue eyes dull. I part my lips, ready to offer up a bunch of silly excuses, anything to make her smile but then it's like a switch turned on. Her face brightens, her mouth stretches into a wide smile and she hauls me into her arms, hugging me close.

"I'm so happy for you two! Wow, Livvy and Dustin sitting in a tree, k-i-s-s-i-n-g. That is the cutest!"

"Um, well we're not a couple or anything like that," I try to say but she's already dancing around, her boobs jiggling beneath her skimpy top. I'm afraid a nipple might fly out.

"Funny how he never told me about you two," she says. "I spent all summer with him and he never mentioned a word about this."

"You don't believe me?" I'm incredulous.

"Of course, I believe you! I'm just surprised. It's so crazy, to think of the two of you together! So fun and crazy." Her smile slips and her eyes dim. "I should go downstairs and check on everyone. See you at the pool?"

"Yeah," I say weakly. "Definitely."

The moment she's gone I sag against the door, staring at my new bikini lying on the counter in front of me. She acted weird. I hope she's okay with this.

I hope we're all okay with this.

chapter five

I'm drunk.

Just like I predicted, it's not even six and I'm already buzzing hard. I'm a happy drunk. Some people are mean when they drink. Mom always accused Dad of being a vicious drunk, but I never really saw it.

Me and Em? We're the happiest little drunk girls you've ever seen. We're laughing and yelling and singing along with the music playing off someone's iPhone. More people showed up, people I don't even recognize, but I don't care. We both greet them like they're our long lost friends and we've been dying to see them for years. We hand them beers because we've gone through all the hard liquor in the house. We invite them into the pool. Someone ordered pizzas and a bunch of boys pitched in their money to pay for it.

When the pizza arrives it smells so good I immediately grab a plate and load it with three slices, not really caring if I look like a pig. Em makes a period hangry issue comment and I ignore her, chomping away on the most delicious slice of pepperoni, olive and mushroom pizza I've ever eaten in my life.

"You've been ignoring me."

I swallow and glance over my shoulder to find Ryan standing there. I thought it would be Dustin, since I sort of have been ignoring him to save any awkward conversations we might have in front of Em.

Though he's been trying to make grabs in the pool all afternoon. Not innocent grabs either—like, his hands hover near my boob vicinity every time he's close. He even grabbed my ass, trying to tug my bikini bottoms down, but I swatted his hand away and called him a pervert.

The hurt look he sent me made me feel bad, but I don't want to make Em upset if she sees us together. Not like I could explain anything to him since I haven't caught him alone the entire afternoon. In fact, Brianne Brown's been cozying up to him, like she always does. She's been after him for a year.

I would love to yank all her pretty blonde hair out of her head.

"I haven't been avoiding you," I tell Ryan. I really haven't seen him much these last few hours. I figured when Em wasn't with me she was with him.

He settles on the edge of the lounge chair beside me, his big, warm body pressed up against mine. I scoot away from him and glance around, discreetly looking for Em but as usual, she's nowhere to be found. No one's really around. We're on the opposite side of the pool from where everyone else is and they're either congregated around the table with the pizza boxes or they're inside getting something to drink.

Meaning we're pretty much all alone.

"Glad to hear it. I thought you were mad at me."

"Why would I be mad at you?" I lift the slice of pizza up to take a bite and he nods toward it, his expression hungry.

"Can I have a bite?" he asks, his voice so low I swear I feel it in the pit of my stomach.

"Um, sure." I hold it up, fully expecting him to take it from me, but he doesn't. Instead, he leans over, so close his body brushes against mine as he takes a bite of the pizza. I'm shocked silent, my entire body going still as I watch him chew. He's so close he could lean right over and kiss me. Touch me.

I scoot away from him even more.

"Delicious," he says, smiling at me. "You have sauce on your face."

Before I can say anything he's wiping at the corner of my mouth with his thumb. My lips part the slightest bit and I swear he gently presses his thumb between them before he pulls away.

Oh. Shit. I'm not stupid. He's totally flirting with me.

This is so not cool. What about Em?

"Thanks," I murmur, suddenly not hungry anymore.

"I should be thanking you, sacrificing your dinner to a guy you just met." Despite the distance between us, he leans his shoulder into mine. "Em said you're a giver."

"I do like to help out my fellow man." Ugh, that sounded so stupid.

"I'm sure." He smiles, tilts his head to the side. "Need something to drink?"

"I'm good." I tell him, balancing the plate of pizza on my knees. I feel extra exposed sitting with Ryan, wearing the skimpy bikini Em gave me, and I swear it feels like my boobs are gonna bust out of the triangles at any given moment.

Ryan's gaze drops to the triangles, as if he can read my mind. "Nice suit."

"Thanks."

"I think Em got you the wrong size."

How did he know the suit was from Em? "What do you mean?"

"Looks like someone's trying to escape." He reaches out, his fingers slipping beneath the triangle of thin fabric covering my right breast and readjusting it.

I swat his hand away. "What are you doing?"

His lazy smile tells me he knows exactly what he's doing. "Trying to help you."

"I don't need your help," I tell him haughtily. "You should keep your hands to yourself."

"Aw, you're no fun." His eyes darken. "Hey, it was harmless flirting. I'm sorry, okay?"

I sit up straighter, appeased by his apology. "Okay."

"You're not mad at me?"

Shaking my head, I admit, "Not really."

He laughs, shaking his head. "I like your honesty."

"Most people don't," I say, thinking of Em. She gets mad at me when I'm honest. She calls it too honest. But I don't like to lie to her so it's like I can't make her happy no matter what I say.

"I like girls who aren't full of bullshit." His laughter dies and he grows serious. "You're not full of bullshit, are you, Livvy?"

I part my lips, ready to say something but before I can get the words out someone else speaks up.

"What's going on?"

We both look up to find Dustin standing over us, his expression thunderous, stupid Brianne Brown standing right next to him, her arm hooked through his.

I want to slap that smug look right off her bitchy face.

"I was just copping a feel and Livvy got mad at me," Ryan says, voicing the one hundred percent truth, his expression solemn.

I start to laugh, shaking my head.

Clearly I'm drunk and stupid right now.

"Seriously, Liv?" Dustin asks, sounding pissed.

"He's joking." I sigh and shake my head.

"Totally joking, bro," Ryan says, devouring another piece of pizza and ending his part of the conversation.

"I haven't talked to you much today," Dustin says, regaining my attention.

I smile prettily up at him, batting my eyelashes. I'm sort of pissed he brought Brianne around. "You've been otherwise occupied."

I'm talking about Brianne. She's tiny with big boobs and pretty blonde hair that is currently caught up in a bouncy ponytail. She's a cheerleader too. Meaning she and Dustin would make a perfect pair.

Seeing them together makes me feel nauseous.

"Maybe we could catch up later?" I hear the hopeful tone in his voice. See the irritated scowl she shoots his way before she glares at me. She doesn't want us to catch up.

"Yeah, definitely," I answer brightly, my gaze locked on them as they turn and walk away.

The moment they leave us, my shoulders sag and I blow out a sigh. Ryan's nudging me with his elbow, that smile on his face unreadable. I have no idea what he's thinking and it's kind of freaking me out. "He's jealous."

"Of who?"

"Of me." Ryan reaches out, his index finger tracing a path along my shoulder. "And us. Sitting together."

I jerk away from him. He needs to stop touching me like that. It's not right, not when he's with Em. "He is not."

"Aren't you two together?"

I shake my head. "We're friends." Best friends. Who want something more.

Maybe?

"Uh huh." The look he sends me is knowing. "So it's like that between you two."

"I have no idea what you're talking about." I refuse to look at him. He'd probably see the guilt in my eyes and I'd be busted. Just like that.

"Right. So tell me." He leans in close, his mouth right at my ear. "You've kissed him."

I remain quiet.

"Sucked his dick?"

He is unbelievable. I send him a look that hopefully is chock full of indignation.

"Jerked him off, then."

The tips of my ears go hot.

"Fumbling fingers in your panties? Did he find your sweet spot or did you have to take care of yourself later when you got home?"

"Ew." I shove him and he nearly topples off the lounge chair. Somehow he keeps the plate of pizza in one hand, never dropping it as he lands on his feet. "You're vulgar."

He grins. "You like it. And I think I've just guessed your darkest, dirtiest secret."

"My lips are sealed." I mime zipping my lips and throwing away the key.

Though he did just figure out my darkest, dirtiest secret.

"Right. Keeping it in the vault and all that." He nods, standing in front of me and blocking my view. As in, he *is* my view.

"No. There's just…nothing to tell." I shrug, all feigned nonchalance.

Ryan settles beside me once more, devouring the last piece of pizza in three bites before he speaks again. "So no jerking off and finger-fucking went down between you two. Got it."

He says the words so casually and I want to die. Just evaporate into thin air. "You are like really…."

When I say nothing else, he laughs. "Go ahead. Say it."

"Crude?"

"Yeah. But does it bother you?" His voice is low, low, low.

I squirm, pressing my thighs together. "It makes me uncomfortable."

"In a good way or a bad way?"

I lift my head, my gaze meeting his. "Would you believe me if I said in a bad way?"

He shakes his head slowly. "No."

Glancing around, I make sure nobody is close and then say, "What about Em?"

"What about her?"

"I thought you two were…"

"Together? Not at all."

I'm startled by the vehemence in his tone. "She said the same thing."

"Really? That's good. Em and I? We see eye to eye." His face comes closer to mine. I can see there are gold flecks in his green eyes. And that he hasn't shaved in a day or two. Stubble covers his jaw. "I don't know if I believe you."

His whiplash change of subject makes me tilt my head. "About what?"

"About you and Dustin." He hesitates, his mouth curving into a lopsided smile. "I think you have messed around with him."

"So what if I have? Does that bother you?"

"No." His smile grows. "Makes me curious."

"Curious about what?"

"Exactly what you two have done together."

I can't tell him. Can I? No. Yes? "We've kissed."

"Big deal."

"Um…touched each other." Why am I saying this?

"Under your clothes? Or completely naked?" His gaze rakes over me, like he's trying to imagine me completely naked. I bet he's having an easy time of it considering I'm barely dressed.

Stupid Em and the stupid bikini she gave me.

"You ask way too many personal questions," I tell him.

"I'm trying to figure out what you like."

I suck in a breath. "Why?"

"Because whatever he can't do for you, maybe I can."

Okay. Okay, okay, okay. This boy is way too forward. I rise to my feet, practically trip over my own flip-flops, and I step away from him, needing the distance. "You're with Em," I remind him.

"It's not serious."

"It doesn't matter," I say firmly. "You shouldn't flirt with me. We shouldn't be talking about any of this," I tell him as I start to walk away.

"Thanks for the pizza!" he yells after me.

But I don't acknowledge him.

chapter six

I t's late, past one in the morning and I'm in Em's bed alone when I feel someone slide under the covers. I go stiff, scared for the briefest moment it's a stranger, but then a strong arm wraps around my middle and Dustin rests his chin on my bare shoulder.

"I can't believe I found you," he whispers close to my ear, his lips touching my skin and making me shiver.

"I've been here the entire time," I tell him sleepily. Well, I've only been here for maybe an hour. Em disappeared a while ago and so did Ryan. I think they're in her parents' bedroom doing…God knows what.

I shouldn't let it bother me. He's sort of a creep, to flirt so heavily with me right before he tumbles into bed with one of my best friends. I should tell her what he said. How he touched me. The words he said.

Everything Ryan says is laden with sexual innuendo. And for one breathless, shivery moment, I wanted him to talk to me like that again. Touch me again.

But that is absolutely crazy. I like Dustin. I should be with Dustin.

Everywhere I looked though, I couldn't find him. My head was spinning and most everyone had already left, so I dragged myself upstairs and collapsed into Em's bed, drunk and tired yet unable to fall asleep. I'm still wearing the bikini.

And Dustin is still wearing his board shorts. Nothing else. We are skin on skin, and his mouth is now on my shoulder, his fingers drifting lazily over my stomach.

I told myself I wouldn't do this again, but wow, his touch feels so good. And I've been so lonely this entire summer. It feels good to be back, in Dustin's arms.

"I missed you," Dustin murmurs, his mouth hot on my neck, his hands wandering up until they're cupping my breasts. His touch is gentle yet with enough firmness to make me crave more. I arch into his hands, gasp when he shoves the triangle-shaped fabric away and he's touching nothing but bare skin. "If you want me to stop, I will."

He always says that. He's considerate. And I really appreciate that. My feelings about him confuse me though. And it doesn't help that Ryan's walked into our lives and sent my head spinning even harder.

Even though I should totally forget about him. He seems...

Dangerous.

"Don't stop," I tell Dustin, turning around to face him when he encourages me with his hands on my waist. He grabs hold of my leg, drapes it over his hip as he leans in and kisses me.

His damp, full lips move over mine hungrily, our tongues thrusting, hands wandering everywhere, the bed creaking as we shift into a better position. I don't want to go too far, but I need to ease the building ache deep inside.

Right now, it's like only Dustin can take care of me.

"Ah, hell," he moans when he slips his hand in my bikini bottoms. "Livvy, you're so wet."

I rock into his hand and kiss him, moaning when his busy fingers hit a particular spot. "Oh God." I want more. More, more, more. If he stops touching me like this, I will die.

And he knows it.

"Missed you so bad, Liv. Missed being with you like this," he whispers, his fingers increasing their pace, his mouth hungrily devouring mine. I move with him, my hands sliding down his chest, loosening the ties of his swim trunks so I can dip beneath and grab hold of him. When I wrap my fingers around him, he groans against my lips, his fingers faltering.

We're a mess. Sloppy. Somehow I end up naked and flat on my back and his swim trunks are around his knees as he hovers above me. I'm touching him and he's touching me and we're kissing. Moaning. Whispering words of encouragement. That ache deep within me grows, consuming me, and my hips rise toward his, seeking fingers like I have no control. I squeeze him tight, his fingers slip over one spot over and over again, and that's it.

The shudders consume me, a soft "oh" falling from my lips as I shake and he follows right after me, a choked moan coming from deep within his chest. Until he collapses on top of me, his forehead pressed against mine, his ragged breath hot in my face. I clutch him close, smooth my hands down his back and he shivers beneath my touch.

"We came—" Dustin pants, like he can barely talk. "—together."

I nod, suddenly feeling shy. It's just so strange to get naked with your best friend. I'm so caught up in the moment it usually doesn't bother me, but afterwards, I feel weird.

Awkward.

He rolls over and pulls me into his arms, kissing my forehead. "Next time I want to go down on you."

Oh, God. I'm not even tempted by the prospect of him going

down on me. I can't imagine Dustin with his face down there. It's too embarrassing.

I just…no.

Pulling away from him, I slide out of bed, thankful it's so dark. I find my bag on the floor and grab an old T-shirt I brought to sleep in. I tug it over my head and pull the tie out of my hair before I gather it all back up and put it into a sloppy bun.

There. I'm ready for bed.

My eyes have adjusted to the dark and I watch as one of his legs sneaks out from beneath the covers and he kicks off his shorts so they land on the floor with a soft plop. The comforter bunches around his waist as he leans against the pile of pillows, curving his arms behind his head and looking as comfortable—and satisfied—as he pleases.

"Come here," he says, and I watch him, hesitant.

The faint smile fades and he sits up straighter, his hands braced on the mattress, the muscles in his arms straining. "What's wrong, Livvy? You haven't acted the same since you came home."

"We've barely talked." I cross my arms in front of my chest.

"Yeah, and whose fault is that?"

"I don't know, Brianne Brown's?"

"Give me a break." He sounds irritated.

"Did you do anything with her tonight?" Totally crazy question I don't want to know the answer to.

"Why? Are you jealous?"

"No!" God, no.

Fine. I'm totally jealous.

"I didn't do anything with Brianne. She left a while ago. I came to find *you*. I'm in bed with *you*." He pauses. Takes a deep breath. "I just made you come with my fingers, Liv. What else do you want from me?"

I stare at him, my heart racing, my mind racing too. I don't know what I want from him. I've been avoiding him since I got home yesterday since I don't know how to ask for what I want. And then he sneaks into bed with me, all warm and big and cuddly. How could I resist?

"I—I don't know what I want," I finally say, my voice raspy, my entire body starting to shake.

"Liv." He sounds different. Like he's not mad or frustrated with me any longer. No, more like he's worried about me and he wants to take care of me. I watch as he slides out of bed, completely comfortable as he comes toward me without a stitch of clothing on. "Come to bed with me."

"No." I shake my head, my entire body going stiff when he wraps his arms around me.

"Olivia." My name is a whisper against my hair and my muscles slowly start to relax at his closeness. The familiar scent of his skin, the way he holds me, close but not smothering. "Come on. Please don't be mad."

"I'm not mad." I'm never mad at him. More like I'm mad at myself.

"I'm a jerk," I say as he pulls away and takes my hands. "A terrible friend."

"No, you're not."

"You deserve someone better than me," I tell him once he leads me over to the bed and guides me under the covers.

He pulls me back into his arms and I go willingly, nestling my cheek against his bare chest. His heart beating so steady and true is a comfort. This is Dustin. *My* Dustin. My eyes close and I start to fall asleep when I hear him say something.

"I don't want anyone else," he whispers. "I hope I deserve you."

I can't answer him. I don't know how.

I fall asleep instead.

chapter seven

"So. You and Dustin."

I shuffle to the kitchen counter and plop down on one of the stools, propping my elbows on the counter. "What are you talking about," I mumble.

"You told me you were on your period."

No need to explain my lie. I shrug instead. "It was nothing." I don't want her to make a big deal about last night. How does she even know?

"Uh huh." The knowing smile on Em's face tells me she doesn't believe me at all. "He was naked in my bed, Liv. And you were snuggled up next to him."

Crap. She saw us. But when? "I wasn't naked," I point out.

Em goes to the fridge and pulls out a jug of orange juice. "Right, but he was."

"What did you do? Peel back the covers and check him out?" I'm grumpy. She's hitting me with stuff I don't want to deal with first thing in the morning.

"No. I saw his shorts on the floor and he'd kicked the comforter off partway. I saw his naked butt." She grinned. "That tells me plenty. So what happened? Did you two have carnal knowledge of each other? You know, s-e-x?"

"Em! Jesus! Don't say things like that." I glare at her, then lower my head to stare at the counter. I have a pounding headache from too much booze.

"Well? Did you?" Em shuts the fridge and turns to face me, the orange juice still clutched in her hand. "How was it? Dustin has nice hands. Long fingers."

I lift my head and gape at her. "What do you mean?"

"You don't notice things like that? You should. Boys with good hands…mmm." She shivers, like that's the only thing she wants in this world. "Does he know what to do with them?"

I say nothing. How can I? To deny it would be a lie.

"Your silence is confirmation. You two got busy in *my* bed." She slaps the edge of the counter. There's a vicious gleam in her eyes and I almost worry she's mad at me. "Dirty girl."

"Shut up. Where were *you* last night?"

The grin on her face is a tell-all. "With Ryan," she says slowly, then sighs. "It was…magical."

I'm tempted to tell her all the things he said to me yesterday, but I keep my mouth shut. "Is he still here?"

"No, he had to get home." She uncaps the orange juice and pours a cup for herself, and then a cup for me. "I was going to sleep in my bed but saw it was otherwise occupied."

"I'm sorry." I take the orange juice she offers me and sip from it, wishing I had coffee. I'll go to Starbucks in a bit and grab myself something. I need to feel like a functioning human being first before I leave, though. "I think Dustin is still sleeping."

"Aw, isn't that adorable?" There's an edge to her tone, one that says maybe she doesn't find his crashing out in her bed that adorable after all.

"I don't know what to think about us. About me and Dustin," I clarify when Em looks at me strangely. "Since I've come home, it's been weird between us."

"Uh huh." Em nods. "Want me to talk to him? Ask how he feels about you and report back?"

"Oh, I don't know..." My voice drifts. I love that she's offering but I'm scared that she might mess it up? That's mean of me to think, but I can't help it.

"I want to help." She smiles. "So let me help."

Dustin chooses that particular moment to shuffle into the kitchen, his bedhead at epic levels, clad in only those maddening swim trunks. Dustin has a nice body. He's lean, with broad shoulders and a long torso.

My gaze drops to his hands. His long fingers, the wide palms. He reaches for me and I watch as he clamps my shoulder and drops a kiss to my cheek before sitting on the stool next to mine.

"Mornin'." His voice is extra deep and scratchy, and he clears his throat. "No coffee?"

"If you want coffee, I suggest you head to Starbucks," Em says snidely.

Dustin's brows rise "Well, excuse me. What crawled up your butt this morning?"

"God, you're so gross. And if you really want to know, *you* did." Em doesn't bother offering him a glass of orange juice. She storms out of the kitchen instead, calling over her shoulder, "I'm taking a shower," as she leaves.

We look at each other the moment she's gone, our eyes wide. "What's her problem?" he asks.

"I don't know. But I'm pretty sure her and Ryan had sex last night." I hate that's the first thing that comes out of my mouth. It's like I can't help it. Why is she in such a snit if that did really happen? She planned on wearing special undies and everything. Now she's all crabby.

It makes no sense.

Dustin's dark brows rise even higher. "Really? I didn't think he was trying to tap that."

"Guys are such pigs," I mutter, shoving his shoulder. I grab my glass, but he snatches it out of my hand, taking a long drink. "Hey!"

"That's what you get for lumping me in with all the rest of them." He hands me back the glass, his gaze warm. "You okay?"

I know what he's asking. And I appreciate that he's so thoughtful.

"I'm fine," I tell him, offering a reassuring smile. "How about you?"

"Freaking awesome." He leans in and delivers a smacking kiss to my lips. "Wanna go grab breakfast?"

"And leave Em alone? We should wait for her to finish her shower first." She'll be mad. I know she will. But shit, breakfast does sound good. There's nothing here but a bowl of stale potato chips and orange juice. I don't even think there's any cereal. The house is pretty much empty of everything.

"Screw that. I've been with her all summer. I need an Emily break." He reaches out and touches my hair, tucking a loose strand behind my ear. "I want to have some time with you alone so we can really catch up."

"I don't have much to tell you. Just the usual. Christine's lame. My dad was never around. Dakota and Sierra were even more annoying than usual." I shrug, noticing the way he's looking at me. Like he really cares. Like he wishes he could take all of my problems and conquer them.

I bet he would if he could. I've known him for what feels like forever. Longer than Em and I have been friends. We grew up together in this neighborhood and he chose me as his best friend. When Em came along, I chose her. We all three chose each other.

So why does he want to get away from her?

"Are you two in a fight or something?" I ask. When he frowns at me, I clarify, "You and Em."

"She's being weird. I think it's that Ryan guy." Dustin scowls. "I don't like him."

"Why not?" Unease slips down my spine. I don't particularly like Ryan either. He's funny and awful and sexy and arrogant, yet…I'm drawn to him.

It makes no sense.

"He's a know-it-all. Thinks pretty highly of himself. You can just tell. I'm sure once school starts he'll ditch us all for the popular crowd."

"Dustin. My friend. My love. We *are* the popular crowd," I tell him in all seriousness, then shove his shoulder, which is pointless. The boy has muscles. He's lean and fast, with the body of an athlete. He's become well known because of his basketball skills and while we're not total losers, we're not super-popular either. "Seriously, why would he ditch us?"

"He's a jock. Played football at his old school. He just started going to practice here." He grimaces. "I hear he's good."

Of course he plays football. Of course he's good at it. He seems untouchable. He'll start school and see all the other girls there and forget all about us…

Ryan will become a football god and break Em's heart. I'll console her with ice cream and '90s movie night and everything will be right in our world. Dustin will want to hang out with us and we'll get drunk on his dad's liquor stash because his parents are never home on a Friday night. They always go out.

It'll be like old times.

"Let's get out of here." He leans in to kiss me again and I dodge him, leaping to my feet and waving a hand at the oversized T-shirt I'm wearing.

"I need to change." I point at him. "So do you."

"I think I have another T-shirt around here somewhere since you're wearing mine." He glances at the mess surrounding us and makes a face before looking at me. "We'll need to help her with this, huh."

"You know it."

Dustin sighs. Runs a hand through his dark hair and messes it up thoroughly. He looks cute like that. For one quick moment, I can forget all about my worry and imagine what it would be like if we were really together.

It would be…nice. I have no doubt Dustin would make a great boyfriend. He's attentive. Caring. Good-looking. A great kisser. Smart. Funny. He makes me laugh.

I want that. I want *him*.

I'm just having a hard time telling him.

"We should wait for her," I suggest, my voice quiet. "We can change while we wait and then all three of us can go to breakfast. Then we'll come back and clean up the house."

"Good idea. I guess." He smiles, his eyes crinkling at the corners. "You always have good ideas, Livvy."

That's not really true.

But I'm not going to correct him.

chapter eight

We end up at a breakfast house not far from our neighborhood, a place I remember going to all the time when I was a kid and my parents and I were still a happy little family unit. We'd go every Saturday morning and I always got the chocolate chip pancakes since they came with a whipped cream face and a cherry nose.

But that was kid's stuff. My past life. I'm different now. Since coming home I *feel* different and I think a lot of it has to do with what happened last night. Between Em and I. Dustin and I.

Even Ryan and I.

If my best friend ever found out how Ryan touched me, what he said to me...

I think she'd hate me forever.

Em's so focused on her phone she doesn't realize the waitress is waiting for her order after Dustin and I already gave ours. I kick her under the table and she glares as I flick my head toward the waitress.

"Oh." Em sits up straighter and sets her phone on the table. "What did you get?" she asks me.

"Bacon, eggs and hash browns. Sourdough toast," I tell her.

"I'll have the French toast." Em smiles at the waitress as she hands over the menu.

"Bacon or sausage?"

"Sausage."

"Didn't you get enough sausage last night?" Dustin asks, his tone completely innocent.

Em narrows her eyes and we all forget about the waitress as she huffs away. "You're disgusting."

"Seriously, Em," I say quietly, gaining her attention. "What happened with you and Ryan?"

She remains silent, her phone buzzing and she picks it up, types out a quick text.

"We're all friends here," Dustin says when she still hasn't answered. "We used to tell each other everything."

The look she sends both of us is full of irritation. And...hurt? "Funny, how some of us are *still* keeping secrets."

Dustin tilts his head so he's staring at the table, like he can't face her. I remain still, fighting the war inside me. I forgot to mention to Dustin that I told Em about us. I hope he won't be mad.

Her expression turns incredulous. "So you two are really together now? After everything we've been through?"

"No," I say just as Dustin says, "Yes."

Our heads swivel in tandem as we both stare at each other. It's his turn to have eyes full of hurt. I didn't mean to deny we're together, but we're not really together. We haven't made it official.

Yet.

"Which is it then?" Em's tone is snide. "Are you with Liv or not, Dustin?"

I frown, my gaze going to her. Why does she sound...jealous? And why are we having this very personal conversation in the middle of a crowded restaurant?

"Keep your voice down, Em. Jesus," Dustin says.

"I deserve to know the truth." Em lifts her chin, her expression completely unreadable. "I'm the one who's going to get left out of this special little relationship if you two turn into boyfriend and girlfriend, so at least tell me what's going on."

"You kind of sound like a jealous bitch," Dustin mutters.

"I don't have any reason to be jealous." Em's brows shoot up. "Do I, Dustin?"

"Oh my God, what is wrong with you two?" I glare at the both of them. "Stop fighting. What happened is no big deal."

"Maybe to you," Dustin retorts.

"Dustin, come on." I reach out, touch his hand, but he snatches it away like I'm made of fire and I just burned him. "I don't want to fight."

"I don't either," he says, though he won't look at me.

"You two lovebirds are gag-inducing." I watch as Em picks up her phone and starts texting once more. She can feel my gaze on her and finally glances up, her expression daring me to defy her I guess. "What? You talk in code and kept your so-called relationship a secret. I'm out of the loop yet again. I always am when it comes to you two."

"Em."

She's focused on her phone once again, her teeth sinking into her lower lip like she's trying to contain a smile from spreading across her face. All around us regular life is happening. Families crowded into booths, their kids babbling nonsense. I hear a baby cry, an older woman laugh uproariously, a waitress asking someone if they want more coffee. I look around, the tension at our table palpable in this sea of normalcy, and I hate it.

I want normalcy. Crave it.

"We're going to help you clean up the house after breakfast," I tell Em, desperate to change the subject. "When are your parents back?"

"Tomorrow night." She sighs and grabs her coffee, taking a big gulp. "They're going to kill me."

"No, they won't. They won't even know you had anyone over," I say firmly, gently nudging Dustin's side with my elbow. "Right D?"

"Right." He nods. Doesn't look at either of us. He's still upset with me, I suppose, studying his phone, his brows furrowed, his other hand clutched around the sweating plastic cup from Starbucks he picked up on our way to the restaurant. They let him come in with the Frappuccino when I told him they'd probably make him throw it away.

The triumphant smile he'd given me when he'd strutted into the restaurant had been…cute. Sweet. Made me smile in return and laugh.

None of us are smiling or laughing right now. And it sucks.

"Hey."

A familiar voice makes all three of us lift our heads to find Ryan standing in front of our table. He's got a giant grin on his face, his golden brown hair damp, and he's wearing a white T-shirt and black basketball shorts. His gaze meets mine and darkens the slightest bit as he drinks me in.

I feel that look all the way down to my toes.

"Ryan!" Em leaps from her seat and wraps him up in a full-body hug. He returns it, one hand briefly skimming her butt as he kisses her cheek before she takes his hand and pulls him into the booth with her. "I invited him to breakfast. Hope you don't mind," she tells us, her tone defiant. As if she wants us to tell her we absolutely one hundred percent *do* mind.

"No, of course we don't," I say, my voice a little too high. A little too bright.

Dustin says nothing at all.

THE PLAN AFTER breakfast was for us to head back over to Em's house in Dustin's Jeep so we could start the cleanup process. But Ryan's thrown a wrench into the mix, since Em wants to ride with him. Meaning she's forcing me to have to ride with Dustin.

Alone.

Which is good, because I need to clear the air and apologize for denying that we're together. Maybe that'll give him the opportunity to ask me to be his girlfriend and I'll say yes. Right?

Right?

It's what I want. I know it's what I want. Though once we agree we're dating, that'll change our entire relationship.

"You have a phone charger in your car, right?" Em asks Ryan as we stand in the parking lot.

"Nope." He shrugs. "Why, you need one?"

Em nods, glancing over at Dustin. "I know you have one."

"I do," he agrees, his expression reluctant. Like he doesn't want to deal with Em.

Not that I can blame him.

"Then I guess we'll all three ride back together and you can follow us, Ryan," Em says.

His expression turns into mock pouting. He even purses his lips, which is, like, the cutest thing ever. "Maybe I don't want to ride alone."

"Aw." Em wraps her arms around his middle and squeezes him. "It's only a five-minute ride."

"I know." His pout vanishes and his gaze clashes with mine. "Maybe Livvy can ride with me."

"Oh, I don't think…" I start, but Em cuts me off as she pulls away from Ryan.

"Perfect! And I can ride with Dustin and charge my phone." She sends me a meaningful look before she glances at her phone, but now it's her turn to pout. "Damn it. It just died."

That meaningful look means she's going to talk to him about me. My stomach immediately starts twisting in knots, making me regret I ate so much at breakfast.

"Come on. Let's go," Dustin says, glaring at me as he grabs hold of Em's hand and drags her to his car.

Leaving Ryan and I standing in the parking lot together.

"You look scared," he says the moment they're out of earshot.

Ugh. I hate how he does this sort of thing. "You don't scare me."

He starts walking toward me, his body brushing against mine as he passes. "Maybe I should," he murmurs. "Come on."

I turn and follow after him, surprised when he whips out a keyless remote and hits the button, a brand-new white BMW's taillights flashing when it unlocks. The car is so new it doesn't even have plates yet.

And it's gorgeous.

Expensive.

"This is yours?" I ask as he opens the passenger-side door for me.

Ryan waves a gallant hand toward the open door. "No. I'm stealing it." He rolls his eyes as I draw closer. "Yeah, it's mine. Get in."

I climb inside, overwhelmed by that new car smell. The black leather seats are butter-soft, the scent strong and rich as it envelops me, and my mouth goes dry when he slides into the driver's seat, his hands reaching for the steering wheel.

Who knew a guy climbing into his car could be so sexy?

"This is really nice," I say as I lean forward and run my hand over the dash.

"It's all right." He starts the car, the engine rumbling to life, and I lean back, trying my best to discreetly watch him as he drives.

He moves with a confidence I've never seen in any guy I know before. Like he's in full command of the car, the space, the parking lot, the road. It all belongs to him and we're just lucky enough to get to cruise along for the ride.

My gaze drops to the cup holders in the center console and I spot the iPhone charger cord resting there. "You lied," I say incredulously.

He sends me a confused look. "What about?"

"You have a charger." I hold it up, let the white cord dangle from my fingers.

Ryan's face breaks out into a devastating grin. "So I did. Anything to get you alone with me in my car."

I drop the cord back into the cup holder and turn away from him, my mind swirling. I can't believe he lied to Em.

I also can't believe he wanted to get me alone.

"You didn't want to ride with me," he says once he navigates out of the parking lot.

"It's not that, it's just…" I watch him, unsure of what to say next.

He sends me a quick look. "What?"

"You and Em." I hesitate for a moment. "I know you're together."

"Just because we messed around last night doesn't mean we're together. It was nothing."

"You shouldn't flirt with me," I remind him.

"What's the big deal? It's just a little harmless flirting between… friends." His lips twitch in the corners and I know he wants to laugh.

The jerk.

"I'm not going to get into the middle of you two," I say.

"There's nothing to get in the middle of."

I'm shocked. He has to be lying. Or he cares way less than Em does about what they're doing. "So what are you two exactly?"

"Friends?" He sends me another cryptic look as he gently presses the brakes. We come to a stop at a streetlight, Dustin's black Jeep is up ahead of us. "Isn't that what you and Dustin are?"

"Well, yeah." I shrug, not wanting to talk about what Dustin and I are.

"And you two messed around last night, right?"

God. Is he fishing for information or does he actually know? "Nothing happened," I mumble, turning my face away so I can stare out the passenger-side window.

He chuckles. "Liar," he murmurs just before I feel his fingers dance across the top of my thigh. I suck in a breath, my gaze meeting his once more, and he's smiling, a freaking devil's smile curving his lips. "You just don't want to admit you got naked with Dustin."

My mouth drops open. The way he describes things…it's like he was actually there. Last night was the first time I actually got naked with Dustin. How does Ryan know this? Or is he just assuming?

"Your face says it all." He squeezes my knee, his palm hot against my skin before he releases me. "How was it? Did he make you come?"

"Stop," I gasp, blown away he would say these things. It was bad enough, what Dustin said to me last night. I'm not comfortable talking about this sort of stuff in the middle of the day in Ryan's car, let alone last night after an intimate moment with Dustin.

"I'm guessing he didn't." Ryan shakes his head and hits the gas when the light turns green and the traffic starts to move. "Too bad. Sexual frustration is the worst."

"Like you know anything about it," I retort, crossing my arms in front of my chest like some sort of shield against his crazy questions and statements.

But it doesn't work. They just keep coming.

"Oh, I know *everything* about it. I'm totally sexually frustrated right now. At this very moment."

"Give me a break." I roll my eyes.

"It's true." Ryan presses a button and the window slides down, letting in warm summer air. He looks over at me, the wind blowing his hair into his eyes. He looks gorgeous, those green eyes of his pinning me in place. "And it's all because of you."

"You are unreal." I start to laugh, shaking my head. I don't believe him. Not at all. He's full of shit. Just saying things to try and get a rise out of me or something. "You were just with Em last night."

"Yeah. So? I mean, it was great and all, but she's not you." The sly smile stretching his perfect lips makes me want to punch him.

I uncurl my arms and raise them in the air, like he just said the most ridiculous thing ever, which he did. "You're insane."

"For you."

"You just met me."

"Yeah, but the attraction was there from the very start." He flicks on his blinker, turning right as he follows behind Dustin. "I shook your hand and I think you electrified me. Short-circuited my brain."

"Shut. Up."

"Dead serious." A hesitation. "You didn't feel it?" His voice softens and I look at him, hold my breath when he reaches out and yet again touches my thigh with gentle fingers. I jerk my leg away from his hand. "I did. I looked into your eyes and thought, 'This girl is gorgeous. I want her.' But then I saw you with Dustin and figured I didn't have a chance."

I'm breathless. Wordless. He can't mean it.

"All I've heard from Em all summer is Livvy this and Livvy that. She puts you on a pedestal, you know. You're her best friend."

"She's my best friend too," I say quietly. "That's why..."

"It was nothing." He reaches out and squeezes my knee, and this time I don't pull away. It's like I can't. "Trust me. Em knows what's up. It's a summer thing."

"Whatever. Maybe you should make that clearer to her."

Ryan removes his hand from my leg as he pulls in front of Em's house and shuts off the engine, turning to look at me. "I may have been with Em last night, but I wanted it to be you."

"You're ridiculous." Please. He's full of it. He has to be. "I don't believe you."

He shrugs. "Believe what you want. It's true. And I'm going to prove it to you."

My hands are shaking as I reach for my tiny purse and sling the strap over my shoulder. I grip the door handle, ready to burst free from the car when he grabs my wrist, stopping me.

I turn to look at him, silent. Waiting.

"She means nothing to me," he says, his expression dead serious.

I make a face. "She should. You slept with her last night. Had sex with her."

"We didn't have sex. We really didn't do anything. She was too drunk and passed out the minute her head hit the mattress." He smiles. "But we're friends. Like you and Dustin." He pauses. "You get it, right?"

Slowly I nod, tug my wrist out of his grip. I'm shocked by his admission but I try my hardest to play it cool. "I get it." I start to climb out of the car and then bend down as I lean against the door. "Oh, and by the way..."

"Yeah?"

"You were wrong. Dustin did make me come." I smirk at him. "Just thought you should know that."

It feels really good to see that stunned expression on Ryan's face.

Feels even better to shut the door before he gets a chance to say anything else.

chapter nine

"Our last weekend of freedom," Em sing-songs as she floats past me in the pool. She's sprawled out on a bright yellow inflatable lounge chair, her golden skin glistening from all the suntan lotion she slathered on earlier. Guess she gave up on sunblock.

Me? I've got on SPF 50 and I'm wearing a hat that belongs to Em while I float on the giant ring that looks like a chocolate donut with sprinkles. "I don't want to go back to school."

"You so do." She splashes me with water, her Ray-Ban aviator sunglasses hiding her eyes, but I know they're flashing at me. "You can't wait to strut your stuff in front of the boys and show off your summer tan."

"Right. Me, tan?" I glance at my body. I do have tan lines, but they're faint. All I see are the new freckles that sprouted up. "Give me a break."

"You're looking so gorgeous right now, Liv. I see the way the boys stare at you."

"Like who?" The early afternoon sun is hot and I close my eyes, my cheap sunglasses I got at Target not enough to ward off the intense glare. It's August and hot as hell and we're counting down the days until we have to be back in school on Tuesday.

Em's parents came back two nights ago and they never said a word about the condition of the house. That's because we worked on it for hours, especially Dustin and me. The kitchen was the absolute worst and we spent most of our time in there. Eventually Ryan and Em took off, claiming they were going to clean her parents' bedroom, but they shut and locked the door and Dustin and I immediately knew what they were up to.

It pissed me off. That Ryan could flirt with me, say such crazy as hell things to me and then go off and bang Em behind closed doors.

What an asshole.

This was my first time hanging out with Em after we cleaned her house, and she's acting so weird. She begged me to come over, admitting the minute I walked into her bedroom that she needed to get high. We passed a joint between us for a couple of minutes, but I never really took a big puff. I didn't feel like getting wasted.

Clearly getting wasted was on Em's Saturday to-do list.

"Liv. I need to know something."

Her tone is deathly serious and I go tense, scared of what she might ask me. If it's about Ryan I'm unsure what I should tell her. Hopefully they'll end it soon and I won't have to tell her anything. Though I should. She's my best friend. I'd want to know if Dustin was acting flirty with other girls.

Even if he doesn't officially belong to me.

"What do you want to know?"

She lifts her sunglasses, her dark blue eyes staring right at me. "You and Dustin. What's going on?"

I sigh with relief. Dustin I can handle. Ryan, I can't. "Well, like I said. We messed around a few times before I left for my dad's." I let my fingers drift in the water, swirling them back and forth.

Her brows go up. "Define messing around."

"We didn't have sex, but…" I wave a hand and she giggles.

"You've touched his dick."

"Stop." I slap my hands on my cheeks.

"You're so funny. What's the big deal?" She splashes me again and I splash her back. "Did you suck it?"

"No! *God.*" I splash her even harder and she laughs, rolling off the inflatable lounger and dunking under the water, her glasses sliding off her head.

I sink under the donut and dive down, snatching her floating glasses up just before they hit the bottom and then I swim to the top, my head breaking the surface just as Em's does too.

We're facing each other, the water dripping over our faces, my sunglasses forgotten but hers clutched in my fingers. "Here," I say, handing them over.

Em takes them. "Thanks."

We tread water as I try to catch my breath and I can feel her looking at me, her gaze searching for…what? I don't know. It's weird. "You had sex with Ryan," I finally say. Wondering if she'll deny or confirm.

She shrugs. "Sort of."

That was the most vague answer ever. "You want details yet you won't give me any?"

"You'll freak out if I give you details." The smile on her face is wicked. "Like, I could tell you he's huge. And he knows what he's doing with his fingers. And his tongue."

"Stop," I whisper, and she laughs.

"See? You definitely don't want details." Her smile fades, as does the laughter. "I don't think he likes me, though."

"What do you mean?"

"Not like you like me. Or Dustin." She presses her lips together, like she wants to say something else, but she doesn't. "Where is Dustin anyway?"

"Out of town with his parents." And he was so pissed about it too. He texted me saying they planned a weekend family trip without telling him and he didn't want to go.

Em blinks rapidly, looking surprised. And hurt. "He didn't tell me that."

"Em..." I can tell she's mad, though I don't really get why. She's been acting weird about Dustin and I since I came home.

"No. Don't make excuses for him. It's like he forgets all about me when you come back home. It sucks." She turns away from me and starts to swim, her lithe arms cutting through the water with precise strokes. I follow after her, irritated by her changing moods, her irrational anger toward me and Dustin and the fact that lately she always has to get high to function.

I don't like it.

The second we hit the shallow end I stand, grabbing hold of her foot and stopping her progress. She swings around, her body making a big wave, and she lands on her feet, shoving her hair away from her face while glaring at me. "What's wrong with you?" I ask.

"Nothing," she bites out, thrusting her chest forward. The black bikini she's wearing barely covers her boobs and her nipples are hard. I can see them strain against the fabric.

Why I notice this, I don't know, but it's like she wants me to see. She is being so weird lately. I don't get it.

"Did you talk to Dustin? In the car that one day?" I ask. I never did find out what she said.

"Not really." She shrugs. "He wasn't very…responsive." There's a sneer curling her lips.

"Are you jealous of my relationship with Dustin? Because don't be. If we get together, I promise we won't neglect you," I tell her.

She laughs, but it's sad. "Oh, that sounds familiar."

I frown. "What are you talking about?"

"Just…" She shakes her head. "Never mind. I don't want to talk about it."

"No. I think we do need to talk about it." I step closer to her, about to reach out and grab her arm when I hear a familiar male voice.

"Please, *please* tell me you two are about to make out."

Ugh. Ryan.

Em's mood shifts yet again. "Who let you in?" she coos as she bats her eyelashes at him, her voice sickeningly sweet.

He kneels down and rests his elbows on his bent knees, smiling at the both of us. "Your parents. They'd freak out if they knew what I've done to their daughter in their bed."

"You are so bad," Em says, splashing him.

I'm disgusted. If Dustin had said that, Em would've called him an awful name. Ryan says it—and what he says is freaking rude but true— and she acts like it's the cutest thing ever.

Ryan rises to his feet and pulls his T-shirt off, tossing it on a nearby chair. His chest is like a work of art and his abs…render me speechless. I try my best not to stare at him. "It's damn hot out here."

"You know, I didn't invite you over," Em says as he walks along the pool's edge, heading straight for the diving board.

"And you know your day is made whenever I show up." He grins, hops onto the diving board and goes to stand on the very edge.

"Maybe I was having an intimate swim with my very best friend,"

Em continues.

"Ooh, that sounds dirty." Ryan laughs, his gaze meeting mine. "Now I'm *really* glad I came over."

I say nothing. How can I? I don't want to give myself away and I don't want to piss Em off. Right now he's her golden boy.

So I have to stay silent and deal with them together. He'll show his true colors eventually and she'll figure out he's not the one for her.

He's a total douche.

A sexy douche, but still.

"Hey, show Liv your cannonball," Em calls.

Ryan bounces a little, the board dipping from his weight. "She won't be impressed. Will you, Livvy?"

He's such an ass. I shake my head once. "Nope."

Em whirls around. "Liv," she hisses.

I shrug. "He's so cocky."

"He has *reason* to be cocky. Trust me." She turns and cups her hands around her mouth. "Show me what you got, sexy boyfriend!"

Her vague reference to *Sixteen Candles* will not make me smile.

Ryan jumps on the edge of the diving board, gaining height, gaining momentum. I watch, trying to fight my fascination but it's no use.

He's gorgeous. Everything he does appears effortless, whether he's driving his beautiful, expensive car or hopping on a diving board with that perfect body of his. Or smirking at me while saying the most inappropriate stuff ever, it all just seems to come so easy to him.

And when he finally hops off the diving board, executing the most perfect dive in the history of teenage kind, his body slicing into the water with hardly a sound, barely a ripple in the water, I tell myself I'm going to have to stay strong.

Withstanding Ryan might end up being the death of me.

chapter ten

Em's parents went out to dinner, leaving the three of us alone in the house with money for pizza delivery. The minute their car pulled out of the driveway, Em dashes off to raid their liquor stash and Ryan runs out to his car, walking back into the house with a giant smile and a joint pinched between his fingers.

"Who's ready for a smoke?" He looks right at me, his gaze so intense it's like he can see deep inside. All of my secrets, all of my fears.

I shake my head. "No thanks."

The smile falters. "You're no fun."

"Aren't you supposed to stay clean, considering you're on the football team?"

"Drug tests already happened. I'm good." He has a lighter in his hand too and his thumb flicks against it. Once. Twice. Until finally the flame is lit and he holds the end of the joint over it until a tendril of smoke rises. "I'm celebrating tonight."

"You're celebrating a clean drug test by smoking pot?" My brows go up and my tone is full on judgmental, but I don't care. "That's smart."

"You don't get it, do you?" He moves closer to me, the both of us seemingly alone since Em is in the giant walk-in pantry looking for liquor bottles. My hands grip the edge of the cool marble countertop and he reaches out, his index finger sliding across my knuckles in a feather-light touch. "I'm celebrating the fact that I get to spend my Saturday night with you, Livvy."

My fingers tighten around the thick marble. I refuse to look up at him. "Don't start this again."

"Don't start what?" His tone is innocent and he removes his finger from my hand. I immediately miss his touch, which is so incredibly pitiful. "You know how I feel about you."

It's bullshit, I want to say, but I don't. I think he's a liar. I think he's totally playing me to…what? Make Em jealous? Drive her insane? Drive *me* insane? "I also know how you feel about Em. You need to leave me out of it."

"You guys like whiskey?" Em calls from inside the pantry.

"No," I yell in reply.

"Damn it," I hear her mutter, and I can tell she's still rifling through the bottles. They clank against each other and I wince, hoping she doesn't drop one.

Ryan says nothing. Just watches me with those green, green eyes, his mouth tilted upward at the corners, appearing as if he has a secret.

In a way, I guess he does.

"You staying the night?" he asks, his voice soft.

I nod.

"Gonna sleep in Em's bed?"

I frown.

"What do you girls do when you're in bed together, hmm?" He

tucks a strand of hair behind my ear, tracing the rounded edge.

"Not what you're thinking," I say snidely as I move away from him, unsure where he's going with this.

"How do you know what I'm thinking?" He touches my cheek. My chin. Places his thumb in the center of my bottom lip and gently tugs until it releases. "You have cock-sucking lips."

I jerk away from him. "You are such an asshole."

His eyes warm, as if he enjoys me calling him names. "It's true. Big lips look especially good wrapped around my…"

"I found gin!" Em emerges from the pantry triumphant in her discovery, the nearly full bottle of gin gripped in her hand as she holds it above her head.

"Got any tonic to go with it?" Ryan asks.

"Oh." She sets the bottle on the counter and hurries back over to the pantry. "Let me check."

The moment she disappears from view, he's turning toward me. Touching me, his hand on my arm, his fingers skimming down, stopping at my wrist. I move away from him, irritated that he thinks he can get away with this. I wish like crazy that Dustin were here. He'd be a good distraction. Protection.

My shield against the potency that is Ryan.

Ugh, that I even think he's potent is so freaking annoying.

"You can call me as many names as you want and try to get away from me, but it's going to happen," he says, his tone assured. Arrogant.

"What's going to happen?" I ask as I go to the sink and turn on the water, pushing the lever to hot. I wash my hands vigorously, scrubbing them like I'm about to go into surgery. Like I can wash away his touch with a few pumps of antibacterial foaming soap.

Do I really want that though? Or am I trying to convince myself?

He stops so he's standing right next to me, his head bent, his mouth close to my ear. "You and me."

His lips brush my temple, and then like a ghost...

Ryan's gone. Barging into the pantry and telling Em that she's blind, there's a bottle of tonic on the top shelf.

I just scrub my hands harder, but no matter how much I try, I can't wash away his touch. His words.

His everything.

"I'M SCARED, LIVVY." Em's voice trembles in the darkness and I blink my eyes open. I'd just about drifted off when she spoke and I'm lying on my back, staring up at the ceiling.

We're in her bed. We've been here for a while, at least an hour, maybe more. Ryan finally left and I'd never felt so relieved. The tension ran high the entire night. We gave up on the gin when we found better stuff and ended up drinking vodka and Sprite. I got a little buzzed. We watched a movie on Cinemax that was basically soft porn and I left the two of them in the living room, not even bothering to say good night.

I figured they would do it on the couch. Figured Em's parents wouldn't come home until late, and I was right. I stayed up in her room and listened to music with my ear buds, scrolling through Instagram until I got sick of seeing photos of everyone having a good time during their last weekend of the summer before school begins.

I miss Dustin. I wish he was here with us. With me.

"Why are you scared?" I finally ask.

She sighs, the sound so forlorn I feel sorry for her. Sort of. She is, after all, the lucky bitch who lives in a gorgeous house, has her own car, a pool, money, all the clothes she could ever want, parents who let her do whatever she wants and a hot guy who's into her.

Oh, and who also claims to be into me.

This is so messed up.

"School is going to start and everything's going to change."

"No it's not," I say.

Em turns and I do too so that we're facing each other. I can see her eyes glittering in the dim light. She's watching me so carefully, in that assessing way she has. "It is. Everything's changing. Can't you feel it?"

"No." I'm lying. I can feel a shift, but I blamed it on the weirdness between Dustin and me. The weirdness between Ryan and me, too.

"Starting our senior year, planning for our future, for college. We have to take SATs and ACTs and pick our majors and all that crap. Plus there are the boys." She ticks those items off like a list. "That's what's messing everything up."

"We won't let any of that mess everything up," I reassure her. "As long as we don't change, everything stays the same, right. We can study for the SATs together. Pick out the same college, live together in the dorms. It'll be perfect."

Em touches my cheek, her hand sliding down to cup the side of my neck. "You're so funny, Livvy. Don't you see? We've changed the most." When I remain quiet, she continues, "You and Dustin together. I don't know what to think about that."

"There's nothing to think about," I say.

She stares, silent, her fingers curling into my neck, her nails scraping my skin. I wince and pull away from her. "Is it that easy to dismiss him?"

"He's my friend," I say, trying to reassure her. "Just like you're my friend."

"So you put me equal with Dustin." Em laughs, the sound soft. "I find that hard to believe."

"I put you above Dustin." The words fall from my lips so easily, but they're a lie. Dustin has always come first. I've known him longer and we have a deeper history. Not having him around this weekend makes me want him around, despite my worry over what's happened between us.

How much we've changed.

I guess Em is right.

"Wow, I can't believe I rate so high." She pulls me into her arms and holds me close, shifting so her head is nuzzled between my neck and my shoulder, her mouth moving against my skin. "I love you, Livvy. So much. Don't ever leave me."

"I won't," I tell her as I kiss the top of her head.

"Don't ever change," she murmurs.

That's a promise I can't make, no matter how much I want to.

chapter eleven

D ustin drives me to school on our first day back because it's a tradition—we always go to school together on the first day. Though Em wasn't ready yet so she didn't go with us. There was no way I would be late on our first day of senior year. Em may not give a shit, but I do.

"Looking good," Dustin says as I walk toward his Jeep Wrangler, my backpack slung over my shoulder. By day's end it'll be full of books and my back will be aching.

I do a twirl, showing off my outfit even though I shouldn't. I'm wearing denim shorts and a cute flow-y cream-and-lace top. Very Coachella, which is still a look to strive for. "You like?" I ask him.

His gaze is warm, appreciative as he leans out his car window. "I freaking love."

Dustin's use of the word *love* takes all the steam out of me and my smile fades. I'm nervous as I walk around his car and get in on the passenger side, slamming the door behind me and letting my backpack drop to the floorboard.

"Why the long face?" he asks as he pulls out onto the road.

"It was hard getting up this morning so early." I stare out the window, taking in my neighborhood, each house as familiar to me as breathing. We go past Em's place and her car is still parked in the front…

And Ryan's is parked behind it.

I face forward, my mind awhirl. So he's taking her to school? That's serious. That doesn't say "just friends". Though Dustin is taking me to school too, so maybe that doesn't say just friends either. Of course, we've been going to school together on the first day—on pretty much every day—since I can remember, so maybe I'm just jumping to conclusions.

"Olivia." Only Dustin says my full name, beyond teachers and my parents. "Did you hear me?"

Shaking my head, I focus on him, smiling brightly. "Sorry. I was thinking. What did you say?"

"I asked if you wanted to get together after school and come to my house." He pauses, his gaze fixed on the road. "My parents won't be there."

He wants to hook up. I know what he's asking. I can tell by the way he won't look at me, the tone of his voice. "Um, I don't know. I might hang out with Em…"

"And Ryan?" His tone is vicious.

Angry.

"Well, probably, if he doesn't have football practice. He's Em's boyfriend, after all," I say, though I don't know if that's necessarily true, from what they both tell me. "You should hang out with us. I think Em wanted to go swimming. It's going to be so hot today." It already was.

"She's having you come over there to be her front, you know. All she really wants is to fuck Ryan," Dustin says.

"Stop talking about them like that," I tell him, my voice low. It's so rude, so...

"What do you want me to say? That they have a *special* relationship?" He sneers. "Give me a break."

"The way you talk about Ryan, it's like you're jealous."

"I've had to deal with his shit all summer. Let's just say I can see right through him," he mutters.

"And what do you see?"

"A prick who uses girls and thinks he's the shit."

I lean back heavily against my seat, staring out the window once more. Dustin's right. Ryan *is* a prick who uses girls and thinks he's the shit.

"So you won't come over."

A weary sigh escapes me. Is it always going to be like this? Me stuck between the two of them and constantly having to choose? "She invited me last night."

"So she comes first."

"Well, you can come over too," I start but he doesn't let me finish.

"I don't want to go over to Em's house and hang out with her and that asshole," he mutters. "I just want to hang out with you."

"I don't get it. Why do you hate him so much?"

"Why do you always want to talk about him?"

I lean back in my seat, shocked by the anger in his tone. "I don't always want to talk about him. But I do want to go over to Em's after school. It's always fun to gossip about everything," I say, my voice small.

"So you're choosing Em over me." He stares straight ahead, never taking his gaze off the road.

"Why does it always have to be a choice? Can't I have you both in my life? Why do things have to change?" I'm not just talking about Em or Ryan. I'm talking about the changes between me and Dustin too.

He sends me a look. "We grow up, we change. It's a part of life."

"Being a grown up means being able to talk rationally and not get jealous over stupid stuff," I mutter, crossing my arms in front of my chest.

"Are you calling me jealous?" he asks incredulously.

"Well, are you?"

Dustin brakes hard and the car swerves wildly to the right as he jerks the steering wheel, cutting off the car behind us. It races by us as he stops on the side of the road, the horn blaring, the driver giving us the finger and yelling obscenities, but I don't even think Dustin notices.

He's too busy staring at me, his expression full of hurt and anger and so much more that I can't even begin to describe. "You're right. I'm jealous. He's a total dick, Livvy. He moved in on Em so fast I got whiplash. And I see the way he looks at you." He hesitates before he adds softly, "And how you look at him."

The pain in his voice, on his face…it makes me feel bad. But I'm also immediately on the defensive. "I don't look at Ryan in any special way."

Do I?

"Do you like him?"

"No, not like that." I shake my head. "Never like—"

He cuts me off by reaching out to grab my hand, and his fingers curl around mine. They're warm, his touch comforting. Dustin is like a cozy blanket I want to wrap myself in when I'm feeling down.

And that's nice. I appreciate cozy. Sometimes, I really *need* cozy.

I frown, the threat of tears pricking the corners of my eyes. No way do I want to cry today. I can't.

"Don't fall under his spell like Em did," he says, his deep voice soft. He squeezes my hand and I meet his gaze. "He'll only hurt you."

My lips part, but I can't speak.

"He's hurting Em right now. Can't you see? He doesn't care about her. And he won't care about you either. Not like I do, Livvy." He brings our linked hands to his mouth and he kisses my knuckles.

"You're talking to me like I'm an idiot," I point out. "I would never make a move on Ryan. Em is my best friend."

"I thought I was your best friend."

Here we go again. I shake my head, feeling like a selfish bitch, but I refuse to have this conversation. Pulling my hand away from his, I look away, not wanting to face him.

"Please, Dustin. Don't do this. Not today. It's the first day of school," I plead.

His frustration and anger suddenly overwhelms the tiny space. "If not today then when, huh? We've been dancing around this for over a year. We've been making out for months, hooking up. I want more. I want…" He clamps his lips shut, his gaze dark as he looks away.

I finally dare to look at him, noting the steely determination of his jaw, his brown eyes turbulent, his hair ruffled by the breeze. He's good-looking—gorgeous, really—and he's *my* Dustin. But I don't want to get together with him like this, when he's so angry. Fighting over Ryan, worried over Em, squabbling over who my real best friend is. This is stupid, and Dustin and I aren't stupid.

Yet we're acting like two jealous idiots who can't figure our shit out.

"What do you want?" I ask softly, selfish enough that I want to hear his answer.

"You," he says, his voice breaking just the slightest bit. Just enough that I can tell. "That's all I've ever wanted. I wanted you to be my first, but…" His voice drifts and he shakes his head firmly. "I wanted us to be each other's first. I want us to finish our senior year together, and maybe even figure out a college to go to. Together."

My heart is cracking wide open yet panic swamps me too. This is exactly what I want, so why am I not answering him? It's just…at this moment, it doesn't feel right. This, how we're coming about it, doesn't feel natural.

It somehow feels…

Wrong.

He plots and plans. It's what he does. And it's like he has our entire lives plotted out for us. That's scary. Maybe I don't want this after all. Nothing against him, but maybe I want a different boy. Maybe I want a lot of different boys. I don't know.

What I do know is that—*oh God*—I'm afraid to tie myself to Dustin. The sudden realization smacks me in the face. He acts like he wants forever and that terrifies me. We're too young. Things can change.

Things always change.

"I-I don't know," I stutter, closing my eyes as the guilt rushes over me. What am I doing?

Why am I messing this up?

He puts the Jeep into drive and pulls away from the curb, saying nothing, and I remain quiet too. Until the silence becomes unbearable and I feel like I'm about to burst out of my skin when we pull into the senior parking lot.

"Don't hate me," I whisper once he parks the car and turns off the engine.

Dustin doesn't look at me. It's like he can't. "I could never hate you, Livvy." He pulls the keys out of the ignition and throws open the driver's side door. "Hope you have a good day."

I climb out of the car, the tears forming in my eyes, my chest so tight I can feel that ache everywhere. "Bye, Dustin." I come way too close to sobbing. Why do those two words feel so final?

The first day of school hasn't even started yet and I'm already trying not to cry.

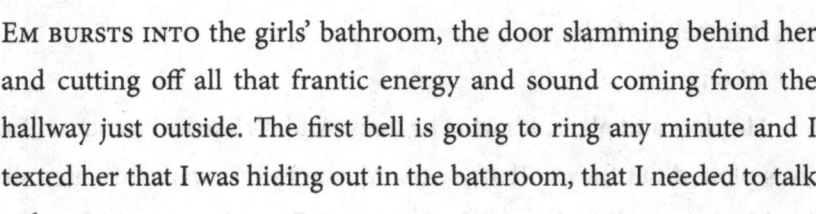

EM BURSTS INTO the girls' bathroom, the door slamming behind her and cutting off all that frantic energy and sound coming from the hallway just outside. The first bell is going to ring any minute and I texted her that I was hiding out in the bathroom, that I needed to talk to her.

"What's wrong?" she asks, sounding winded.

I spill my guts about Dustin, how jealous he acted, how much he hates Ryan and how badly he wants to be with me. My thoughts are a confused, jumbled mess and I swear I'm going to cry, but I don't want to ruin my makeup. I worked on my eyes for twenty minutes this morning. I wasn't about to screw up a good cat eye and decent contouring.

"He'll get over it," she reassures me, drawing me in for a hug, clutching me close before she releases me. She looks amazing wearing a little blue-and-red plaid pleated skirt and a white T-shirt that clings to her chest, the fabric so thin I can see the bra underneath is black. She wears the schoolgirl sexpot look well. "I know he will. He gets over everything and moves on. He always does."

"Maybe he won't," I practically wail, sniffing loudly. Damn it, I cannot cry.

Em goes into a bathroom stall and pulls off a wad of toilet paper, handing it to me. I blow my nose, dab at my eyes and go to the mirror, checking on my makeup. Still looking good.

"He will. He did with me. He forgot all about me," she says, her voice small.

My eyes go wide and I turn to her, tilting my head to the side. It's like my heart is in my throat at her words, the meaning behind them. "What did you just say?"

"I didn't know how to tell you this." She crosses her arms in front of her, in full on defensive mode, her expression contrite. "But when you were gone this summer, Dustin and I...we messed around a couple of times."

"*What?*" My ears are ringing. My head is spinning. It's like I can hear the words she's saying, but I don't understand them. They can't be true. What she's saying—I don't know why she's lying to me.

"It was no big deal at the time, or so I thought. We were drunk and feeling stupid and horny, I guess, and he just...kissed me. Next thing I know we're wrapped around each other and our hands are everywhere. I finally had to shove him off of me."

"You're lying," I accuse. She has to be. I can't compute this.

I don't *want* to compute this.

"I'm not, I swear! It happened a couple of times over the summer, while you were gone. Sometimes it got—out of hand, and he didn't want to stop. I told him we shouldn't, but he kept pushing and I gave in. He even tried to turn it into a serious thing, but I told him no way. I couldn't do it. I couldn't do that to *you*." She grabs my hands and I jerk away from her, backing up, needing the distance. "It's been so hard to keep this from you, Livvy. That's why I was so upset when I found out you were hooking up with him, too! It's like Dustin was bouncing from you to me and back to you again."

I can't believe her. I don't *want* to believe her. Dustin would never do that to me. No way, no how. I just...

I can't wrap my head around it. And she wouldn't do that to me either. My two best friends messing around after he messed around with me?

No, no, no, no.

"He told me not to tell you. Made me swear on it, like he *forced* me to agree to keep this secret. It's been so hard, that's why I didn't talk to you much when you were gone. I felt so terrible. I never want to hurt you. Ever." She hesitates. Winces a little. Why does it feel like such an act? "You're my best friend, Livvy."

Right. Sure. She's carving my heart into tiny little pieces with her words, yet she doesn't want to hurt me. I wish I could hate her. I think I'm in shock.

"So you two hooked up." My voice is flat. My emotions, my heart, my everything is…flat. Unfeeling. A mess. I'm a riotous mess inside and I'm trying my best to keep my cool.

"It was nothing." She waves a hand.

"You and Dustin had—sex." I choke the last word out. It hurts, saying it. So stupid, considering I keep pushing Dustin away, but he gave me that whole "firsts" speech not even an hour ago and now Em is telling me they were together.

Meaning I came second. I might've asked for it by leaving, but he couldn't even wait for me.

"One time. Just…it was only once. To get it over with, you know? Now we're not virgins anymore." Em smiles, but it's fake. I can tell. It doesn't quite reach her eyes, which look frantic. Nervous. "But now I've told you everything and we can move on, right? Put this all behind us." Her lips quiver at the corners, like she's going to what? Cry? Give me a break. "Forget boys. Forget Dustin. It's just the two of us, together. I matter more than he does. You told me that. You *promised*."

"That's before I found out you were two were together," I say, my voice raspy, my stomach roiling. I feel like I could throw up. Just puke up my breakfast along with all the horrible images her words conjure up.

Dustin and her. Together. Dustin kissing Em. Dustin touching Em.

Dustin naked with Em and actually having *sex* with her. Did he do it to her in her bed, like when we were together last?

I close my eyes against the thought and blindly run into a bathroom stall, retching into the toilet.

"Livvy!" Em pushes the door open and I can feel her behind me, her hands going to my hips, then tugging on my hair. I jerk away from her hold, afraid she'll try and help me. I don't want her help. "Oh my God, are you all right?"

"Get out," I gasp, running my hand over my mouth, the taste almost unbearable. I need gum. I need to brush my teeth. I need my mom.

The bell rings, the low, familiar tone loud in the bathroom, but I don't turn around. Don't make to leave.

But I definitely want Em to leave. I'm desperate to get away from her.

"We have to go to class," Em says, her voice quiet.

"Just go," I sob, my stomach pitching and rolling again, and I lean over the toilet, bracing my hands on the edge of the seat as I purge my guts. My stomach cramps and my head swims. My eyes are filled with tears and I don't know if it's because I threw up or because I'm sad.

Devastated.

"I can't leave you here," she says, and I whirl on her, knowing I look like hell, that my makeup, everything is shot to shit, but I don't care. Let her look, let her judge.

"I don't want you here. Leave. Go!"

She flinches, as if every word I hurled at her was a physical blow, and she backs out of the stall, pushing the door open with her butt. "You're mad. I get it. We'll talk later."

"No. You *don't* get it. I never want to talk to you again," I whisper, shaking my head.

"Come on, Livvy. You're making such a big deal about this," she whines, still just inside the stall, the metal door at her back.

"You fucked Dustin!" I scream at her, the tears streaming down my face as my stomach rumbles. I rest my hand over it, wishing it would stop. I don't want to throw up anymore. I want to go to the office and go home. Mom will flip since it's the first day, but I don't care. If you vomit at school, they send you home. It's a guaranteed pass, like a fever.

"It meant nothing. We're just friends fooling around, right? Like you two were. Are. Whatever." She shakes her head, looking about as pissed as I feel. "And you always told me he was just your *friend*. You never wanted more from him. You always told me that!" she yells back.

"It doesn't matter." It's a betrayal, pure and simple. Though how can it be if she didn't know Dustin and I hooked up in the first place?

Whatever. She messed around with him. He played us both.

She's a fool.

But then again, so am I.

chapter twelve

"You sure you're feeling better?" Mom asks as we sit at the table eating breakfast.

Well, she eats. I'm pushing around my yogurt in its cup, the slices of honeydew melon she cut for me a few minutes ago sitting neglected on my plate. I haven't regained my appetite thanks to my stellar first week at school and how I lost my two best friends since they couldn't keep their hands off of each other.

The only bright side is that betrayal is an excellent diet. I've barely eaten anything and I'm guessing I've already lost a few pounds.

"My stomach is still queasy," I tell her, which isn't a lie. I feel sick over everything that's happened. I'm so freaking grateful it's Friday. I can stay home over the weekend and not face everyone at school. Like Em.

And Dustin.

And stupid, irritating Ryan.

I've barely seen Ryan, which is fine with me. Though every time I pass him in the hallway he smirks at me, like we share a naughty secret. He's in my government class, but I always get there early and he arrives just as the bell rings, sitting in the back so I don't have to see him.

I can feel his gaze on me, though, practically burning a hole in my back for the entire period.

It's annoying.

Dustin is in my trig class, but so are a bunch of his friends and he sits with them, sending me hurtful looks every time I catch his eye. I'm so mad at him I'm afraid I might scratch his eyes out. What's crazy is I've never even talked to him about what happened between him and Em.

I don't think I can. I don't want to hear his explanations, his excuses. Just thinking about the two of them together hurts my heart.

And I don't know what to think about that. Or how to handle it.

I have no classes with Em, thank goodness. She's sent me what felt like a billion texts on Tuesday after the bathroom incident, all of them basically saying the same thing.

I'm sorry. I'm sorry. I'm sorry.

Forgive me.

He's nothing. Our friendship is everything to me.

Please talk to me Livvy.

PLEASE!!!!!!

They changed tone when I ignored her.

Answer me.

You can't ignore me forever Liv.

Are you really going to ruin our friendship over a stupid guy?

Really?
FUCK DUSTIN! He's an asshole!
YOU are the asshole for letting him ruin everything!!

I finally had to block her. I felt like a bitch doing it, but I couldn't take the texts anymore.

"Olivia."

I look up, see the scowl on Mom's face, and my stomach clutches with worry. "What?"

"I need to ask you a question." She takes a deep breath, her expression...nervous? Oh, shit. "Your nausea. How you're tired all the time. There's no way you could be *pregnant*, is there?"

"What? *No!*" The word explodes out of me and the relief on her face is obvious. I push back my chair, rise to my feet as I glare at her. "I can't even believe you asked that!"

"You're a seventeen year old girl who's been moody and distant ever since you got back from your father's. Then you complain of nausea and you throw up on the first day of school. I'm sorry if I jumped to conclusions," she says, not sounding sorry at all.

"When would I have got pregnant in the first place, huh? I was at Dad's all summer!"

She shrugs. "Maybe you met a boy in Oregon."

That's freaking laughable. "He keeps me under lock and key there. Most of the time I was stuck hanging out with Christine."

Mom makes a disgusted face. "I didn't know what to think. You've been so distant. And then when you kept throwing up..."

"I'm not pregnant, Mom. Okay? So don't worry about it."

"Are you on birth control? Because you should be. Condoms aren't one hundred percent effective, you know. Maybe you should get on the pill."

I so do not want to be having this conversation right now. My cheeks are on fire hearing Mom talk about condoms and birth control and the pill. "I'm not having sex, Mom, so don't worry."

Her eyes look ready to bug out of her head. "You're a virgin?"

My glare is murderous. "Mom. Please."

"Well, it's just I was having sex at your age." She pauses, takes another deep breath, all while I'm dying because she just said that. I don't want to think about my mom having *sex*. Gross. "Olivia, I want you to know that you can come to me for anything. Anything at all. I don't want us keeping secrets. We never have before. I know we haven't talked much lately because I've been busy with work—"

"And with Fitch," I add like a sniveling little brat.

"Right, and Fitch." She clears her throat. I'm sure she hates me throwing him in her face, but he's there. Wedged right between us. He spends the night at least three times a week, and between him and work, it's like she has no time for me. Which was fine when I first got home and wanted to be with my friends. But this week, I'm hanging out with no one and feeling terribly alone.

I would never say this out loud, but I kind of need my mom. And she's not there for me.

"If I need you, don't worry. I know where to find you." I slam back the rest of my coffee, setting the cup on the table before I grab my backpack off the chair, slinging it over my shoulder. "See ya."

"Have a good day, honey!" she calls after me, the slamming door cutting her off.

I walk through the garage and emerge out into the warm morning. It's been ninety-plus degrees all week and today is no different. I've given up trying to look cute. Now I'm just trying to get through the day before I can hide out in my room for the weekend. I'm wearing a pair of army-green shorts and a white sleeveless T-shirt, with little lace detail around the neck. My thick hair is in a ponytail and I didn't even bother to put any makeup on beyond a quick coat of mascara.

I'm so over my senior year and we're barely a week in.

The school is close to my house, so I'm walking there when I hear a car come up just behind me. The engine slows, its rumbling purr loud in the otherwise quiet morning, and I glance over my shoulder to see a sleek white BMW following me.

And Ryan is in the driver's seat.

Turning away, I increase my steps, not wanting to talk to him. The car pulls up alongside me, and he rolls the passenger-side window down. "Livvy," he calls, his deep, familiar voice making my stomach twist.

"Go away," I tell him, staring straight ahead. If I look at him, something bad will happen. Like my knees will get weak or my heart will trip over itself. He's so good looking and it's like he uses his looks as a weapon. Forget that. He's trouble I don't need.

"Em mentioned you two are fighting." His words make me want to break out into a run, but I don't. I just walk even faster. "Want a ride to school?"

"No thanks." I shake my head.

"You can't ignore me forever."

Watch me. "Go hang out with Em. I'm sure she needs you."

"There's nothing between us. We haven't even talked that much the last few days. Only when I was asking about you."

His words enrage me. I stop walking and he hits the brakes, his car idling. I dare to turn, to look at him, glare at him, hope like hell he can see all the anger and frustration and pure irritation in my gaze. I wish he would leave me out of their supposed discussions. "You always say that yet you two are always together."

"Not anymore. I haven't seen her since Wednesday."

"Big deal."

"Get in the car, Livvy."

I shake my head. Cross my arms in front of my chest. Glancing up, I see another car pass us by.

It's Dustin's Jeep.

My stomach drops into my toes. Someone is with him in the passenger seat. A girl.

It's Em. And they don't even notice us. She's looking over at Dustin, talking animatedly, her hands gesturing wildly in the air.

I feel like I've been sucker punched in the gut.

Growling under my breath, I stalk toward Ryan's car and open the door, practically throwing myself into the passenger seat. I shrug my backpack off my shoulder and hold it in my lap, turning to look at him. "Happy now?" I ask snidely.

"Immensely," he says, his smile wide. Like my crap mood doesn't even bother him. "Shut the door and put your seatbelt on, babe."

Ugh. I should sock him for calling me babe, but I don't. Instead, I do as he tells me, pulling the door shut and locking my seatbelt into place. Once he hears that click, he shifts the car into drive and pulls back out into the street, driving slow, like he wants to savor this moment of the two of us alone in his car.

"You never talk to me in class," he says, his deep voice all soft and melty.

I refuse to let that voice melt me.

"You're always late," I say with a shrug.

He grins. "So you *do* notice me. I figured you didn't even realize I was in government with you."

I can't not notice him. And that's what's so hard to deal with.

"What are you doing tonight?" he asks.

"Nothing," I automatically answer.

"Jordan Tuttle is having a party at his house." Ryan pauses. "Want to go?"

I shake my head.

"Not even with me?"

"Especially not with you," I mutter. "Your flirty ways aren't going to work on me, Ryan. Quit while you're ahead."

"So the hottest girl at school won't go with me to Tuttle's party." I turn to stare at him, shocked by his comment. "I'm trying to gain some street cred with my new team here, Livvy. Throw a guy a bone."

Jordan Tuttle is our varsity quarterback. He's also outrageously good-looking, outrageously talented on the field and an outrageous asshole. Much like the guy whose car I'm currently sitting in. "You don't have a game tonight?"

Ryan shakes his head. "Not for another two weeks."

"So you definitely made the team?"

The arrogant smile he sends my direction is bone melting. Thank God I'm sitting down. "Of course I made the team."

I shove his shoulder, unable to resist. "You are so full of yourself."

"That's your favorite quality of mine."

"Not even."

He pulls into the senior parking lot, slowing down to look for an open space. "So? Will you go to Tuttle's with me tonight?"

"I can't," I admit softly, shaking my head.

Ryan guides the car into a spot and shuts off the engine. "Why not? Embarrassed to be seen with me?"

Not even close. "I don't want the hassle."

He frowns. "The hassle of what?"

"Fighting you off. Dealing with Em." Dealing with Dustin if he's there, which he might be. Though he really doesn't hang out with the football crowd since he's on the basketball team. There's some sort of weird divide there, but he is friends with Tuttle, so maybe he'll be there.

And I don't want to risk running into him.

"Don't say no yet." Ryan grabs my hand and brings it to his mouth, dropping a kiss on my knuckles. "Think about it."

He's being extra sweet, not as cocky. But why? What's his motive? A guy like him has to have a motive. I don't trust him.

I need to remember that. He's not to be trusted.

Ever.

chapter thirteen

"Where's your other half?"

I glance up to find Amanda Winters standing in front of me. It's lunch period and I'm sitting against a tree, my ear buds in, though I don't have any music playing. I use them as a defensive method to keep people from talking to me.

Looks like it didn't work with Amanda.

Pulling the right ear bud out, I squint up at her, the sun shining above her head making it hard for me to see. "Who are you talking about?" I have two former other halves, after all.

"Emily." Amanda makes a face. "You two are usually always together."

"Yeah, well, now we're not." Amanda is only in one class with me this year. I've known her since kindergarten, and while we've never been close, we're not what I'd consider enemies either.

"You guys have a falling out?" She plops down on the ground beside me even though I didn't invite her to. Looks like I'm not having lunch alone after all, which is what I've been doing the last two days.

"I guess." I offer her a halfhearted smile. "I don't really want to talk about it."

"No problem." Amanda nods toward my neglected sandwich sitting next to me, still encased in Ziploc. "Whatcha eating?"

I study Amanda, wondering at her motives. Ever since I got home from Oregon, I feel like people are saying one thing but they mean another. As in, I can't trust anyone. And I definitely don't trust Amanda. I don't even really know her that well. "Ham and Swiss on sourdough."

"Not hungry?"

"Not really."

"Me either." Amanda scans the quad, much like I do. This is the social hour, when everyone gossips, flirts, makes out, fight, whatever. Couples come together or they break up. Friends have arguments that result in a temporary falling out. Or even a permanent falling out. Someone gets suspended at least once every couple of weeks and it always happens out here in the quad.

Yet I have no desire to be a real part of it. Not anymore. I feel anchorless, adrift at sea without my friends on either side of me. I see Em off in the farthest corner of the quad with a new squad of girls. I'm sure that's what she calls them too, her squad. She always did have Taylor Swift aspirations.

Dustin is sitting at a table with his basketball buddies, and every once in a while he lifts his head in this certain way, his gaze intent as he scans the area. I may be totally reading too much into it, but I think he's looking for me.

Right. In my dreams.

And then there's Ryan, holding court in the center of the quad, surrounded by the other football players and their hangers-on, every one of them girls. Cheerleaders, the popular girls, the ones who smile brightly and twirl their hair around their finger while they flirt with the boys and look perfect. These girls are the ones he has to choose from, and every one of them is prime.

Jordan Tuttle is sitting to his right and he doesn't look too thrilled with all the attention the new boy is getting. No surprise. Jordan wants to be king of his court, not share his throne with the new guy.

Jordan and Em would probably make a perfect couple, though he's not one to dip below his social level. Em would be considered slumming for Jordan.

Harsh but true.

"Why aren't you hanging out with your friends?" I know Amanda has a huge social circle. She's in band and they're all kind of weird—well, at least our high school band is. Not that they're freaks or anything, but they spend most of their time together, and they rarely date outside of the music department, so it all feels rather…incestuous.

"I quit band," she admits, turning to look at me. "I was sick of their shit."

"Really?" I frown. "But you've been in band since, like, fifth grade."

"Yeah, well, it sucks. I'm so over it. My parents are flipping out, like I'm throwing everything away, including a band scholarship, which is nuts. Hate to disappoint them, but playing the clarinet isn't my ideal career choice, so I'm giving up on that dream," Amanda says sardonically.

I burst out laughing. "You don't see yourself playing the clarinet in a smoky jazz club wearing a fedora and drinking scotch on your break?"

Amanda grins. "Not really. And you have a vivid imagination."

"Sorry." I stop laughing, feeling stupid. "Got carried away, I guess."

"I don't mind." She smiles, leans her shoulder against mine briefly before shifting away. "I'm sorry if you and Em are in a fight. That's hard."

"It's okay," I say softly, touched by her apology. "I'm realizing that maybe she wasn't a good friend after all."

"I'm having the same problem," Amanda says.

"What do you mean?"

"Tara Knudson. You know her, right?"

Vaguely. Fellow band geek along with Amanda, she's a member of student council, and a total brainiac—also like Amanda. "Yeah, sort of."

"She was my best friend." Amanda plucks at the dead grass we're sitting on, pulling blades of it out so hard the roots and dirt still cling to the ends as she tosses it on the ground. "Until I found her in a bedroom at one of Jordan Tuttle's parties, wrapped around my boyfriend like a pretzel."

"Get out."

"I'm serious," Amanda says with a nod, her eyes sad. "I hate them both. Broke up with him *and* her on the spot."

"Who was your boyfriend again?" I feel like a jerk for asking, but I honestly don't remember.

"Thad Billings. He's in band, though he's a junior." Amanda makes a face. "That's what I get for dating a younger man."

I giggle. I can't help it—the way she said that was kind of funny. "How long were you two together?"

"Almost four months. We started dating right before school was finished." She shakes her head, stares off into the distance. "I'm starting over. Clean slate. No more band, no more best friend, no more boyfriend."

Sounds familiar, not that Dustin was my boyfriend.

"Aren't you dating Dustin Henry?"

Is she in my head or what? I scoff. "No, we're just friends."

"Just friends. Cheaters love to use that term." Amanda's eyes go wide. "Not that I'm calling you a cheater. I'd never say that about you. I don't even know you that well, but—you know what I mean."

"I do. Don't worry, I didn't think you were calling me a cheater." I'm definitely not the cheater. I may've kept secrets from both Em and Dustin, but I definitely didn't cheat on them. They're the ones who were messing around behind *my* back.

"You're on the yearbook staff, right?" Amanda asks, clearly trying to change the subject. So I let her.

"Yeah, I am." It's my one thing. The only thing I have that doesn't involve Em or Dustin. "Why do you ask? And please don't ask me to take photos out or insert photos of you. That's out of my control." Somewhat.

She laughs and shakes her head. "I don't care about that stuff. I was just wondering. I need something new to focus on. Now that I'm not in bad my counselor keeps telling me I need to find other extracurricular activities so I look good on my college applications."

"We'd love to have you." So many people sign up for yearbook thinking it's an easy class. But it's also hard work, so we tend to lose people too.

"Olivia Hudson, what are you doing all the way over here?"

Dread slithers down my spine. I know that voice. Was just riding in his car this morning. Now here he is standing in front of Amanda and me, that typical self-assured smile curling his perfectly kissable lips, his hands on his hips as he stares down at the both of us. "Hey Ryan," I say stiffly.

"Who's your friend?"

His question makes Amanda sit up straighter. "Amanda Winters, meet Ryan..." I am having a total blank moment. I hear his full name every day in government when our teacher takes attendance and now

I can't remember it.

Not that he offers it up either. "Nice to meet you." He smiles down at Amanda, one of those dazzlers that's probably making her melt inside. Poor Amanda. She has no idea what or who she's dealing with. At least I can prepare myself to withstand the potency. Sort of. "You two look lonely."

"We're fine," I say quickly before Amanda can say anything. Not that she's speaking. I think she's become mute in Ryan's presence. "Don't worry about us."

"Come sit at our table." He flicks his head in the direction of his precious centerpiece table.

"Thanks, but lunch is almost over." I smile, wishing he'd leave.

He frowns, looking like he's going nowhere, damn him. "Come on, Livvy. What do I have to do? Beg?"

I laugh. "Please. You're not the type to beg.'"

"Watch me." Without warning, he falls to his knees and I scoot my legs up, my bent knees pressing against my chest, my mouth falling open when he curls his hands together like he's about to pray. "Please, please, *please* Livvy. Come sit with me for the rest of lunch. And bring your hot friend."

The smile on Amanda's face is so wide I bet it hurts.

No way can I allow myself to be swayed by his cuteness. Life is so not fair. "Won't the queen bees be pissed if we sit with you?" I nod toward the table.

Every one of the girls sitting at his table is watching us, their disgust obvious. I'm sure they're all secretly vying to be the first to sink their claws into Ryan and snatch him up as their boyfriend.

Ryan glances over his shoulder for all of about two seconds before he returns his attention to me. "I don't give a shit if they're pissed or not. Come on, Livvy. I'm feeling like an asshole right now."

"You *are* an asshole, didn't you know?" I laugh when he clutches his heart like a lovesick cartoon character. He is so full of crap.

But he's also cute. And kind of funny. I like funny. I usually find it irresistible, so if he proves to have a good sense of humor, I'm probably done for.

"Then do this asshole a favor and come sit with me. And you too, Amanda. Come on." He stands, offering his hand to Amanda, and she takes it, popping up to her feet. She sends me a look, one that says, *don't be stupid, let's do this!*

Reluctantly, I put my hand in Ryan's and he tugs me to his feet, pulling me in close so he can whisper in my ear, "Knew I could convince you."

I raise a brow. "You're that confident."

"With you? Always." He steps closer, his body brushing against mine and making a million tingles scatter all over my skin. "I bet I could convince you to do just about anything I want you to."

That sounds like a promise—or a threat. "Don't be too sure," I say, my voice shaky. I can feel Amanda's gaze on us and I'm sure she's curious to know what he's saying.

It's like I can feel everyone's eyes on us. They're probably all wondering what Ryan wants with me. He's out of my league. I know it. He probably knows it too.

But he doesn't really seem to give a shit.

"By the time I'm finished with you, I'll have you eating out of my hand," he says, his words oozing with confidence.

And for some reason, his words conjure up all sorts of dirty thoughts. Maybe it's the way he said *eating* and *hand*. Out of his mouth, he makes the words downright wicked.

"Come on." He turns so he's between Amanda and me, and he slings his arms over our shoulders, dragging us both into his body. He's solid and warm, muscular and tall. I fit perfectly just beneath his arm, but so does Amanda. "You know those bitches I'm sitting with, right?"

I laugh as he leads us toward the table and so does Amanda, though she sounds a little nervous. "Not really," I confess, and Amanda mumbles her agreement. We're not privileged enough to sit with the popular girls.

"Well, let's bring you into the fold. Girls, meet Livvy and Amanda," Ryan says as we all three stop at the head of the table.

They all mutter hello, their gazes narrowed as they blatantly scan both of us. Probably sizing up the competition, not that I consider myself real competition with them. I'm just...a girl. Who happens to be on the yearbook staff and gets decent grades and is desperate to get out of this hellhole otherwise known as my hometown.

The guys are checking us out too, with interest in their eyes, the words *fresh meat* most likely floating in their brains as they study us. Amanda's not a bad looking girl. She has shiny brown hair that's cut bluntly just past her shoulders and expressive brown eyes. Her nose is a little big, but she's tall and willowy, though she doesn't have much in the boob department.

"Sit down," one of the guys offers, nudging the boy next to him to get him to move over and make room. "Join us."

I'm about to sit next to Amanda when Ryan snags my hand, forcing me to sit in between him and stupid Tuttle. I look at him, the determined line of his jaw, his icy blue eyes staring right at me. Hardly anyone calls him Jordan. They all just call him Tuttle, even the teachers.

"This is Livvy," Ryan leans over to tell him, his shoulder brushing against my chest as he does so.

The smirk he sends in my direction when he shifts away tells me he did that on purpose.

"I know Olivia," Tuttle says, his voice full of irritation. "We've gone to school together forever."

"We played a married couple in the sixth grade play," I remind him. One of my more mortifying moments that I don't like to remember. Back in sixth grade, the last person any girl wanted to be married to was Jordan Tuttle. He'd gone through an awkward stage back then, with a mouth full of braces, pimples already dotting his face and a weird, gangly body that seemed to grow extra fast. I think he was close to six feet tall by the beginning of seventh grade.

He'd filled out just fine and was now a freaking superstar. Everyone wanted a piece of Jordan Tuttle.

"Didn't we have to kiss at one point? In the script?" Jordan asks, his eyebrows rising.

I shake my head. "Um, no. We were only twelve. I'm sure you would've rather spit on me than kiss me." At the time Tuttle hadn't seemed interested in any girls, least of all me.

Ryan laughs. "Missed opportunity, bro."

"I was trying to make you jealous, asshole," Tuttle says, leaning over so now his shoulder was pressing directly against my boobs. I am surrounded by two large, muscular boys, and it's like I'm the tasty center of a football-playing sandwich. "Considering she's all you've been talking about the last few days."

My head swivels to Ryan, shock coursing through me. "No way."

"Way," Ryan says, reaching out to dab the tip of my nose with his index finger. "I'm telling you, Livvy, I'm going to make this happen."

I lower my voice. "Really? So what's going on with you and Em?"

He waves a hand, seemingly dismissing her. "She's old news. I hate what she's done to you."

He does? I watch him carefully, trying to see if he's sincere or not. He stares back, his expression never wavering. Maybe he is being truthful.

"You should come to my party, Olivia," Tuttle says, making me turn away from Ryan.

I make a face as I look at Tuttle. Why does he keep calling me by my full name? It's weird. "I don't think…"

"Don't think. Just say yes," Ryan says, interrupting me. "Bring your friend if that makes you feel more comfortable."

How is that going to make me more comfortable if I barely even know Amanda? This entire situation is getting completely out of hand. "Ryan…"

"Don't argue. Don't protest." He rests his finger against my lips, silencing me when I was fully prepared to argue and protest. "Come on, Livvy. We really want you there. You and Amanda."

"What about Em?" I ask, my voice small, my brain fully prepared for another one of his bullshit answers. But I have to ask again. I have to make sure.

"What about her? I already told you. Forget that chick." His lips quirk up. "Oh, wait, I already have." He holds up his hand and Tuttle gives him a high five as they both laugh.

"You two are pigs."

"Give me a break. You're mad at her. I know you two had a falling out. You and Dustin too." He skims his fingers down my cheek, the feather-light touch sending my senses into overdrive. "What better way to get revenge on them than to come with me to the party tonight?"

I would never consider myself petty. I'm not one to stoop low and I don't like playing games.

But at this very moment, I feel like my life has turned into one giant game, and I need to stay ahead in order to not get burned.

I was already burned by Em and Dustin, and their betrayal cut like a knife.

Maybe now I can finally even up the score.

chapter fourteen

When school lets out I walk home, texting Amanda along the way. I'm reluctant to go to the party. What if Em's there? Worse...what if Dustin's there? I don't want to deal with either of them, and I definitely don't want to deal with the both of them.

I won't go to Tuttle's party if Amanda can't make it. And for a minute, I think she's going to back out, what with the text she sends me.

Tuttle is an asshole. He made fun of me in eighth grade.

Laughing, I type out my reply.

He makes fun of everyone at some point in our lives. Now you're just part of the club.

The summer afternoon air is hot. Stifling. I think of Em's pool. Of jumping into the water, feeling it wrap around me and cool my skin, ease my thoughts.

I frown. I should forget all about Em's pool. Me hanging out at her house is never going to happen again. Our friendship is over. And no matter how much it hurts, how much I might miss her, I can't forget that she betrayed me.

My phone dings again and I read the texts from Amanda.

So you're going to force me to go to Tuttle's party? Fine.

I'll go. I'll even drive. What time should I pick you up?

Let's go late. The less time I spend with Tuttle, the better.

I'm relieved she offered to drive. Though she keeps mentioning Tuttle, which is somehow...telling? Maybe?

Pick me up around nine? My mom probably won't let me leave the house if it's any later.

Sounds good.

I shove my phone into the back pocket of my shorts. I'll tell Mom I'm spending the night at Amanda's. Or maybe even Em's. She won't check on me and anyway—she doesn't have a clue we're fighting. I didn't want to tell Mom about any of it. She'd ask too many questions, questions I didn't want to answer so I remain quiet.

It's easier.

As I approach my house, my heart falls into my toes when I see Dustin's familiar black Jeep parked in the driveway. I stop in front of our neighbor's house and look around, trying to figure out if I can make my escape without Dustin seeing me, but it's too late.

He's climbing out of the Jeep, looking good in a pair of jeans and a black T-shirt that hugs his lean torso, his expression contrite when he faces me. I stay rooted to the spot, unable to move, unable to tear my gaze off of him. My heart is racing. My head is spinning.

And the anger begins to simmer to a low boil.

"Go away," I yell at him.

"We need to talk, Livvy. You can't avoid me forever," he says, his voice washing over me and reminding me for a brief second that I still care about this boy, despite what he's done to me.

"Watch me," I say, my tone defiant as I dart across the lawn and make my way toward the front door. I fumble with the zipper on my backpack, undoing the small pocket in the front so I can yank out my keys. My hands are shaking as I try to unlock the door and then he's there, standing directly behind me, his hand on my upper arm as he tries to turn me around to face him.

"Come on," he pleads. "Look at me."

"No." I finally succeed in opening the door and I squeeze inside, trying to shut the door on him, but he thrusts his shoulder forward and blocks me, pushing his way in.

I fight against him, but he's stronger than me. He sets me aside and shuts the door, locking it behind him. He's angry too. I can tell by the way the corded muscles in his neck stand out in stark relief, how he glares at me with those dark, all-knowing eyes.

He has almost a dangerous air about him and my traitorous body responds. Dustin's…hot like this. Mad at me. Frustrated with me.

The feeling is mutual.

"You're going to believe Em over me?" he says as he leans against the front door. "After everything we've been through? Seriously?"

"I don't want you in my house." My voice is shaky. I curl my arms in front of my chest so he can't see that my hands are shaky too. "Go home, Dustin."

"We need to talk."

"There's nothing to say!" The words burst out of me like I can't control them, and it feels like I really can't. "You had sex with Em and kept it from me. Oh, and we messed around with each other too, but we also kept it from Em. How messed up are we, huh?"

"Livvy…"

"You can't have your cake and eat it too, Dustin." I never really understood that cliché before, but now I totally get it. Dustin wants us both hanging on a string, tied to him, so he can yank us back in whenever he chooses. He can't have both of us.

He can't have me.

"What happened with Em…" He takes a deep breath and expels it slowly, tilting his head back so he's staring up at the ceiling. "Nothing much happened at all, I swear. It meant nothing. It was a mistake."

"A mistake that happened a couple of times," I remind him and the miserable expression he wears confirms what Em told me, though he doesn't answer me.

It wasn't just a one shot deal. He'd messed around with her multiple times. The realization settles like a rock in my stomach.

"Like you and I were a mistake. Right?" I throw out on purpose, hoping it'll hurt him.

The wounded look he sends my way tells me I made a direct hit. "You don't believe that."

"Oh, but I do." I turn and walk deeper into the living room and he follows me, his hand hooking around my arm. I tug out of his grip and he grabs me again, spinning me around so I have to face him. "There's nothing left to say, Dustin. I want you to leave."

His expression hardens, his mouth thinning into a straight line. "I can't believe you'd be this heartless."

"Heartless? *Heartless?* I can't believe you have the nerve to say that to me! *You're* the one who asked me to be your girlfriend, all while you *knew* you'd hooked up with Em and kept it from me! You're the heartless one, asshole," I bite out that last word, and I'm so angry, I'm breathing hard.

"You don't think I feel bad for doing that? I never wanted to hurt you—"

"Too late!" I lunge toward him, my hands landing on his chest as I give him a hard shove. He goes stumbling back, the look of shock on his face almost comical.

But I'm not in the mood to laugh.

"I messed everything up. I'm sorry," he whispers, rubbing at his chest like I might've hurt him. Maybe I did, I don't know. It's wrong, but I wouldn't mind making him hurt just a little. Payback for what he did to me. "I'm so sorry, Livvy."

"Fuck you." I've never said those two words and really meant them before.

I do now, though. I mean it with every fiber of my being. Fuck Dustin. Fuck Em. Fuck the both of them for keeping their secrets and ruining everything.

They ruined everything.

Everything.

The tears slip down my cheeks before I even realize I'm crying. I wipe at them furiously, feeling weak. The last thing I want in front of Dustin. He'll jump on that. I know he will.

And then he's right there, standing directly in front of me, and I don't fight him. I don't push him away.

"I'm sorry." He says those two words so softly I barely hear them. He says them again, cupping my face with his big hands as he tilts my head back so my blurry gaze meets his, his thumbs gently wiping away my tears. He stares into my eyes, his gaze dropping to my lips, and then his head descends. I stretch up on my tiptoes…

We're kissing. And the kiss is wild. Hungry. Hot. He pulls me into him and I collide into his chest with a whimper, my lips parting and his tongue sweeping into my mouth. We cling to each other, his hands falling from my face to land on my hips. His fingers curl around the belt loops on the front of my shorts and he yanks me closer, as close as we can get. A mixture of fear and excitement grips me and I struggle against him, tear my mouth away from his, and then he's kissing my neck, his mouth wet, his teeth nibbling my skin and making me shiver.

"Don't fight it," he whispers close to my ear. "Don't fight me, Livvy."

He kisses me before I can say anything, and I let him. I get lost in the taste of his lips, the sensation of his hands roaming beneath my shirt and touching my bare skin, his tongue tangling with mine. I'm so angry yet I want him. It's the craziest, most confusing thing I've ever experienced, and I don't know how to stop it from happening.

So I let it happen.

I let him guide me to the couch.

I let him pull me onto his lap so I'm straddling him.

I let him kiss me so thoroughly I'm left breathless. His mouth breaks away from mine to move down the length of my neck, his hand curved around one breast, my hands in his hair, the both of us panting, our bodies trembling with anger. Passion.

I let him take my shirt off, his fingers skimming over my collarbone, down the valley between my breasts. His attention is fixed on my chest, as if he's enraptured, and without thought I reach for the tiny clasp on the front of my bra, undoing it with a quick flick of my fingers.

And oh God, I let him touch my bare skin, his fingers shoving away the cups of my bra impatiently, his mouth eager as he kisses me there. Licks me there. Sucks me there…

"Stop." I shove at his shoulders and he leans back, his eyes glazed as he stares up at me with swollen, damp lips and ruddy cheeks. "Dustin. What are we doing?"

He shakes his head. Swallows hard. Tentatively reaches out to brush the back of his fingers against my left breast. I shiver at the gentle touch, telling myself I can't do this. I can't fall into this trap.

"You should go." My voice is low, my gaze never wavering from his, and he touches the side of my face, his fingers brushing my cheek before he drops his hand.

"Get off me, Liv."

His voice is steel. Hard. Demanding.

Without a word, I do as he asks, turning away from him so I can fix my bra, snatch my shirt off the couch and slip it back on. I take a shuddery breath and turn to find the living room empty.

He's already at the door, his broad back to me as he runs a hand through his hair. I watch with held breath as he opens the door, pauses, as if he might turn to face me or say something.

But he does none of that. He slips out of the house, shutting the door behind him quietly, and I fall onto the couch the moment I hear that click, my legs giving out, my heart thundering as I think of his mouth on my skin, the anger I felt toward him.

The pleasure that I let consume me for one delicious, crazy moment.

I slap my hands over my eyes, waiting for the shame to wash over me.

Yet it never comes.

chapter fifteen

"Want to pre-party?" I ask Amanda as I slide into the passenger seat.

She sends me a confused look. "With what?"

"This." I pull out a bottle of vanilla-flavored vodka Mom had in her stash. I remember that she didn't like the taste. She bought it last Christmas. I'd bet money she forgot it was in the back of the pantry.

Amanda's face brightens. "Sweet." She reaches for the bottle and takes off the cap, then tips it to her lips. The moment she takes a swallow she grimaces. "This stuff is awful."

I laugh and take the bottle from her, gulping a few swallows down. She's right. It's horribly sweet yet burns like acid as it slides down my throat. I can feel the alcohol working its magic within minutes, though, coursing through my veins, leaving me warm and tingly.

I take another drink. Then another. Not giving a damn that we're sitting in my driveway at nine o'clock at night. Mom isn't even home.

She left a few minutes ago with Fitch. They were going to the movies like they were a young couple in love or something gross like that.

"Slow down there, cowgirl," Amanda says, amusement lacing her voice, her arm stretched out toward me as she waggles her fingers. "Don't polish it all off in one swallow."

"You said it's awful," I point out, giving her the vodka.

"Doesn't mean I won't drink it. Beggars can't be choosers."

We polish off the bottle within twenty minutes. Well, I mostly polish it off. Amanda takes a few sips, but otherwise she's trying to be good as our designated driver for the night. She only has to get us to the party, though. Tuttle's parties are known to go on all night, with lots of people leaving in the morning after they've slept off their drunken night. His parents go out of town on a regular basis and somehow they never find out about the big parties he has.

Or if they did know, they never protested.

"I can never remember how to get to his house," Amanda says as she puts Tuttle's address in her maps app.

"You've been to his house before?"

"Well, yeah. I've been to exactly one of his parties." Her eyes get this faraway look as she stares into the distance. "It was a crazy night."

"It's always a crazy night at Tuttle's," I joke, though it's true. The last time I went there Dustin and I had so much fun—

No. I push the thought of Dustin out of my head. Forget him. I'm with Amanda tonight. I need to focus on that.

Off we go to his house, me giggling and desperate to talk about what happened between Dustin and I earlier. But I don't know if I can trust her with my secrets yet, so I remain quiet. She cranks up the music and is singing along with the radio, her voice actually pretty good and then I'm singing along too, only I sound awful.

"Your talents don't lie in your voice," Amanda says not too kindly once the song is over.

I laugh and shove at her shoulder, which makes her hands jerk on the steering wheel, the car swaying. This only makes me laugh harder. "You're mean."

"Honest," she points out. "There's a difference."

Maybe she's what I need in a friend. Someone who's painfully honest, who will tell me when I'm screwing up and being an idiot. Clearly Em let me fail on a daily basis. Now look at me.

I'm the queen of the idiots. It's like I can't control myself when I'm around boys.

Especially Dustin.

It's weird because I never let boys distract me before. Have my hormones kicked in or what? I've been focused throughout high school. Involved in a few clubs, mostly yearbook-related. Was on student council last year, but only as part of the junior prom committee. I didn't party much, but then again neither did Em, not until near the end of the last school year did she start getting a little crazy.

We all started getting a little crazy.

Leaning forward, I slap the dash of Amanda's tragically average car, desperate not to think tonight. I need to just enjoy and…feel. "Hurry up. I need a drink."

Amanda presses on the gas, gunning it, and my body snaps against the seatbelt, jerking my head back. She laughs when I glare at her.

"You told me to hurry," she points out, and I give her the finger, making her crack up.

I'm not acting like myself. I could blame the booze or my earlier encounter with Dustin but I don't think that's why. I feel…freer somehow. Like I can do and say and be whatever I want, whenever I want. I don't have Dustin and Em holding me back.

I don't care what anyone thinks.

We arrive at Tuttle's house in less than twenty minutes, so it's almost ten o'clock by the time Amanda pulls into the long gravel driveway. He lives out in what we call the country, where the lots are bigger and the houses are grander. Tuttle's family is loaded. His dad is a big shot corporate lawyer and his mom comes from money, so they live in a freaking mansion.

And by the looks of all the cars parked along the driveway and out in the fields that surround the Tuttle house, it looks like practically the entire senior class is here.

Amanda parks the car out in the field and we make the long trek down the driveway to the house. The night air is warm, a cool breeze washing over us every few minutes, and I spot a few familiar faces as we walk. A small group of guys stand in a circle passing around a joint. A cluster of girls console one who stands in the center, her hands pressed against her face as she cries.

I look away, hoping like crazy I don't end up like her tonight. I've cried enough this week already.

Ryan's car is parked right in front of the four-car garage, the half-moon shining from the sky above making the BMW's pristine white paint gleam. I didn't notice Dustin's Jeep anywhere, but that doesn't mean he's not here.

I have a feeling he is.

And I don't want to see him.

"Should we just open the door?" Amanda asks as we walk up the steps that lead to the entrance.

I'm guessing she hasn't been to a lot of house parties. The music playing inside is loud, the throbbing bass seeming to pulse within me. So many people are talking and yelling it's like a dull roar, where you can't make out what they're even saying.

"No one will hear us if we knock," I say as I grab the handle and push open the door. I stop in the entry as Amanda shuts the massive door behind us, taking it all in.

The living room is huge—and it's crammed full of people. Some are sitting on the overstuffed white couches. Most are in the middle of the room dancing to the music blasting from invisible speakers, cups clutched in one hand, smiles pasted on their sweaty faces. It's blistering hot despite the giant fan circling frantically above us.

"Let's look for something to drink," Amanda yells close to my ear, and I nod, taking her hand as I lead her through the crowd.

We push our way through the crowd, Amanda and I a united front. I see the curious looks on everyone's faces as we pass. They're probably wondering when did we start hanging out, and I have a feeling some of them will ask where Em is.

Or maybe they know. Maybe she's already here.

My stomach twists at the thought of seeing her.

We make our way to the kitchen, which is three times as huge as my own. The room isn't as crowded and the air is much cooler. I sag in relief against the shiny black granite countertop as Amanda grabs two bottles of beer from a giant bucket of ice that sits on the floor.

"Tuttle's so high class he doesn't even have a keg?" Amanda asks as she twists off the cap of her beer.

I do the same and pitch it into the nearby garbage can that's already overflowing with trash. "I guess so."

Amanda brings the beer to her lips, her wide-eyed gaze darting everywhere, taking the kitchen in. "I think I could fit my entire house in here."

I smirk at her. "Whoever marries Tuttle is going to live the high life."

She grimaces while I chug half my beer. "Who'd marry Tuttle? Talk about setting yourself up for misery."

"And here I thought you were madly in love with me." Tuttle comes up directly behind Amanda, and the look on her face is straight out of a cartoon. All bugged-eyed and gaping mouth and flushed cheeks. She stiffens when he wraps his arm around her neck and pulls her in close, her back pressed against his front. He presses a sloppy kiss to her cheek and she sends me a look. One that says, *save me*.

I just laugh and shake my head.

"What exactly did you hear?" Amanda asks him cautiously. She looks frozen in place, like she might shatter at any moment, and I'm starting to suspect she might like Tuttle more than she's letting on.

"Enough to know you think you'd be miserable if you married me." Tuttle kisses her cheek again, his mouth drawing closer to her lips and she leans away from him. "Aww, what's wrong, Mandy? You don't like it when I kiss you?"

"Get off me." He loosens his hold on her and she turns around, her hands going to his chest to push him away. He goes easily, the smile on his face downright unreadable. I never know what Tuttle's thinking. It's like no one does.

His gaze shifts in my direction and he slowly approaches me, his arms open wide as if he expects me to walk into them. So I do, a surprised huff of breath escaping me when he hugs me tight. I return it, careful not to spill my beer before I disengage from his hold.

"Ryan will be glad to see you." Tuttle's gaze eats me up yet I can't look away. "Lookin' good, Olivia."

I tell myself not to be excited by the mention of Ryan, but I can't help it. I'm pitifully excited. "You realize no one calls me Olivia but teachers and my parents," I point out, finishing off my beer. I set the empty bottle on the counter and Tuttle grabs a fresh one from the bucket of ice.

"And Dustin." Tuttle smirks, like he knows my secret. "He's allowed to call you Olivia."

I say nothing as he twists off the cap on the beer and then hands the bottle to me. His fingers graze mine and I meet his gaze, wondering why he's bothering with us when he has hundreds of other people to choose from.

He's barely said ten words to me the past three years of high school. He runs with a different crowd. But he's eyeing Amanda and me like he's interested, though he tends to focus more on Amanda. All while she's doing her very best to ignore him completely.

This is going to be a weird night.

"Tuttle!" A curvy blonde appears out of nowhere, curling her arm through his as she stares up at him with adoration in her eyes. "I've been looking for you everywhere!"

"I've been here the entire night, doll." He leans in and drops a kiss to her over-glossed lips, his hand smoothing over her ass in a blatant possessive gesture. I stare at both of them, at the display they're putting on, at the obvious way Tuttle's laying his claim on some girl, like that's supposed to make us feel…what?

Jealous?

"Who are your—friends?" the blonde asks with a sneer, glaring at Amanda and me.

"She's Olivia." Tuttle smiles as he points at me with his beer bottle. "And that's my future wife, Amanda."

Amanda's eyes bug out of her head yet again.

The girl sniffs, her eyes narrowed as she contemplates us. "Huh."

"Who are you?" Amanda asks.

The blonde's thin eyebrows rise. "You don't know who I am?"

"Um, no." Amanda's trying to contain her smile, but it's no use. It breaks free and wow, when the girl smiles? She's knock-em-dead gorgeous. From the stunned look on Tuttle's face, I believe he thinks the same. "I've gone to school with most everyone in this house since I was five. And I've never seen you before in my life."

The blonde makes an irritated noise and glances up at Tuttle. "Tell them my name, sweetie."

He makes a face, one that says he's busted. "Uh…"

She pulls away from him, her glare icy enough to freeze hell. "I give you the best blowjob of your life and you can't remember my name?"

"Aw, babe, you should know better. I say that to all the girls," Tuttle drawls as the blonde storms out of the kitchen.

We still never find out her name.

"Do you really say that to all the girls you've been with?" Amanda asks when the blonde is gone. "That they just gave you the best blowjob of your life?"

Tuttle shrugs, looking completely at ease. The little argument didn't faze him one bit. "Yeah, probably. I'll say pretty much anything when a girl lets me come in her mouth."

"Ew," Amanda says as I start to laugh.

Big, warm hands land on my hips and I go hot when lips brush against the side of my neck. I could smell him before he touched me and I glance over my shoulder to see Ryan standing there, a satisfied smile on his too-gorgeous face.

"I figured you wouldn't show up," he murmurs.

"I'm here, aren't I?"

He shifts so he's standing at my side, and I can't take my eyes off of him. He's wearing a charcoal gray T-shirt and a pair of jeans that fit him to perfection. His brown hair is artfully mussed, his mouth damp from the beer he just took a drink of, and my heart goes pitter-patter the longer I stare.

"You've made my night." He shifts his attention to Tuttle. "Hogging her already?"

"Keeping her by me since I knew you'd come back for another round." The boys grin at each other and I wonder what they're talking about.

Maybe it's best I don't know.

chapter sixteen

"Tuttle slid his hand between my legs," Amanda announces when I find her hours later.

Yes. *Hours* later, I finally stumble upon her on the crowded back patio. I lost her somehow and ended up wandering all over Tuttle's house, both inside and out. Talking with people I don't know, telling more than a few people *no, I didn't come here with Em* and *sorry, I have no idea where she's at.* I also drank lots of beer. Did a round of tequila shots with a group of cheerleaders including Lauren Mancini, queen of the student body, who called me over and offered me a glass.

That was a surreal moment.

I spotted Dustin about an hour ago. Chilling outside with his basketball friends and sending me hot looks, all while ignoring Brianne Brown, who'd planted herself right next to him, her arm linked in his.

It was difficult, but I looked away. I'm not going to be lured in by him again. It doesn't matter how good his hands felt on me earlier. Or how frantic yet delicious his kiss had been. None of that matters, not when I know he—he *cheated* on me (I have no idea what else to call it) with Em.

I haven't seen her all night.

But back to the matter at hand. Amanda is watching me, an expectant expression on her face. She looks excited about her revelation. What she expects me to do with her announcement, I'm not sure but I'll try my best.

"And?" I send her a pointed look. "Did you like it?"

Amanda rolls her eyes, her face flushed, her eyes sparkling. She's buzzing, I can tell. "It happened so fast, and with nothing leading up to it. Just one moment we're sitting there all cozy in an overstuffed chair sharing a bottle of whiskey and the next, his hand is between my legs."

"Did he at least kiss you?"

"No, but he said it was like we were kissing because his lips touched where mine touched on the whiskey bottle." Her expression is full on dreamy.

That's either really romantic or a total line. I'm not sure which one yet. "And then he groped you."

"Not really a grope." She taps her finger against her lips. "More like this sly touch. Like one minute he's passing me the bottle and the next his hand drops to the middle of my thighs, his fingers creeping in."

"You never answered my original question." At Amanda's frown I continue, "Did you like it?"

"Oh. I don't know." She wrinkles her nose. "I don't know how to feel about Tuttle. He confuses me."

Welcome to the club, I want to tell her, but I don't. I'm confused too. Ryan's running hot and cold, as usual. He'd seemed so happy to see me earlier in the kitchen, but then we got separated and it's like he's avoiding me. I don't understand. Maybe he's playing hard to get.

I frown. Pretty sure I should be the one who's playing hard to get. How do I mess this stuff up every single time?

"Boys are confusing in general," I tell her, reaching out to touch her arm. "Want something to drink?"

Amanda shakes her head. "I need to find a bathroom first."

We end up back in the house, pushing through the throng of bodies that crowd every available space, making our way to the bathroom. We find it blissfully unoccupied and I stand watch outside the door, deciding I'm going to use it too when Amanda finishes.

"Did you come with him?"

I look to my right to see Dustin standing there, his expression unreadable, his arms crossed in front of his chest. The position makes his biceps bulge attractively and I tear my gaze away from his arms to glare at him. "Who? Oh, you mean Ryan? Why do you care?"

"You know why I care." He drops his arms and his hands curl into fists at his sides. "This is so stupid, Livvy. Just talk to me. Let me explain."

"So what? You can talk yourself out of it and earn my forgiveness? Nope." I look away from him, but then he's there. Right in front of me, in my face and not going to budge.

His voice drops and he has the nerve to touch my cheek. And God, his fingers feel good on my skin. "What happened earlier didn't mean anything to you?"

I shake my head, my defiant gaze meeting his. "We got caught up in the moment."

He blows out an exasperated sigh and his hand drops from my face. "It's more than that and you know it."

I'm about to say something else, maybe even tell him to back off, but then Ryan's looming behind me, acting like the Big Bad Boyfriend who will throw down on anyone—just for me. "Leave her alone, asshole."

"Who the hell are you to tell me what to do?" Dustin asks, his temper showing.

"The same guy who'll beat the shit out of you if you don't quit harassing Livvy." Ryan stands taller, his shoulders, his chest going wide. But no matter what, he'll never beat Dustin in height.

I wonder if that bugs him.

"Come on, Ryan. Back off," I start, but Ryan glares at me, that look saying more than words ever could.

Let me handle it.

Amanda chooses that particular moment to open the bathroom door. She stumbles out and comes to a stop, looking from me to Dustin to Ryan before looking at me once again. "I think I interrupted a love triangle," she says with a hiccup.

Truer words were never spoken.

I take my opportunity and start toward the bathroom, ignoring Dustin when he calls my name. Slipping out of Ryan's hold when he tries to grab my hand.

It's not until I shut and lock the door behind me that I'm able to take a full, decent breath. I'm shaking. I don't know how I've become so completely caught up in this love triangle, as Amanda calls it, but I hate it.

Turning on the faucet, I cup my hands and let it run for a while, finally leaning over the sink so I can splash the cool water on my flushed cheeks. I close my eyes, letting the water drip from my face, but after a while my head starts to spin so I open my eyes. Reach out for the faucet and turn the water off before looking at my reflection in the mirror.

I look like hell—smudged eye makeup. My cheeks are still flushed despite the water dripping on my skin. I grab a towel and dry my face. Take a deep breath and turn to unlock the door.

Ryan shoves his way into the bathroom the moment the door cracks open.

"You took forever. Jesus," he mutters as he locks the door before he turns to me. The wicked smile on his face makes my blood chill. "Finally we're alone."

"You've ignored me all night," I say, clamping my lips shut the moment the words leave me. I sound like a jealous girlfriend, which is ridiculous. There's nothing going on between us.

Not really.

He tilts his head to the side, leaning against the door. "Aw, Livvy, don't be like that."

"Be like what?" I lean against the edge of the counter, waiting to hear his explanation. My head won't stop spinning. I've had way too much to drink.

"Like…that. You know. Like you own me." His smile doesn't fade as he pushes away from the door and starts to approach. "Let's keep this simple."

"Keep what simple?" I ask warily.

"You and me. We're…friends." This sounds vaguely familiar. "We don't need to define what's happening between us."

"Right now, a whole lot of nothing is happening between us."

He grabs hold of my upper arms and lifts up. I end up sitting on the bathroom counter, and I spread my legs when he shifts to stand in between them.

"Well, I can make a lot of *something* happen if you want." His voice drops about ten octaves, low and rumbly and sexy. I tilt my head back and stare at his gorgeous face, wondering how in the world I found myself in this situation.

I go from having zero prospects to two hot boys who are practically fighting over me. I feel like I'm in some sort of weird dream state. Things like this don't happen to me. They just...

Don't.

"I don't want to be another hookup at Tuttle's house," I whisper. It's true. I've heard endless stories of various hookups at one of Tuttle's parties. If I mess around with Ryan tonight, my name will be added to a long list of girls who've hooked up with Tuttle's friends on a Friday night.

"You're not hooking up with Tuttle." He smiles. "You're with me."

"I know that." I roll my eyes and his smile fades. I think he realizes he's going to get nowhere with me tonight.

And he's right. He's not. First, I'm not about to give up that easily. And second...I'm still a mess from what happened with Dustin.

Stupid Dustin.

"You're going to make me work for it, aren't you?" He touches the corner of my mouth with his thumb, drifts it across my bottom lip.

"Every girl should make a boy work for it," I murmur as his hand falls away from my face.

"Most don't." He leans in close, his mouth just about to land on mine. "Em sure as hell didn't."

Okay. That is the dose of cold reality I really didn't want to hear. I shove at his chest and he takes a faltering step back, the potential kiss ruined. Glaring at him, I hop off the counter and start for the door, but he darts in front of me, blocking me from going for the door handle.

"I shouldn't have brought her up," he says.

"No shit," I mutter.

"I don't even know what I was thinking."

"Clearly." I sigh and cross my arms in front of my chest. "Let me out, Ryan."

He slowly moves away from the door and I unlock it before throwing it open, striding out into the hall to run smack dab into...

Em.

Could my night get any worse?

Her gaze goes wide when she sees Ryan emerge from the bathroom just behind me. "What are you two doing together?"

I go into automatic "placate Em" mode, which is what I've been doing for years. "It's not what you think—" I start.

"None of your damn business," Ryan tells her, interrupting me. He stands just beside me and slings his arm around my shoulders.

Em wrinkles her nose. "Well, don't you two look cozy."

I can't stop staring at her. She looks...crazy. She has tons of eyeliner on, yet her face is pale. Her lips are blood red and she's wearing a black tank top and the shortest denim shorts I've ever seen in my life, black fishnet stockings and Doc Marten boots completing the look.

She looks like every punk goth girl come to life.

I have to remind myself I'm mad at her. That she had sex with Dustin and they kept it from me. They betrayed me, and I know my logic is messed up because essentially I did the same thing to her with Dustin, and I don't even know how to keep any of this straight anymore.

We're all messing around with each other.

And it's a freaking disaster waiting to happen.

chapter seventeen

"Are you so stupid you're really going to fall for his crap?" Em asks, waving a hand in Ryan's direction.

I step out from under Ryan's arm, needing the distance. I thought seeing Em tonight would only make me angry, but instead I feel bad. I feel sad too. We're letting boys get in the way of our friendship and that's so dumb. Even if that boy is Dustin.

Who is now standing directly behind Em, like they're together or something. They look so much like a couple I'm filled with the need to lash out.

"Are you so stupid that you're going to believe everything *he* says?" I point at Dustin and he takes a step back, looking offended and wounded all at once.

Ugh. Tired of him trying to get me to feel sorry for him. It's bogus. The anger sweeps back over me, swift and deadly, and without a word, I turn and make my escape.

I hear Ryan call my name. Dustin does too. Even Em yells after me. But I don't answer them, I don't turn around—I just keep walking, pushing past people, earning a few rude remarks for my equally rude behavior. My head is still spinning, the music is so loud and I find myself outside, on the front porch, heaving my guts out in the bushes near the door.

Oh God, this is so freaking gross. I hate puking and I keep doing it this week.

"Hey." Amanda lightly touches my arm once I'm finished, her voice laced with concern. "Are you all right?"

I turn and wipe my hand across my mouth. She takes a step back with a grimace. I'm sure I look just fantastic. "Have any gum?" I ask, my voice hoarse.

"In my car." The look on her face is complete sympathy. "Did you drink too much?"

I nod.

"It was the vanilla vodka," she says solemnly.

My stomach lurches at the memory and I turn back to the bush, afraid more might come back up. But it was a false alarm.

Thank God.

"Are you ready to go?" she asks.

"You want to leave?" I'm surprised. I thought the plan was to stay the night. Which was a stupid plan when I think about it, but still. "Are you drunk? Should you drive?"

"Trust me, I'm completely sober." Amanda shakes her head, then looks around. "I need to get out of here."

"Why?"

She grabs my hand and leads me down the front porch steps. "I'll tell you when we get to my car."

We hurry back to the car, both of us shivering since the temperature has dropped dramatically. There are still so many cars parked along the driveway, in the field. There are also more than a few cars occupied with couples inside doing God knows what. A few of them look to be rocking.

That could've been me tonight. Though most likely on a bathroom counter—or Ryan would've had me on my knees. I have no idea exactly what he wanted to do, but I could take a guess or two.

I sort of regret pushing him away, but dude—he brought up Em. That ruined my mood completely. And I'm not going to give Ryan a blowjob in Tuttle's bathroom. Forget that. He probably has cameras in every room so he can capture special moments and use them against people later.

Probably not, but it's fun to think about.

"Okay, listen," Amanda says the second we pile into the car and she shuts her door. She turns my way, pointing at me. "You can't breathe a word of this to anyone."

"Breathe a word of what?" I ask.

She digs through the center console until she finds a pack of gum and she offers it to me. I take a piece with a murmured "thanks" and tear off the wrapper, popping the minty gum into my mouth. I nearly moan it tastes so good—and it takes away that nasty barf vanilla vodka flavor.

"What I'm about to say. I don't want anyone else to know." Amanda looks away, blowing out a harsh breath. "I shouldn't even tell you. I don't know you. Not really. Who's to say you won't run and tell your friend Emily and then the two of you will laugh at me every time you see me?"

"Amanda." I reach out and touch her arm. She turns to look at me, her dark eyes wide, her expression—scared? "Em and I are pretty much through. And I swear I won't tell a soul. I promise. You can trust me."

I really want her to trust me. I need a real friend. I think she does too.

She swallows hard and I drop my hand from her arm, waiting to hear what she's going to say.

"Jordan kissed me," she whispers.

I frown. "Who?"

An exasperated noise escapes her. "Jordan Tuttle!"

"Oh. You threw me by calling him Jordan."

"He asked me to call him Jordan." She hesitates, a dreamy look crossing her face. "He says he doesn't like it when girls whisper Tuttle when they're doing…whatever it is they're doing to him."

"He actually said that to you."

Amanda nods.

"And you fell for it."

She frowns and turns away, her long dark hair shielding her face. "There's nothing to fall for. He kissed me. That's it."

"And he told you to call him Jordan."

"Don't you see?" She turns to look at me again. "No one calls him Jordan. Not even the girls who do him or give him blowjobs or hand jobs or whatever."

I hate to break it to her, but he probably uses that line on every girl he tries to get with. I'm not going to tell her that, though. I'm not going to be responsible for Amanda's broken heart. I still think she's trying to mend the pieces back together after her ex cheated on her.

"Your ex wasn't at the party, was he?" I ask.

She shakes her head. Laughs a little. I feel like my question lightened the mood, just like that. "No way. He's not cool enough to get an invite from Tuttle ever again. Last time was just a fluke thing."

Right, because she caught her ex with her best friend at Tuttle's. Crap always goes down here. And seriously, I'm almost relieved to hear her call him Tuttle instead of Jordan. "So how was it?"

"How was what?"

"The kiss you shared with Tuttle."

"Oh." The dreamy look is back. "It was—nice."

"Nice?" I arch a brow.

"Yeah." Her gaze meets mine. "It was sweet."

"*Sweet?*" Come on. Tuttle is not known for being sweet or romantic or nice. He's the guy who gropes you and somehow convinces you to get naked so he can have his way with you. I've heard enough stories the last few years to know at least half the shit that's said about him around school is true.

"He didn't really try anything. He seemed almost nervous," she admits.

"With the exception of the crotch grab," I point out.

"That happened before I went to the bathroom. The kiss came after."

"What happened after you left the bathroom?"

"We ran into each other and he took my hand and started leading me up the stairs. I asked where we were going and he was being all mysterious, telling me I'd find out when we got there. I started to get frustrated and tried to leave, but he wouldn't let me." She hesitates, a slow smile spreading across her face. "I'm glad he wouldn't let me."

Oh God, I'm envious of her romantic moment with Tuttle. While I would normally find it hard to believe under normal circumstances, I think I'm just drunk enough to believe in true love.

"So he took me to his bedroom and I was ready to bail, you know? I wasn't about to become another Tuttle party conquest."

Pretty much what I told Ryan in the bathroom.

"But he didn't want to stay in the bedroom. He has a balcony off his room and he took me outside so I could see the view. And it was gorgeous. Then…he kissed me." Her tone was wistful.

"That's…sweet." I can't believe that word left my mouth in reference to Tuttle.

"Right?" She turns to me excitedly. "It was so crazy. Yet nice. But I have no idea if we'll see each other again, you know? We probably won't. He's, uh, done this sort of thing before. I think he's just drunk and he didn't know what he was doing. He rarely talks to me at school."

"He talks to no one at school except his closest friends."

"We have three classes together this year." She bites her lip, then releases it. "We've always had a class together. For, like, ever. He's actually really smart."

"You want to go back inside and look for him?"

"No. I don't want to ruin the moment. He'll probably say something awful and I'll hate him forever." Amanda shakes her head. "Tell me what happened with the new guy. And Dustin."

"There's nothing to tell," I say, the words practically tripping over themselves I said it so fast.

"Right. Give me a break. I'm sure something happened. That's why you had the both of them looking ready to fight over you." She rolls her eyes. "Besides, I thought you and Dustin were together."

"We're not." Everyone thinks we're together. We both thought we'd end up together eventually. "We're just friends. And Ryan…" I sigh. "I don't know how I feel about him. He's confusing."

"They all are," she says with a nod. "You can talk about it if you want. I won't tell anyone."

I'm not comfortable telling Amanda anything about Ryan and Dustin yet. And half my problem is I don't know what to say, how to explain all the stupid, insane things I've done these last few weeks. I have no excuses and I don't want Amanda to hate me for what I've done. "We should go. Maybe?" I squint my eyes and peer at her. "Or are you drunk?"

"Jordan's kiss and this conversation sobered me up completely," Amanda says firmly.

"Are you sure? I don't want to ask you to drive me home and then you get a DUI or whatever." That would be awful. I don't want to put her at risk.

"I'm good. I promise." She starts the ignition. "Let's get out of here before we both do something stupid and go back inside that house."

I laugh. "Good idea."

We're just pulling out of the driveway when I get a text from an unfamiliar number.

> **Did you leave? Where did you go?**

Frowning, I reply:

Who is this?

"Isn't that Dustin?" Amanda asks.

I look up from my phone to see Dustin standing in front of his Jeep, talking with someone. More like yelling at someone.

It's freaking Em. And she's yelling at him too.

"My life has turned into a bad TV movie," I mutter under my breath. "Like Lifetime on steroids."

Amanda bursts out laughing. "No joke." Her laughter dies. "Do you think they're fighting about you?"

I glance down at my phone when I see the text reply.

> **It's Ryan.**
> **I miss you. We didn't spend enough time together tonight.**
> **What happened in the bathroom earlier was a disaster.**
> **I should've never brought up Em.**

"I doubt it," I say as we drive past them and Amanda guides the car onto the road. "I'm sure they've already forgotten about me." Maybe.

Maybe not.

I decide to answer Ryan's texts.

You just brought up Em again.

His reply is immediate.

> **Sorry.**
> **Forgive me?**
> **Talk to you later?**

Smiling, I tap out a quick response.

Okay.☺

chapter eighteen

I waste most of my Saturday sleeping, which pisses Mom off. Not that I care. I have a raging hangover that only sleep, four ibuprofen and two bottles of water can finally ease.

Mom forces me out of bed around three, demanding that I do my laundry and help clean up around the house. I start my laundry and clean my bathroom before hopping into the shower. The hot water feels good and I soak under the spray longer than usual, and the bathroom is completely steamed up by the time I finish. Mom hates it when I take long showers.

Lately it feels like she hates pretty much everything I do.

I'm sneaking back into my room wrapped only in a towel, my hair falling against my back and dripping wet when I collide with freaking Fitch in the hallway.

Like full on run into him so hard my boobs bounce against his chest.

"Oh my God!" I practically shriek. My shrill voice makes Fitch jump about a mile.

He grabs hold of my upper arms, his fingers squeezing into my flesh. "Jesus, Olivia. You scared the hell out of me."

"Let me go," I demand, unable to pull out of his grip for fear my towel will slide off and show him everything. I'm completely naked and Mom's boyfriend is way too close. And he's actually *touching* me.

I'm trying my best not to completely freak out.

"What are you doing?" His gaze skims the length of my body and it's not necessarily creepy, but it's not on the up and up either.

As in I think Fitch just checked me out.

"What do you think? I just got out of the shower." I pull away and his hands fall to his sides, his expression a little dumbfounded. What, hasn't he seen a teenage girl in a towel before?

Probably not.

"Where's Mom?"

"She ran to the supermarket." He runs a hand over his very short brown hair and I flatten myself against the hallway wall, edging closer to my open bedroom door.

Weird. I swear I closed it before I went into the bathroom.

"I didn't mean to scare you," Fitch says when I remain quiet.

I meet his gaze, my fingers curled around the edge of my bedroom doorframe. I'm close to making my escape and I can't wait to get away from him. "It's okay," I say shakily.

"We don't need to tell your mom about our little—run in, do we?" He smiles nervously. "Maybe it can be our little secret."

"Sure," I say as I slip backward into my bedroom and practically slam the door in his face.

Sagging against the door, I lock it as quietly as possible so it's not obvious and I glance around my room, checking to see if anything out of place.

But it doesn't. Everything looks exactly the same and I tell myself I'm just being paranoid. Maybe I did leave my bedroom door open. Why would Fitch want to search my room anyway? There's nothing interesting in here for him.

I frown. Well, there is that tiny baggie of weed I have buried deep in my underwear drawer. Oh, and then there *is* my underwear drawer. Fitch has never given me a creeptastic vibe before, but I don't know him that well. They started dating before I left for the summer yet Mom never brought him around.

Now she's leaving him at the house with me while she goes shopping.

I don't like it.

With a sigh I push away from the door and go to my dresser, grabbing clothes to change into, which I do hurriedly. I wrap the towel around my head and grab my phone, checking to see if I have any messages, and I'm all sorts of excited to see that I do.

One is from Amanda.

Do you have a hangover?

Another is from…Ryan.

What are you doing tonight?

My heart skips a giddy beat. Amanda's text came in ten minutes ago, Ryan's almost fifteen. I decide to answer Amanda first to prolong the anticipation.

I'm better now. Slept most of the day and just took a shower.

Amanda's reply is immediate.

I had to get up early to go do a family thing. I'm in bed now. I feel like a zombie.

Poor Amanda.

Have you heard from Tuttle?

OMG no!!!!! Why would you even think that???!!!!???

Lots of exclamation points and question marks—Amanda's being a little over the top.

Well, he did kiss you…

I'm deleting these texts! I told you I don't want anyone to know what happened last night.

Okay. Chill. This is just between you and me.

Right. Someone will find these texts and then I'm ruined. No way. *delete delete*

She's even more dramatic than I thought.

A secret isn't a secret when more than one person knows about it.

Amanda doesn't reply, and I guess I can't blame her. Mom told me that a long time ago, warning me that's what makes secrets so dangerous.

Following Amanda's wishes, I delete any and all texts that mention

Tuttle and then I respond to Ryan.

I think I'm stuck at home tonight. ☹

It's like he's sitting on his phone, he responds so quickly.

On a Saturday night? Harsh.
My mom got mad at me when I tried to sleep most of today.

You should've stayed the night with me at Tuttle's.
Are you still there?

Nah. But I did stay the night.
You could've been cozy in the guest bedroom with me.

My face is on fire and all he's doing is telling me we could've slept together.

Though come on. We wouldn't have just slept together. Something else would've happened. Something I might not be ready for.

But then again, maybe I am.

Sounds like I missed out.

You did. But you can have your chance again with me.

More like you should be asking if YOU deserve another chance with ME, after what you said last night.

He doesn't reply, and I grab the brush on top of my dresser, parting my hair in the middle and then running the brush through it again and again until it's sleek and straight. It's easiest for me to braid it when it's still wet and I twist one side into a French braid and then the other side before Ryan finally responds.

Let me make it up to you.

I bite my lip, thinking of all the ways he could do exactly that.

How?

                                        Go out with me tonight.

Where?

                                        It's a surprise.

The door leading out to the garage slams and I lift my head, listening for Mom's voice. I hear it, along with Fitch's, and I wonder if she'll let me go.

I can almost guarantee she won't. She'll want to play happy family tonight and it's going to suck. I'd rather be stuck in my room doing homework than hang out with them.

Unfortunately, I have no homework.

"Livvy! Come help me unload the groceries!" Mom calls, and I grimace.

Why can't stupid Fitch help her out?

Grabbing my phone, I send Ryan a quick text before I go help her.

Sorry. I'm in prison tonight. Probably for the rest of the weekend. But I'll see you Monday, okay?

Not waiting for his reply, I go to the kitchen to help Mom.

"YOU WERE WITH Em last night, right?" Mom asked just after we sit down to eat dinner.

I pause in bringing the fork to my mouth, then slowly set it down on my plate. It's best that I don't totally lie because she's on friendly terms with Em's parents and she could find out with a simple phone call if I was with her or not. "Um, no. I was with Amanda, remember?"

She frowns, sending a quick glance at Fitch before looking at me. "Who's Amanda? I don't think I've ever heard you mention her before."

"We've been hanging out lately," I explain before I shovel food in my mouth. Fitch barbecued steaks and I have to admit, they're pretty delicious.

"What did you do?"

"Oh, we went to miniature golf." No one I know goes to miniature golf anymore, but what else could I say? If I told her a movie, she'd ask which one and then want details. Plus, she was at the movies herself just last night.

No way could I tell her the truth. Hearing I went to a giant party at Jordan Tuttle's house would make her lose her shit.

Mom's face brightens. "How fun! But what's going on with you and Em? You haven't talked about her all week."

I chance a look at Fitch, who's acting completely oblivious as he eats everything on his plate. "It's…complicated. Can we talk about it later?" I don't want to share my best friend troubles with Mom's boyfriend. He doesn't need to know my private business despite the fact he almost saw me naked.

I'm still a little mortified by that.

"Oh." Mom looks surprised. "Well, maybe tomorrow you can tell me what's going on."

I offer a weak smile. "Yeah. Tomorrow."

We finish eating and I help clean up the kitchen like usual. Mom slips outside to talk with Fitch and I can hear her giggle through the partially open window above the sink. Hear the sound of lips connecting and her gently chastising him for who knows what.

Best if I don't know at all.

The kitchen is clean by the time it's dark outside and I'm dying to leave. Mom and Fitch are cozied up on the sectional couch in the living room, scrolling through the Netflix menu together and trying to decide if they want to watch a comedy or an action film.

"You should come join us, Livvy," Mom calls from the living room.

I'm lingering in the kitchen, contemplating if I should reach out to Ryan again or not. I don't want to seem like I'm trying too hard. Or being too pushy. He worried me after saying last night I should be chill and not be the overbearing friend.

I need to back off. But I don't want him to forget that I exist.

"I'm not in the mood for a movie," I tell her before I dash off to my bedroom to grab my phone. I purposely left it in my room so I wouldn't be tempted to look at it. When we have these ridiculous family dinners she gets mad if I keep checking my phone and has threatened to take it away more than once.

I can't risk losing it, so I stash it away and pray I don't miss anything major.

Of course Ryan texted. And of course he's saying exactly what I want to hear.

> **I don't think I can wait until Monday.**
> **I want to see you tonight.**
> **Livvy? Where are you?**
> **Playing hard to get?**

> **I'm cruising around the neighborhood if you want to come with.**

The last message is time stamped less than five minutes ago. My fingers fly over the keyboard as I send him a message.

Are you still in the neighborhood?

A few minutes pass and I chew on my thumbnail, afraid I missed my opportunity. But then he replies and I practically start to bounce.

I'm right outside your house if you wanna come see.

Without thought I stash my phone in the back pocket of my tiny denim shorts and race through the house. My hair is in braids, I have no makeup on and my outfit is sort of lame, but I don't care.

I stop near the living room and say, "I'm going out."

Mom nudges Fitch in the ribs and he pauses the movie they just started. "Where? And with who?"

"With a...friend. And I don't know. We're just going to hang out around the neighborhood." I shrug, glance at the front door. I need to go. Get out of here before Ryan gives up and leaves.

"What friend? Don't be sketchy with me, young lady, or else I won't let you go at all."

I blow out an exasperated breath. "His name is Ryan. He moved into the neighborhood over the summer. He's friends with Dustin." That last bit I added is a complete lie, but I'm trying to make her feel better.

"Oh. How is Dustin? He hasn't been by much either lately," Mom says.

"Mom, can I go?" I'm jittery with impatience. And I think Fitch can see it. He reaches out and touches Mom's arm.

"Let her go. It's early yet," he says.

I hope he realizes I'm giving him a mental high five. "I promise I'll be back by midnight."

"Ten."

I roll my eyes. It's already a little past eight. That's less than two hours with Ryan. "Eleven."

Mom sighs. "Fine. Eleven. And when you go out with this boy again, I want to meet him."

"Okay, okay," I tell her, hoping like crazy we do go out again but not really wanting Ryan to meet my mom.

"Be careful. Make sure your phone's charged."

"It is," I yell as I make my way to the front door.

Mom's biggest fear is if she can't get a hold of me. I hate that she can keep tabs but love that I can call someone if I need to be rescued.

I open the door to find his car parked in front of my house. I can hear the low rumble of the engine, the dark-tinted windows obscuring Ryan from my view, and I tell my heart, my entire body to calm the flip down.

This is no big deal. Just the two of us. Alone. Together. I can handle it. I can play it cool. If Em can be with this guy, then so can I.

I think of her, a disgusted look on her face. Of her saying I'm taking her sloppy seconds. I can literally hear those words come out of her mouth and I...

Hate them. Because they feel true.

What am I doing?

Pushing all thoughts of sloppy seconds and Em out of my head, I walk calmly across the lawn toward Ryan's car. The passenger-side window slides down and there he is, bending over to peer out at me, a cute smile curving his too perfect lips.

"Hey. So you made it after all," he says when I reach the passenger door.

"I did." I lean down so our faces are level. My smile can barely be contained. "I broke out of jail."

"Then it's my lucky night." He flicks his chin at me in that wholly masculine way boys do. "Get in."

I open the door and slide into the passenger seat, Ryan's clean, citrusy scent wrapping all around me once I shut the door. It's like the world ceases to exist when we're in his car. "Where are we going?"

"A surprise. Remember?" Grinning, he guns the engine and we tear off down the street, into the dark, dark night.

chapter nineteen

After Ryan pulls his car into a church parking lot and we share a joint, he takes me to Sonic to get milkshakes. Sonic is like a kitschy drive-in and they have delicious ice cream and slushy drinks, though I'm not big on their food. Of course, since we smoked that joint we both agree that we're starving and pretty much anything sounds good.

We park and are discussing milkshake options when Cannon Whittaker approaches the car and chats up Ryan. Cannon is another senior football player on the varsity team, a big hulking mass of muscle with dark blonde hair and a baby face that's oddly out of place with his giant man body.

"Who you here with?" Ryan asks him, and Cannon mentions some girl's name I don't recognize. Waves a nonchalant hand in her direction and I crane my neck to check her out. A petite yet busty girl with long, straight platinum blonde hair is sitting on the tailgate of his tricked out silver truck, sending Cannon a pouty look that she believes will entice him, no doubt.

"Wasn't she with Tuttle just before school started?" Ryan asks.

Cannon makes a dismissive noise. "I guess. I don't know. She's like the team mascot, if you catch my drift. Knows how to keep her mouth shut, too, which is why we keep her around. If you ever…" His voice drifts as his gaze meets mine and he clamps his lips together.

I'm glaring at him. I know what he was about to say. And Cannon is an idiot to say it in front of me.

"I appreciate the offer, but I'm good." Ryan places his hand on my thigh and gives it a squeeze before he releases me.

I say nothing, though my skin goes hot where he touched me. Should I be insulted? Probably. Yet for some weird reason, I'm not. Maybe it's the weed. Maybe it's the fact that I'm with a hot guy who makes me tingle with just a glance, and I have no idea what that's like, being with someone so incredibly popular yet also mysterious. No one really knows anything about Ryan.

Maybe I could be the first person to really get to know him.

Or maybe Em was the one he confessed all of his deep, dark secrets to.

Frowning, I push all thoughts of Em out of my mind. I hate how she always creeps up on me when I'm with Ryan. It's probably guilt, though I shouldn't feel guilty for being with Ryan. They were never really together in the first place.

Cannon and Ryan perform one of those complicated handshakes boys always do and then he's gone, headed back to his little blonde fairy so they can cuddle on his truck's tailgate and she can spoon-feed him ice cream.

No joke.

"I didn't know you were friends with Cannon," I say once he's gone.

He's one of those guys who struts around campus like he's the shit.

Well, really the entire football team does that, including Ryan.

"Only because of football," Ryan says with a little shrug, smiling up at the carhop girl when she suddenly appears with our order.

The second she's gone I'm talking again. Saying things I probably shouldn't say.

"You've barely been at school a week and you're already making lots of friends." I'm trying to sound casual. Like I'm not digging for information, though I really am.

"Guys from the team, that's it." He smiles, slow and sexy. "Oh, and you." His gaze drops to my lips.

They're tingling like he actually touched them. And now I'm giggling, my cheeks warm, as usual. I hate that I blush so easily. "You're such a flirt." I gently shove at his shoulder, but it's like trying to push a boulder.

"You love it," he says, his voice dripping with confidence as he snatches my wrist and drops a quick kiss on my hand before dropping it. I can't react, since he did it so fast.

But he acts like it's no big deal. Instead, he's leaning forward and messing with the sound system settings before music starts to play. "You like rap?" He turns to look at me.

Not really, but I nod eagerly just to see him send me that pleased smile yet again.

"This is my favorite song," he says as he sinks into the black leather seat, his fingers tapping on his knee to the heavy bass beat.

"Um, so how's practice going?" I ask after too many minutes of silence between us. I didn't want to interrupt his favorite song, but I also don't want him to think I'm boring or that I have nothing to say.

"It's good. We're looking all right. The team I was on at my old school was better. Hate to say it." He grimaces and lowers the stereo volume with a button on the steering wheel. "But we'll catch our rhythm eventually. Get better."

"I'm sure."

"And it's hot as hell here, so that kind of sucks. Makes practicing after school miserable. I'm not used to the California heat." He traces the steering wheel with his index finger and I become fixated on that finger, imagining it's actually touching me. "Thank God we have a pool."

"I'm sure it's much cooler in Washington," I say.

"Definitely." Ryan runs a hand through his hair, messing it up adorably. Boys and messy hair—they just get me every time.

"Do you miss Washington?" I ask.

"Yeah, sometimes. I miss the weather. My old house too, because it was the only place I ever lived until now. Sometimes, change is hard, you know?"

I do know. I'm living through massive change at this very moment.

"But it's good here. I like California." He smiles softly. "You'll come to our first game, right?"

We were good little students with loads of school spirit the first couple of years, but Em and I gave up midway through our junior year. Football games became boring, especially when they started doing awful—with the exception of Tuttle. We barely paid attention and would rather work the social angle. Though now that I'm helping with the photos for yearbook, I'll be going to all sorts of games. "You really want me there?"

"Hell yeah I do. I'll need a good-luck kiss from you to make sure we win." He flashes me a smile and I roll my eyes, giggling when he moves in closer and makes a kissy face at me.

The roller-skating server chooses that moment to show up by Ryan's window. "Doing okay?" she asks, her tone flirtatious. I've never seen a Sonic carhop check up on customers like this before. "Need anything else?"

I just want her gone. "I'm good," I tell her, lifting my vanilla shake.

Ryan shrugs and when he says nothing else, she skates away, glancing over her shoulder one last time. I sort of wish she'd run into a pole.

I'm going to hell for my jealous thoughts, I swear.

"We should've ordered food," he says as he stirs his spoon in his chocolate shake.

"Do you want to call her back?" I hope he says no.

"Nah. I'm fine." He grabs the cherry that sits on a cloud of whipped cream in his cup and pops it into his mouth. "Can I have your cherry?" he asks after he swallows.

Um. Well, that could be taken a different way. Cheeks hot, I nod. "Sure."

Ryan shifts so he's sitting closer, his face practically in mine. "Feed it to me," he says.

With shaky fingers I pluck the cherry from the top of my shake and hold it out toward Ryan. His mouth opens and I set it between his lips, tugging the stem off before he starts to chew. "Mmm, delicious," he murmurs once he swallows.

I look away from him and take a few sips of my milkshake, savoring the icy cold deliciousness. I hear Ryan shift in his seat and I glance over at him, my lips still wrapped around the red straw.

He sends me a pointed look, his eyebrows raised. "So vanilla, huh? Do you consider yourself pretty vanilla?"

I let go of the straw, tilting my head to the side. "What do you mean?"

He stirs the long-handled spoon in his cup before pulling it out and licking the chocolate ice cream slowly. My body goes warm at seeing his tongue and I squirm in my seat, waiting for his answer. "Never mind," he says after a few licks of ice cream. "I think I have my answer."

He chuckles. I giggle. Again. We quietly half-eat, half-drink our milkshakes, and I chance the occasional glance at him, taking in everything that makes up Ryan. The navy blue T-shirt he's wearing and how it stretches across his shoulders and chest. His arms are like masculine works of art and his fingers are long. Memories rush over me, the night at Em's house, when he slipped those long fingers beneath my bikini top.

I wonder if he'll touch me like that again. I wonder if he'll do it tonight.

If he tries, I'll let him. I won't push him away. I'll want more.

"I like the braids." He tugs on one and our gazes meet. "Cute."

"I didn't want to blow dry my hair," I say with a shrug. His gaze is intense as he watches me, curling the end of one braid around his finger again and again, pulling me closer and closer to him. Until we're so close our breath mingles together and I can see those little flecks of gold in his green eyes.

"So you're lazy," he teases, his eyes sparkling as they search my face, settling once again on my mouth. "Is that what you're telling me?"

"I—" I'm about to defend myself when an ear-splitting horn honks, startling us both. We jump away from each other, my back brushing against the passenger-side door, and I glance out the windshield to see Cannon's truck idling in front of Ryan's car.

"See ya later, Bennett!" Cannon yells before he hits the gas and tears out of the parking lot.

"Is that your last name?" I ask him. "Bennett?"

Ryan laughs. "Well, yeah. You didn't know? I thought you knew everything about me."

"Definitely not everything," I mumble, setting my near-empty milkshake into the center console cup holder.

Not even close. The guy doesn't talk much. We flirt. We say stupid things to each other. I swear he was about to kiss me before we were so rudely interrupted by Cannon.

"Wanna go to the carwash?" he asks, knocking me from my thoughts.

"Right now?" I send him a questioning look.

"I like to keep my baby clean." Ryan strokes his hand across the sleek dashboard almost lovingly. "I go to this one that's open late on Saturday." He pitches his cup into the nearby trashcan and closes his window before starting the car. "Ready?"

I nod, and then we're speeding out of Sonic so fast the tires squeal when he turns onto the street. Ryan hits a button and a panel above our head slides back, revealing a sunroof. I glance up at it in wonder, a little sigh escaping me as he hits another button and the tinted glass opens up, letting in a rush of warm night air.

My braids are flying in the breeze, and when Ryan accelerates harder, I lean back and laugh. My head is fuzzy from the joint we smoked earlier and I'm buzzing. Happy. I close my eyes and savor the sensation of the wind rushing over me, Ryan's scent, the soft sensation of the leather seat cradling my body. Ryan touches me, his fingers burning the skin of my thigh, and I shift under his touch, spreading my legs a little bit.

He takes the unsaid invitation seriously, sliding his fingers between my legs, so close to that low point where I throb for him, and I suck in a gasping breath. I keep my eyes closed, sink my teeth into my lower lip when his fingers tease the frayed hem of my denim shorts, and then I swear I feel his fingers barely brush against the front of my very plain, very boring cotton panties.

I can't look at him. I can't watch what he's doing but oh, I can feel it, and his fingers feel…

So. Good.

Ryan snatches his hand away unexpectedly and I'm so disappointed, so on freaking edge I almost want to yell at him. My eyes fly open and I see he's half hanging out the driver's side window, punching buttons on the pay machine at the car wash. He slides back into his seat and puts the car into gear, sending me a knowing smirk as he pulls the car around and lines it up properly to go through the carwash.

"You really know how to show a girl a good time," I tease as he hits the button and the sunroof slides closed, as do the car windows.

"Carwash on a Saturday night, nothing better," he says with a mischievous smile. "Reach for the button on the right side and put your seat back."

I frown at him. He sure is bossy, always telling me what to do. Though I never protest. "Why?"

"Just do it. I'll show you in a minute."

I do as he says and so does he after putting the car in neutral, both of us flat on our backs once the seats can go no farther. The car jerks forward onto the automatic mechanism and I stare up at the sunroof window as white bubbly soap coats it completely.

Ryan rolls on his side, getting as close to me as possible. "Watch," he murmurs, and I do, entranced by the water rinsing away the first layer of soap before a new, thicker layer is squirted on.

And then he's right there, his head blocking my view, his face in mine. I lick my lips, part them as if I'm about to say something, but he doesn't give me a chance.

He's kissing me. His lips are warm and firm, and the moment they touch mine, a million butterflies flutter in my stomach, making my entire body shake. I reach for him, my hand going to the back of his head, fingers sinking into his silky soft hair as he kisses me again and again. Our mouths becoming more and more open until finally his tongue sweeps in and tangles with mine.

Only a handful of guys have ever kissed me. And most of the kisses were quick and boring and…lacking. Completely lacking that certain something I always saw in movies or read in books.

Dustin brought me to that point. We may have our moments and right now I'm super pissed at him, but the boy can kiss.

Ryan kisses even better. It's like his mouth fits perfectly with mine. His fingers gently stroke my cheek as he keeps kissing me until I'm breathless. Weightless.

Until we suddenly stop moving.

"Shit," Ryan mutters as he brings his seat back up, throws the car into drive and pulls away from the carwash.

I start to laugh as I push the button and my seat slowly rises to an upright position. My entire body is shaky and my head is spinning more from that kiss than the weed I smoked a while ago. Frustration is etched into Ryan's handsome features, his jaw like granite and his eyes turbulent. I study him, think about actually reaching out and touching him, but I don't.

I curl my hands together and rest them in my lap instead.

"I should get you home," he tells me through clenched teeth.

"What time is it?"

"Almost eleven." He glances at me, though mostly keeping his attention on the road. "Wouldn't want you to turn into a pumpkin."

Mom and her stupid curfew. "My mom really wanted me home by ten."

"You got her to change her mind?"

"I wanted it to be midnight. But her, uh, boyfriend got her to compromise."

"A champion on your side?"

"I don't know why. I don't like him that much." I think back on the weird way he looked at me when he found me in my towel. How he asked to keep that encounter between us. Why? What does it matter? Not like he yanked off my towel and tried to do something skeevy with me.

Though he might've…wanted to?

A shiver moves down my spine at the realization.

"Maybe he just wanted to get you out of the house," Ryan suggests.

"Yeah. Maybe," I agree, my voice distant. I guess that could be the reason, but I don't know why. Mom could go to Fitch's house too, though I have no idea where he lives or if it's even nice. He has that forever bachelor-type vibe, so maybe he lives in a shit hole.

More like Mom doesn't want me alone. She probably thinks I'd be up to no good.

She'd be right.

Within minutes we're back at my place and he leans over to press a quick kiss on my cheek. "I had fun, babe," he murmurs against my skin.

My skin goes hot at him calling me babe. "I did too."

"We'll have to do it again sometime."

I nod, afraid I might say something that sounds too eager and crazy.

"I'll see you Monday?"

I nod again, reaching out to open the passenger-side door. He doesn't offer to walk me to the front door and I don't ask him to. What's the point? I guess he could kiss me on the front porch, but he could've very easily kissed me just now too.

Yet he didn't. I don't take it as a bad sign, but Ryan is definitely sending me mixed signals. Kissing me in the carwash so thoroughly we forgot where we were, and now he's practically shoving me out of his car?

It makes no sense.

I climb out of the car and slam the door, offering him a little wave before he drives off down the street. I remain on the sidewalk, my arms wrapped around my waist as the BMW gets smaller and smaller in the distance until it's finally gone. I drop my arms to my sides and am about to turn to go up the walkway to my house when I catch a glimpse of movement to my right.

"Liv!"

My knees go weak at the sound of that familiar voice. "What are you doing?" I ask irritably.

"I live on this street too, you know. Or am I not allowed to be here?"

chapter twenty

"Why are you here anyway?" I ask. We may live in the same neighborhood, but Em's house isn't this close to mine. She has no reason to be out here at this time of night.

Unless...

I glance over my shoulder, spotting Dustin's house, which is just across the street and five houses up from mine. Maybe she just came from his place. Oh God, if that's the case, I swear I'll lose my shit.

Though really, I shouldn't care. It's not like I'm with Dustin. I just came home from a date with Ryan. I have no claims on Dustin. I have no claim on Em either.

Em shrugs, tucks a thick lock of dark hair behind her ear and pulls a pack of cigarettes from the front pocket of her black skinny jeans. She puts one in her mouth, pulls a lighter out of her other pocket and starts smoking. "Couldn't sleep," she says after blowing out a stream of smoke.

"Since when did you start smoking?" I ask incredulously. Yeah, we've passed a lot of joints to each other over the last few years, but I've never seen her actually *smoke* before.

She takes another drag and blows the smoke straight at me, a wicked smile on her face. "Since this summer. It was stressful not having you around, Liv."

Whatever. I'm not about to get into some stupid conversation with her where she blames me for abandoning her. "I should go inside. It's late."

"Come on. Your mom won't care if you're outside talking to me." Em's right and she knows it. "Let's catch up."

"I have nothing to catch up on with you." I start to turn away from her, but she grabs me, her fingers tight around the crook of my arm.

"Don't leave, Livvy. Please." Her voice is a hoarse whisper, and I face her once more, frowning as she drops her hand from my arm.

"Are you okay?"

She shakes her head, yet her smile is bright. "Why wouldn't I be?"

"I don't know," I say carefully. "You seem…moody. And you changed your entire look. Why?"

"I did." She tugs on a strand of her hair, her smile faltering. She's not answering my question either. "You are too sweet, you know that? I mess around with your best friend, the boy you like, and it upsets you so much I make you puke. Yet here you are talking to me like nothing ever happened, just after I snuck out of his house."

My frown deepens and I fight the urge to shove her. Hard. "I figured that's where you were coming from," I say, my voice flat.

"We didn't do anything, though." She sucks on that cig like it's her lifeline. "He just wanted to talk. He's having a tough time of it, not that you care. He's so bummed you won't give him the time of day."

It's weird. Dustin is the bad guy in this situation yet I miss him. I'm mad at Em for keeping their secret, yet I can't stop missing her either. Almost even more than I miss Dustin. I don't have a lot of girlfriends and Em is my closest one. "He'll figure out how to survive without me."

"He doesn't want to. He's really sorry that he hurt you," Em says.

"Then he should tell me, not you." My spine goes rigid and my voice is stiff. I don't need to hear his supposed apology come from Em. How screwed up is that?

"He can't since you won't talk to him." The wry smile she sends my way makes me automatically smile in return, and I don't try to prevent it.

This is…insane. I don't know how to *not* be Em's friend. Yet I can cut Dustin off so easily. It hurts, though.

It all hurts. Being with Ryan tonight eased the pain temporarily, but now that I'm looking at Em, talking to Em, and thinking about Dustin, all that pain comes rushing back, bleeding into my skin, soaking into my bones.

"You should go home," I tell Em as she drops her cigarette onto the ground and mashes it out with her flip-flop. "Your parents are probably wondering where you are."

"They won't even notice I'm gone." She waves a hand, her eyes narrowed with disgust. "They aren't paying much attention to me lately."

"Is everything okay?" Again, my question is automatic, like I can't help but be concerned with Em and her family troubles.

"It is what it is. You know how they are." She shrugs, the spaghetti strap of her red tank top sliding off her shoulder, reminding me that she's not wearing a bra. Easy access for Dustin, I presume?

Ugh. I hate even thinking about the two of them together. I need to stop.

"You were with Ryan," Em says, her voice breaking through my thoughts. "I saw you get out of his car. Don't bother denying it."

I meet her gaze head on, deciding to own my shit. "I was. Does that bother you?"

"No. Yeah. Sort of." She shrugs again, staring off into the distance. "I feel like I should warn you."

My skin prickles at the words. "Warn me about what?"

"Ryan." Em sighs and looks at me once more. "He's just using you."

"For what? To get back at you somehow?" The idea is almost laughable, though I don't say it out loud.

"No. He's just…a user. They all are. The popular guys. The ones who believe their shit don't stink. He doesn't care about you, Livvy. Not like I do. Not like even Dustin does. Ryan will just work his hardest to get into your panties, and once he does? He'll toss you aside. Tell all his friends you were a lousy lay and they'll laugh about it, then move on to the next one."

I flinch at her harsh words. See the misery in her gaze. "Like he did to you?" I say, my voice flat.

Em nods silently.

I take a deep breath, mentally telling myself that I'm different. That Ryan would *never* treat me like that.

But I don't know him very well. I have no idea if he would really treat me like that or not. Look at Dustin. I thought he cared about me. He claims he wanted me to be his girlfriend yet he fooled around with my very best friend. He's been with the both of us.

That's something I don't think I'll ever be able to get over.

DREAD CONSUMES ME as I approach campus, and I slow down, reluctant to go to school. Sunday was a total wash and that was fine with me. I slept in, I ate one too many donuts from the box Fitch went out and picked up while I was still sleeping, and I essentially avoided Mom and her boyfriend all day.

Not that she cared. She gave up on trying to get me to hang out with them and eventually left the house with Fitch. They didn't come back until I was about to go to bed. I had my chance to break free and hang out with…someone. Anyone. But I stayed home instead and caught up with my favorite YouTubers before I put a movie on Netflix and zoned out.

Now it's Monday morning and this is the last place I want to be. Trepidation fills me as each step takes me closer to school. Right about now I would rather be homeschooled. But I know Mom would drive me crazy, so that's out.

Someone shouts my name and I turn to see Amanda hurrying toward me, a giant smile on her face. "Hey, Amanda."

"What's up? Did you just get here?" She sounds breathless when she finally reaches me, little strands of dark hair flying in her face, which she impatiently bats away. "The gossip is rampant this morning."

I grin at her. "What about? You and Tuttle?"

"Oh my God, no. Stop!" She glances around, like she wants to make sure no one is paying us any attention. "About what happened at Tuttle's party after we left."

I frown, my stomach twisting into a giant knot. "What are you talking about?"

"I guess the police were called and they shut the party down and sent everyone home? And a fight broke out between some guys? And Dustin was involved?" Amanda makes a little face.

"*What?* Are you serious?" My Dustin was in a fight Friday night? He's never been the violent type. He gets along with everyone. He's so easygoing I can't imagine him wanting to beat up anyone.

"As a heart attack. I don't know all the details, but I got a Snapchat story from Lauren Mancini—"

"Wait a minute," I interrupt her. "You're Snapchat friends with Lauren Mancini?"

Lauren is one of the most popular girls at school, if not *the* most popular. Student body president, head cheerleader and assistant editor on the yearbook staff, Lauren can do no wrong.

"I'm friends with her brother." Lauren has a twin brother, Sam. "We've been in band together since middle school." Meaning Sam Mancini is the farthest from popular.

"So what? She posted photos of Dustin and someone else getting into a fight on her Snapchat story?" I never even bothered to follow Lauren or friend her on Snapchat. We move in different stratospheres. She probably doesn't even realize I exist.

Out of the corner of my eye I see Tuttle approaching us, and so does Amanda. I can tell by the way she just suddenly gripped my hand so tight I think my fingers might fall off.

"Ladies." He smiles, but his gaze is only for Amanda. "Love of my life." His voice softens and I swear he sounds downright...

Sincere?

She rolls her eyes, her fingers still clinging to mine. "Quit with the over the top declarations."

He rests his hand to his chest as if she just wounded him. "What? You don't believe me?"

"Not really." Amanda shakes her head, a little smile curling her lips.

"What happened at your party, Tuttle? Was there really a fight?" I ask.

His gaze drops to where Amanda's and my hands are connected.

"Have you gone to bat for the other team and forgot to tell me, Mandy? My heart is breaking right now."

She lets go of my hand with a frustrated little growl. "God, you are so annoying."

Tuttle grins. "You love it."

"Seriously. Tuttle. Was there a fight at your party or what?" Now I'm the irritated one.

"Yeah. No big deal, though. Just between your boy and...your other boy." Tuttle laughs. "You're getting as bad as me, Olivia. Breaking hearts all over this school."

Ugh. He's annoying. And I can only focus on his saying my boy and my other boy. What a mess. "Are you saying that Ryan and Dustin got into a fight? Like...a *physical* fight?"

Tuttle nods, smirking like the smug bastard he is. "You're really coming at your senior year with both fists swinging, aren't you?"

I'm so mad I can't even speak. I chance a look at Amanda and her gaze is full of sympathy. "Did you know?" I ask her, hating how hostile I sound. But if she did know and never told me, how can I trust her?

She shook her head, her eyes wide. "No. Like I told you, I only found out last night on Snapchat thanks to Lauren."

I blink up at the sky and tell myself to get a grip. But I can't. Em never mentioned it when I saw her after sneaking out of Dustin's house. And Ryan definitely never mentioned the fight to me. Not once while we were together Saturday night and he had plenty of opportunity to tell me.

God, did he hurt Dustin? Did Dustin hurt him? I never saw one mark on him, not that I was able to inspect his body up close...

"I'll see you at lunch, okay?" I tell Amanda, not giving her a chance to respond before I'm taking off, leaving her alone with Tuttle. I hear her call my name but I ignore her, running up the steps and pushing through the doors of the school's main entrance, heading straight for Dustin's locker.

The hallway is packed and I shove my way past everyone, my backpack nailing more than one person, earning an irritated "Hey!" or "Watch it!" for my rude efforts. I don't bother apologizing or smiling at anyone. I'm a girl hell-bent on making her way to the senior wing and no one is going to stop me.

"Dustin!" I yell his name when I spot him standing in front of his open locker and he whirls around to face me, his expression one of pure happiness for all of about a millisecond.

And then he becomes pissed off, scowling at me, his gaze going blank. That's when I notice the purplish bruise ringing his left eye. A gasp escapes me and I rush toward him.

"Are you okay?" I try to touch him, but he takes a step back.

"Well, I look like a loser who got his ass kicked thanks to your new boyfriend, but otherwise I'm fine," he says, his voice painfully sarcastic.

"He's not my boyfriend."

"Right." He turns his back to me and grabs a book out of his locker before shutting it. "I'm sure you two had a good laugh over what happened."

"Dustin, I didn't even know *anything* happened." I don't want to admit Ryan didn't tell me about their fight, but it's pretty much assumed by what I said, right? God, I'm so furious Ryan didn't tell me he got in a fight with Dustin. He had to think I'd find out somehow. Wouldn't it have been better to come from him? "What were you two fighting about anyway?"

He slings his backpack over his shoulder, his expression incredulous. "Come on, Liv. Give me a break."

"I didn't know this happened, okay?" His eyelid is a little swollen, but I'm guessing it looked even worse on Saturday. The bruise is a vivid combination of purple and yellow hues, and I wish I could give him comfort. Tell him I'm sorry. That I never meant for him to get hurt, all because of me.

"I find that hard to believe." His jaw goes firm as he stares at me hard, like he can't stand the sight of me. My heart cracks at the look in his eyes, how stiff he is, like he's afraid to get too close to me. "Move. I need to get to class."

"Dustin, please." I reach for him again and he jerks away from me. "Talk to me."

The warning bell rings right on cue. "I can't. We have class." The hardness leaves his face and his gaze turns pleading. "There's nothing left to say, Liv. You've made your point. I'll give you what you want and leave you alone."

"But—" He walks away from me before I can say anything else, his back and shoulders rigid with tension. I watch him stride down the hall, my heart racing, my mind spinning with all the supposed reasons Ryan didn't tell me about his run-in with Dustin.

I can't think of a single valid reason for Ryan to keep this from me. Not a one.

chapter twenty-one

I have trig with Dustin the period before lunch and I leap out of my seat the second the bell rings, buzzing over to where he sits with his friends and cornering him before he can leave.

"Can we talk?"

He sends me a wary look, ignoring the low oooohs his friends are murmuring. One of them even says, "Dustin's in trouble," drawing the words out, and I glare at him until he shuts up.

"Please?" I add when Dustin still hasn't said anything. He's calmly stuffing his book into his backpack, taking his time to pull the zipper closed while I'm practically bouncing up and down waiting for him to give me an answer.

"You gonna sic your boyfriend on me again?" He finally lifts his gaze to mine and I see the anger in his eyes. The irritation.

"No." My stomach flutters with nerves. Dustin looks...hot in tough mode, with the black eye and in his full on I-don't-give-a-damn attitude. I'm sick for thinking this way but I can't help it.

His attitude is a total turn-on.

"You buying me lunch?" He rises to his feet, towering over me, and I drink in his lean frame. Why am I suddenly noticing just how tall he is? And how big his hands are? This is ridiculous—I stay away from him for a few days and he's turned into a totally different person in my eyes.

"I can buy you lunch," I offer tentatively. "As long as you drive."

He cracks the barest smile. "I definitely don't want you buying me cafeteria food."

"Then let's go. Time's a wastin'," I say, falling into my old habit of teasing him and acting like everything's fine when it is so not fine.

It's a mess. We're a mess, but maybe…

Just maybe we can fix this.

It works to our benefit that we're leaving late for lunch. The senior parking lot is mostly empty and I don't even see Ryan's car, which is a good thing. I don't want him to see me with Dustin. More like I don't want to cause any more fights or problems.

I just hope that wherever we go to eat, Ryan's not there either.

As we drive we don't really talk. Just about lame stuff like how hot it is and the trig homework looks impossible. I worry it might be too hard for me and he smiles that familiar you'll-be-fine Dustin smile, reminding me that I'm smart.

Then he clamps his lips shut like he didn't mean to say that.

We end up at Pieology, where they make custom pizzas with really thin crust. I love their pizza and so does Dustin because we have distinctly different tastes when it comes to pizza and this way we can choose our own.

I get a mostly veggie pizza with chicken and an herb butter sauce mixed with a little bit of red sauce. Dustin grimaces when I make my order and I roll my eyes when he orders the very unoriginal Mad to Meat You pizza.

"You're going to give yourself a heart attack," I tell him as we go over to the fountain and fill our cups with ice. I get Sprite and he gets Dr. Pepper. "And Dr. Pepper is disgusting."

"You've been insulting Dr. Pepper for years. Your opinion isn't going to make me stop drinking it," he says as he calmly fills his cup with that vile soda.

"It's gross." I snap the lid on and push a straw through the opening.

"And so is your veggie pizza with chicken." He mock shudders. "Who puts chicken on pizza? It's just…wrong."

"You're ridiculous. Everyone loves chicken on their pizza." The restaurant is packed and we find one very small table tucked into the very farthest corner. We head toward it and sit across from each other, so close our knees brush against each other.

I shouldn't let it bother me. It's not like he's touching me sexually. But every time our knees collide I feel a buzz just under my skin, like electricity shooting through me, so light I'd almost miss it.

Yet I feel alive. Everywhere.

"What did you want to talk about, Liv?" he asks once we're settled in.

"Tell me what happened Friday night," I say, wanting to get right to the point. We only have so much time and I refuse to get in an argument with him.

He drops his head to stare at the table, pinching a napkin between his fingers. "Ryan really didn't tell you?"

I shake my head and say no when I realize he's not even looking at me.

"Such bullshit," he mutters under his breath. "Well, I got into an argument with Em first."

"With Em?" I remember seeing them outside when we left the party, both of them yelling at each other.

He nods as he starts to tear the napkin into shreds. "She was being...weird. Clingy. I think she was trying to make Ryan jealous, kind of rub it into his face about what he was missing."

"I can't even believe you're mentioning her right now," I whisper, my stomach roiling. Looks like my appetite is fading thanks to Dustin.

My emotions are so all over the place when it comes to my supposed best friends. It's confusing. They confuse me.

Especially my feelings for Dustin.

"I'm trying to tell you what happened, okay? It's not easy for me to tell you all this." His gaze meets mine and I nod, not wanting him to stop talking.

He returns his focus to the napkin shredding. "Em ends up getting so pissed at me and everyone else in the house that she leaves."

"With who?"

Dustin shrugs. "I don't know. She texted me that she got a ride. She asked me for one, but I wasn't ready to go. I thought you were still in the house, so I went looking for you."

My heart cracks. "You did?"

"Yeah. Found Ryan instead. He said something stupid. I said something stupid back. We started pushing each other and next thing I know we're going at it."

"I can't believe he gave you a black eye." I also can't believe Dustin went back into Tuttle's house looking for *me*.

Why?

I almost don't want to know.

"He sucker punched me. One of his stupid bros called my name and got my attention. Your Ryan punched me in the eye when I was distracted." Dustin stares off into the distance, his jaw rigid. "The pussy."

"Dustin." I rest my hand over his, ending the shredding. "You should've never got into a fight with him."

"You don't understand." Dustin pulls his hand from underneath mine. "I couldn't let him get away with what he said about you."

Unease settles over me like a dark, foreboding cloud. "What did he say?"

Dustin shakes his head. "I can't tell you."

"Come on. Please?"

"I shouldn't." His voice is firm. "But you deserve to know." He hesitates for the quickest second. "He was joking, saying he would take bets on how fast he could get into your pants."

"Take *bets?*" How disgusting. "Are you serious?"

"He's a jerk, Livvy. That asshole doesn't deserve you."

"He doesn't have me," I murmur. Dustin's head jerks up his eyes wide and I try to smile but fail. Maybe smiling isn't the right thing to do at this moment. I'm pissed that Ryan would say such a thing. What a pig. "We're not together."

"You were with him at the party."

"I didn't come with him. I went with Amanda Winters."

Dustin leans back in his seat. "I didn't know you were friends with Amanda."

"We've been hanging out." Now it's my turn to shrug.

"But you went out with Ryan Saturday night."

I frown. "How do you know that?"

Our pizzas are delivered to our table and the server guy is over-the-top attentive, asking us if we need anything else and wanting to make sure our pizzas were properly cooked to order. I practically want to throw a napkin at him to get him to leave, and finally whatever Dustin says works because the guy is gone and now it's just the two of us once more.

Alone.

"Em told me she saw you two together. Well, that she saw Ryan drop you off at your house," Dustin says before taking a giant bite of his pizza.

I watch him eat, picking a piece of chicken off my pizza and popping it into my mouth. "We just hung out Saturday. It wasn't anything major."

"But you like him."

I duck my head, my cheeks hot. "I shouldn't."

"No, you really shouldn't," Dustin agrees a little too passionately.

"Why does everyone hate him?" I lift my head, hoping I'll get a straight answer. An honest one.

"He's a douche. I think you know it too. You're just attracted to him or whatever." Dustin's cheeks turn ruddy, making me realize this conversation is just as awkward and weird for him as it is for me. Despite our being friends for years, he likes me. We've been intimate together. And now here we are at a crossroads, with neither of us knowing which way to go next.

"So you're seeing Em now." When he sends me a questioning look, I continue. "She told me she was at your house."

"You *talked* to her?" He sounds shocked, but I guess I shouldn't blame him.

"She didn't give me much choice. You know Em." We share a secret smile because boy, do we both know Em. Though he knows her a little more intimately now...

Ugh. My wayward thoughts make me crazy.

"Nothing happened between us. I was still really pissed off about Friday's fight and she was just trying to make me feel better," he says, his voice calm and reassuring in that typical Dustin way of his.

Yet his words don't calm or reassure me. They make me anxious. It feels like Em has taken my place. I normally would've been the one who went to Dustin's house to make sure he was all right. Now she was doing it. She was being his safe place and I'm the one he got into fights over.

I'm selfish for feeling this way. For thinking this way. I miss Dustin. I want to keep our friendship. Maybe deep down inside I like that he's always there for me, that he has a crush on me and that I'm so comfortable with him. That I know if I wanted to, I could tell him I want to be with him and he'd agree.

But then I remember he's been with Em and I can't believe she broke Girl Code so easily and that he sort of cheated on me with her. Or she sort of cheated on me with him.

God, see? It makes no sense. My positive thoughts and silly hopes all go to shit as reality smacks me right in the face.

I finally nibble on a piece of pizza, full of regret over my appetite leaving me. I watch as Dustin basically inhales his pizza in a matter of minutes and starts staring longingly at mine.

"I thought you hated veggies and chicken on pizza," I tease him as I pluck another piece of chicken off my pizza and eat it.

"Normally I do, but I'm starving. You gonna eat it?"

I shake my head and he slides my plate on top of his, digging in. "If I ate as much as you, I'd be as big as a house."

"You would not," he says between mouthfuls.

"Would too. You're a human vacuum." We've fallen into our natural habits and it feels so right. Talking with him, watching him—despite the black eye, it all seems so normal.

"Livvy." He shoves the plates out of his way and reaches across the table, taking my hand in his. "I'm sorry for what happened between Em and I. I don't expect your forgiveness or expect you to say that everything's okay, because you shouldn't say that. And if you're not over what I did, I totally get that too. Just know I feel bad. I never meant to hurt you. It was all a...terrible mistake."

Sounds familiar. I called us a mistake. And at the time we felt like one. I didn't want to tie myself down to just one guy. More like I didn't want to tie myself down to Dustin, and I know that's what he wants. He thinks I'm it for him. He'd never say that out loud and holy shit, I sound like a total egotistical asshole, but it's true.

Dustin has our lives planned out. And I want to try to take a different road. I still want to. That hasn't changed.

"Does Em feel the same way?" I pull my hands out from under his but keep them on the table, and he does the same.

He hesitates and I take a sip of my soda, hating how my anxiousness feels like it's eating me alive. "I don't know how she feels."

"Do you like her?" Oh God, I can't believe I just asked him that.

"Not like I like you," he murmurs, stretching out his index finger to gently rub it across mine.

I feel that tiny touch like he stroked my entire body.

chapter twenty-two

I'm sitting on the bleachers after school, a cool breeze washing over me and sending my hair flying across my face. I push it out of my eyes, my gaze zeroing in on Ryan out on the field. Their coach is yelling at the top of his lungs, blowing his whistle what feels like every two seconds, and his barking voice is giving me a headache.

But I'm not going anywhere. I need to talk to Ryan and it's like he knows. He knows he's done wrong and he's avoiding me like I'm an ultra-contagious sexually transmitted disease.

The boy is going to have to face me sometime. I need to ask him if he really made a bet he could get into my panties.

Boys are so awful.

The varsity cheerleading team is on the sidelines, running through their routine and shouting constant positive reinforcement statements at each other like, "You've got this!" and "Don't give up now!" They're working on their stunts as their sassy and perfect ponytails bounce in the wind, and honestly? They're fascinating to watch. All kicking tanned legs and precise head movements, their arms sharp as they swing through the air. They are the complete opposite of the football team—which looks like a scrambling mess—and I can't help but find it amusing.

Even the band is out on the opposite end of the field, running through drills and formations, the tuba players colliding with each other every single time, making the band teacher lose his shit as he yells himself hoarse. Everything that's happening now is so straight out of a teen movie it's not even funny, and I sit there on the cold metal bench, a secret smile curling my lips despite my irritation with Ryan.

"What are you doing here?"

I look down to see Amanda waving at me as she runs up the steps, her pounding feet loud on the old bleacher steps. I'm the only one sitting this high and she scoots in right next to me, flashing a giant smile in my direction as she blows out a long breath.

"I'm waiting for Ryan to finish practice," I tell her as she runs both hands through her long hair, tugging out the tangles. "What are you doing here?"

"I was missing being in band so I thought I'd come out and watch them," she says, though her gaze is fixed on the football players.

Specifically Tuttle.

"Uh huh." I nudge her with my shoulder. "More like you're spying on Tuttle. What did you two talk about after I left you this morning?"

"Nothing." Her cheeks turn the faintest pink and I know she's full of crap. "He just flirted with me like he always does and then I went to class."

"You like him."

She shakes her head, her gaze meeting mine. "No, I don't. He's awful. He screws anything that moves. And if he's not having sex with a girl, he's asking for a blowjob or a hand job or God knows what."

"Then why does he seem so interested in you?" I wasn't saying it to be mean, but seriously. Why did Tuttle seem so into Amanda?

"I don't know." Amanda's gaze returns to the field, to the football players, to Tuttle. "I think he just likes to give me a hard time. That's all."

There's more to it than that, but if she's not ready to admit anything, then I'm not going to pry. She'll open up to me eventually.

Hopefully.

"What are you going to talk to Ryan about? The fight?" she asks.

I nod. "I went to lunch with Dustin."

"You did?" She sounds shocked. "What did he say?"

I fill her in on what happened, what Dustin said. She listens quietly, her expression equal parts sympathetic and indignant on my behalf. I love that I can talk to her and she seems truly interested, when Em would always get distracted or even out and out tell me she was bored.

"Why do you think Ryan kept it from you?" she asks once I'm finished.

"Probably because he knew how pissed I'd be when I found out."

"He seems like the type who wants to cause trouble though, you know?" She makes a little face. "From everything you've told me and what I've witnessed, he doesn't act like he'd care if you knew or not. Actually, I think he'd *want* you to find out."

My gaze goes to Ryan just as he tears his helmet off in obvious anger and it goes flying across the grass. His hair is a mess and he's covered in sweat, his scowl noticeable even from the nosebleed seats. He lifts the hem of his practice jersey to wipe at his face and I catch a flash of his perfect abs.

I squeeze my thighs together to ease the sudden ache there. I'm so mad at him yet he's so freaking *hot*.

"He sends me mixed messages," I tell her, my gaze still fixed on Ryan as he grabs a water bottle and chugs it. "One minute he acts totally into me and the next he's avoiding me. He's…weird."

"Hmm." She presses her lips together like she's repressing what she really wants to say.

"What do you mean, hmm?" I turn to look her.

"I don't know. When guys act like that they're usually hiding something. Like my ex Thad. He would play that game with me and it turned out he was trying to hide the fact that he was messing around with my best friend." The bitterness in her tone is obvious.

"Not every guy cheats, Amanda," I remind her gently.

"Yeah, but a lot of them do. And I don't want to be mean, but I wouldn't put it past Ryan to cheat, not that you two are even really together. Didn't he say that to you?"

Yeah. He did.

"Look at him. He's gorgeous and rich and already part of the popular crowd, and he's only been at school for a week. He's going to surpass Tuttle soon for the most popular senior boy," Amanda continues.

"I don't think Tuttle likes him," I say.

"I *know* Jordan doesn't like him." When I look at her, her cheeks are rosy. "What? He told me."

"When?"

"Just watch out for Ryan," Amanda says, like she knows what she's talking about. "He's probably up to no good."

She's most likely right, but she's talking with all the authority of a girl who's in with the popular crowd and she's not. She's just Amanda Winters, former band geek, current smart girl and possible crush object of one Jordan Tuttle.

Hmm. Maybe I should give Amanda more credit.

We stay pretty quiet through the rest of practice. The cheerleaders leave first, and then the band clears the field. But the football coaches won't let up. They're relentless in demanding the boys run through a play again. And again.

And again.

Never once does Tuttle make a mistake. The guy launches the ball like it's a missile, spiraling through the air, his aim true. It's everyone else who needs work. They all look like they scramble on the field, running into each other, fumbling the ball. I knew our team wasn't the best, but I didn't realize they were that bad.

Finally, when the boys are dragging and look ready to collapse, the head coach calls practice to an end.

"Did you see how good Tuttle played?" Amanda asks me as we rush down the steps toward the field.

"Yeah. I stayed quiet so I wouldn't disturb your moment." And Amanda was totally having a moment. She watched Tuttle move across that field in awe. You could hear his deep, rough voice calling the plays, and she leaned forward every time, like she wanted to savor the sound.

"Shut up," she says good-naturedly over her shoulder. We land on the ground and she starts to go in the opposite direction. "Hope your talk with Ryan works out."

"Wait a minute." I snag hold of her wrist, stopping her, though I keep my gaze focused on the field. The players haven't gone back into the locker room yet and I don't want to miss my opportunity to get to Ryan before he tries to avoid me again. "You aren't going with me?"

Amanda slowly shakes her head and I let go of her. "I don't want Tuttle to know I was watching him practice. That'll just feed his already massive ego."

"He'd probably *love* knowing you were watching him." Yeah, it would feed his ego, but it also shows she cares about him playing the game. Girls don't come to watch Tuttle play football. It's more about the status he'd bring if he ever allowed any girl to actually be seen with him.

Normally, he doesn't. He's a lone wolf who runs on hookups and booze and nothing else.

"Whatever." She laughs. "Go chase down Ryan before he makes his escape."

Ugh. That's exactly what I end up doing, which is stupid. I jog across the field, hating how out of breath I become. I'm not taking P.E. this year since it's not required and I probably should've. I need to get back into shape.

Other guys on the team spot me first and they get Ryan's attention by calling his name and pointing at me. He turns to watch me approach, his hair damp with sweat and his eyes blazing with...

Anger? Irritation? I can't even tell anymore.

"What are you doing here?" he asks when I get in hearing distance.

"We need—" I stop in front of him and try to catch my breath. "—to talk."

He grimaces. "If this is about me kicking your little friend's ass, trust me. He had it coming."

My mouth drops open in shock and I hear more than a few snickers come from the other boys. I ignore them and thankfully they all start to walk off the field. "Why didn't you tell me?"

"I knew you'd be mad at me." He shrugs, his expression completely blank. "So what was the point?"

"But you also had to know I'd find out...right?"

He sighs wearily, the tension seeming to leave his body all at once and making his shoulders sag. "Right. And you're reacting just like I thought you would."

"How exactly am I reacting?" My voice rises and I sound the slightest bit shrill.

Like a jealous, put-out girlfriend. Exactly what Ryan didn't want to deal with.

The rest of the team has left the field and are headed for the locker room, until it's just Ryan and me. He doesn't look thrilled to be left with me, and honestly? I'm not too thrilled to be left alone with him either.

"Like a bitchy girlfriend. And I haven't even got you naked yet." He shakes his head, muttering, "I don't know if it's gonna be worth it either."

Icy cold shock combined with boiling hot rage washes over me and I blink up at him, dumbfounded by his cruelty. "What did you say?" I gasp out.

His mouth thins into a firm line. "You heard me."

What an asshole. "Is it true that you made a bet with your friends about having sex with me?"

He throws his hands up into the air. "Seriously? No, I didn't make a bet, Livvy. Who'd you hear that from? Your little puppet, Dustin? Or maybe Em? Like they care about you."

Oh, that is *it*. I turn on my heel and run off the field, past the bleachers, out toward the parking lot. Until my lungs are burning and I'm halfway home before I finally stop to rest, bending over and resting my hands on my knees as I try to calm my breathing, my racing heart.

Everyone keeps warning me about him. Amanda, Dustin, Em. And for some stupid reason I kept thinking I was different. I was special. He'd treat me better. He'd fall for me and we'd become a real couple.

Clearly I'm delusional.

chapter twenty-three

I'm going to be totally lame right now and pull the PMS card. That's why I've been acting so insane lately. Why my emotions have been all over the place. On top of the unusual amount of turmoil I've suffered through since school started, I was also experiencing a raging case of premenstrual syndrome.

It's been almost two weeks since the infamous football field argument with Ryan, and Aunt Flo's visit is just about to come to an end. Meaning I am finally feeling back to normal.

"I hate being on my period," I say as I come out of the bathroom stall. The first bell is going to ring in a few minutes, so we need to hurry.

Amanda is leaning over the counter, closely examining her face in the horribly dim light of the senior hall girls' bathroom. Big mistake. I always look like hell in this room. I end up with weird shadows on my face and what looks like giant bluish-black bags under my eyes.

"How long does yours usually last?" she asks, her gaze meeting mine in the mirror.

"Four or five days." I stand at the sink next to her and wash my hands, then grab some paper towels. "How about you?"

"Three days. I used to be super irregular until my mom put me on the pill." She pulls a Fresh tinted lip balm out of her purse and applies it quickly, rubbing her lips together before shoving the balm into her backpack.

"You're on the pill?" I sound shocked. I try to act casual, but it's no use. I really am shocked.

"Yeah, though it's not like I'm having sex on the regular." The moment the words fall from her lips in walks Em, along with two other girls, one I recognize but whose name I don't remember and the other...

Brianne Brown. The girl who is trying her best to sink her claws into Dustin and make him hers. Why are the two of them hanging out?

"Livvy." Em's upper lip curls and her gaze slides to Amanda. "And Livvy's friend."

Amanda sends her a pointed look. "Amanda."

"Right. Amanda. AKA clarinet fourth chair?" Em laughs and so do her friends. More like Brianne titters and the sound is so annoying I want to shove her head into the toilet and flush about ten times.

Dude. Maybe the PMS is still lingering. I feel a little ragey just looking at Brianne.

"More like second chair, but thanks for noticing. Though I'm not in band any longer, so yeah." The smile Amanda sends her is saccharine sweet and I cover my mouth with my fingers, not wanting Em to notice me holding back my laughter.

The one girl locks herself away in a stall while Brianne goes straight to the mirror and starts messing with her hair. She's always been incredibly vain, so that's no surprise.

What is a surprise is Em's behavior. Since we encountered each other that one Saturday night almost two weeks ago, we haven't really talked, or even seen each other at school. This past weekend I ended up staying home and helping Mom with yard work. I got a sunburn, blisters on my hand and an extra seventy five dollars in my pocket that I plan on using for new clothes.

But when we last talked, I figured Em and I were cool. Not like we were on best-friends-till-the-end terms, but we had come to an unspoken truce.

Or so I thought.

"You haven't been hanging with Ryan much anymore, huh?" Em smacks her gum as she smirks at me.

"Keeping tabs on me?" So annoying that she knows. And now she's rubbing it in my face.

"I don't have to. Ryan's been spending all his free time with me." She blows a bubble and pops it so loud, she startles Brianne at the mirror. She sends us a dirty look before she starts reapplying her lip gloss.

I go rigid with anger. Ryan and I have made idle small talk in class but not every day. We've texted a few times, nothing serious. A couple of nights ago he sent me a shadowy dick pick on Snapchat that I couldn't even really see. I even screenshotted that sucker so I could zoom in, then sent it to Amanda so she could examine it, and she agreed.

We couldn't see…dick.

Ha ha.

"That's nice," I say just as Amanda grabs my arm and propels me out of the bathroom. I can hear Em yelling "Bye!" as we walk out, but Amanda doesn't give me a chance to respond.

"Why do you even engage with her, huh?" Amanda asks as she hustles me down the hallway.

"I seriously don't know." Em knows just how to get to me, too.

That's what you get for breaking up with your best friend. They use all of your weaknesses against you.

"Well, stop. Besides, she's lying."

I come to a halt, making Amanda stop too. The crowd just parts around us as they keep going. "What exactly is she lying about?"

"Being with Ryan. I know for a fact he's been living and breathing football, this last week especially." She starts walking again and I grab hold of her hand one more time, causing her to stop again. "Stop doing that."

"Tell me exactly how you know this."

There go Amanda's cheeks again. Turning a pretty shade of pink. That only means one thing.

Tuttle.

"I just know, okay? Their practices are intense. They're not allowed much free time beyond the field. Tomorrow's game is huge. They want to come at it hard." Amanda makes a little face. "They're playing the league champions, so they're probably going to get their butts kicked."

"I had no idea." We start walking once more, my thoughts filled with Ryan. Why he was so rude to me that night on the field—yeah, I still haven't let it go—when he was probably frustrated over the team. They'd played like shit during that practice. I'd been a witness.

"I'm not saying that's an excuse for the way he's treating you, but the pressure is seriously on," Amanda explains, smiling and waving at someone we pass. It feels like she knows everyone, though they're mostly people she knows from band.

"So he was distracted."

"They're all really grumpy."

"And you know this how? You've been hanging with the team?" I shoot her a curious glance because seriously. What is Amanda up to?

She shrugs, trying for nonchalant, but it's not working. "I've been watching them practice."

"Oh really? Why?" Now I'm trying for innocent and from the shrewd look she sends my way, I know she's not buying it.

Amanda rolls her eyes. "I don't think I have to answer that."

"Whatever." I nudge her and she nudges me back, a sly smile on her face as she quickly changes the subject.

"Do you want to go to the game with me tomorrow?"

"Sure. I should go so I can take some photos for yearbook."

"Perfect! Plus you can be at the game to support Ryan."

"I guess." I shrug. I'm still hurt by how he treated me. And the bet thing. I still don't know if that was true or not. Yeah, I know Amanda just gave him a great excuse for his bad behavior, but that doesn't mean I have to accept it.

"Come on, Liv. Show Ryan you can be a cool girl who doesn't have any expectations." She lifts her brows as we stop in front of her classroom. "He'll be impressed you showed up for him."

"You really think so?"

"He will! Guys like that sort of thing." She talks like a girl with plenty of knowledge, but most of the time I think she's just winging it. "Don't chase after him, don't ask him what's wrong. Just show up, cheer on the team, congratulate him if they win afterward or tell him good game if they lose. The important part is you're there for him."

"Okay." I nod, encouraged by her words. She's right. I should be there for him. "Yeah. Let's do this."

Amanda's smile is one of those doozies she's so good at delivering. "Perfect. I'll pick you up and we can sit together. Do you know this is the first time I get to sit in the stands like a normal person instead of always being with the band in those hideous, sweaty polyester uniforms?"

"Do you miss band?" I ask her just as the warning bell rings.

"I definitely don't miss having to wear polyester," she calls over her shoulder as she darts into class.

chapter twenty-four

"Oh God." I cover my eyes with my hands, peeking through my spread fingers so I can still keep track of the madness unfolding out on the field. "I can't watch."

"Stop." Amanda pokes her very sharp fingernail in my side and I shift away from her. The girl is forceful when she wants to be. "It's not that bad."

"They look like they're murdering each other!" I drop my hands, and hold the camera up to my face, trying to search for Ryan. But I can't find him in the tangle of players. You can hear the boys grunt and groan and every time it's our turn to try and score, Tuttle screams all of these numbers and weird terms to the rest of the team.

I don't get it. Amanda's trying her best to explain everything, but I think I'm driving her insane. "They're fine. They wear protective gear so they won't get hurt," she reassures me.

"Huh." I've read stories where players are paralyzed. Where they suffer one concussion after another and are messed up. This game is freaking dangerous. She can't convince me otherwise.

The referee blows his whistle and talks about personal fouls and everyone in the bleachers starts yelling and complaining. Including Amanda. She's really into this game.

Like, *super* into it.

Not me, though. I don't watch a lot of football. Dad left and took his Sunday ritual with him. Mom hates all televised sports and I guess her feelings rubbed off on me. I'd rather be hanging out on the upper field where everyone else is gossiping and waiting for this game to finish.

Instead I'm sitting with Amanda, who's glued to the hard, metal seat, her expression rapt as she watches our varsity boys scramble like lost puppies out on the field.

"What happened? Why'd he say personal foul?" I ask, wincing when she immediately launches into a long, detailed explanation that I don't really care about because I don't really get it. I have no idea if they're doing good or bad or worse. Amanda keeps reassuring me they're holding their own and they look better than they did two weeks ago, but I don't know.

The minute it's halftime, I'm dragging Amanda away from the bleachers so we can go buy a soda and maybe some nachos. The line is long at the snack stand and I whine a little at Amanda about having to wait and how starved I am, but she seems distracted.

"We're missing the band performance," she tells me when I ask her what's wrong. She waves a hand toward the lower field and I can hear the band start playing.

"So? Aren't you glad you're not in band?"

"Well, yeah, but it's weird. I've been performing out on that field for the past three years and now I'm not. It feels…strange." She shakes her head, offering me an apologetic smile. "I should go watch."

"No, you shouldn't." I'm being selfish, but I don't want her to leave me alone.

"I should." She nods, her expression firm. "I'm going to."

My mouth drops open, but then I snap it shut. Maybe she misses band after all. "You should take photos of the band."

Her face brightens. "You really think so? You'd trust me with the camera?"

"Totally." I have faith that Amanda won't break it. "Do you know how to work a Nikon?"

"My mom has one." She takes the camera I hand over to her and slips the strap around her neck. "Wow, thanks. This will be fun."

I'm glad she's excited about it. "You want me to get you something at the snack bar?"

"No, I'm good. Thanks, Livvy! I'll take good pictures, I promise!" She takes off before I can say another word.

I stand in line alone, hoping I don't run into anyone I don't want to talk to. I smile and wave at a girl from my English class before I pull my phone out of the back pocket of my jeans and check it for...anything. Maybe a quick text from Ryan? I'd sent him one right before the game, wishing him good luck tonight, but he didn't respond.

Wishful thinking. He still hasn't responded. And there's nothing really happening on Snapchat either. I briefly scroll through Instagram as the line inches forward, distracted by the two girls behind me who keep droning on and on over how hot all the players are on our football team.

"I mean, Tuttle is freaking gorg, but he won't even look our way," one girl says.

"He doesn't do freshmen. He's turning eighteen soon and he has a strict no freshmen rule," the other girl says with all the authority of a stupid freshman.

I almost start laughing but restrain myself.

"What about the new boy? He's hot."

"Which one?"

"Ryan Bennett."

If my ears could perk up, they so would. When the line shifts forward I take a tiny step, keeping myself close to the gossiping girls.

"He's totally hot. Flirts a lot too."

I frown. How would she know that?

"Would that make him a fuckboy? Those types are the worst." Both girls giggle and I'm tempted to turn around and ask them what they know about fuckboys, but I restrain myself.

"Hey, if he wanted to be my fuckboy, I'd take him on," the other one says between giggles. "Is there a dance tonight?"

"Yeah, but do you really think the football team will come to the dance?"

Ha, no. They're notorious for bailing on school activities unless they're forced to attend them. They're always at the homecoming dance only because so many of them are nominated and their head coach forces them all to go.

"Maybe! Wouldn't it be amazing if they showed? Oh my gosh, maybe we could talk to one of them!"

They sound so excited, so young and naïve and hopeful, I have to cover my mouth with my hand so I don't burst out laughing and say something rude like "keep dreaming."

"What's so funny?"

I turn to find Em standing before me, her brows raised, her ruby red lips formed into a contemplative pout. I smile at her automatically, immediately hating how I fall back into old habits every time she comes around.

"Nothing." I tilt my head toward the girls behind me. "What are you up to?"

"Not much. Wishing I could get out of here, but I'm with Brianne so..." Em makes a face. "She likes these sorts of things."

"You hate these sorts of things."

Em smiles slowly. "I know. Yet here I am."

I say nothing. There are a thousand questions running through my mind, but I don't know where to start and besides, I don't think she'd answer seventy-five percent of them. It's hard to remember I'm mad at her when she's been such a big part of my life for the last six years.

"Who did you come to the game with?" Em asks when I don't say anything.

"Amanda Winters."

She wrinkles her nose. "Since when did you start hanging out with Amanda Winters?"

"Since when did you start hanging with Brianne Brown?" I throw back, my tone snotty.

"Since we basically broke up."

The line shifts forward and I realize I'm the next one up. "Give me a break. We were never together."

"You're my best friend, Liv." Em steps closer, sinking her teeth into her blood-red bottom lip. "I've missed you so much. Brianne isn't as much fun as you."

I'm not going to say Amanda isn't as much fun as Em because that isn't necessarily true. Amanda is a different kind of fun. She's smart and funny and we have a good time together.

Frowning, I sneak a look at Em to find her already watching me. She looks so different. Her gaze is hazy, like she smoked a little something before coming to the game. Her eyeliner is thick and smudged and that lipstick she's wearing makes her mouth look huge.

"Have you seen Dustin?" I dare to ask her.

"No," she says flatly.

Huh. I go up to the tiny window of the snack stand and Em goes with me. I order nachos and a Coke, then look at Em. "Want something?"

She shakes her head and pulls a cigarette out of the pocket of her tiny denim shorts. The booster parent helping me thrusts her arm out the window, waving her finger at Em. "No smoking on school property!" the woman yells.

Em laughs. "I'm not smoking it. See? It's not lit."

The woman glares and I glare back, irritated. "My nachos?" I remind her.

She pushes away from the counter with a withering stare and goes to make my nachos and get my Coke. Em cracks up, the cig still dangling from her mouth as she laughs.

"Who got her panties all twisted in a bunch?"

"Who knows?" This moment right now feels like old times. Em and I, when we're together, we're not always the best influence on each other. I know this. So does Em. We don't outright get into trouble, but we push each other beyond our limits. Meaning usually Em pushes me and I restrain her. I never really noticed our push-and-pull relationship until I stopped hanging around her and started spending time with Amanda.

It feels good, to have that rebellious little push back again. I'm thinking Em feels the same way.

Once I pay for my food and drink I go sit at a nearby bench and Em joins me, exchanging her phone for her cigarette. She sends a text to someone before smiling at me. "Give me a nacho."

I hand her an extra cheesy one, her favorite. She bites into it, murmuring a little as she chews. "God, it's so good. Hanging out with

Brianne and Naya is exhausting. They're always on diets. They force me to watch what I eat and they keep food journals. When I told them I don't count calories they about died."

"That sounds awful," I say before I take a big slurp of Coke.

"Right?" Em reaches out and snags her own chip coated with processed cheese. "The only reason Brianne wants to hang out with me is because I'm friends with Dustin."

"Do you really believe that?"

Em nods, licking a glob of cheese from the corner of her mouth. "Totally. She's hoping I'll put in the good word with Dustin."

"You two are still hanging out?" Ugh, it hurts just saying it. Dustin tells me he wants to avoid her. Em acts like they've never stopped seeing each other. I don't know who to believe.

"Sort of? I don't know. You should've seen the disappointment on her face when I told her we haven't hung out much lately. Now Brianne is stuck with me." She grins and snags the cup out of my hand. "She's so hot for him it's pitiful."

I tell myself not to feel jealous, but it's no use. I'm half tempted to go find Brianne and pull all that perfect blonde hair out of her head. I hate how she chases after him. "Is he hot for her?"

"He's not talking to me, so how would I know?" Em shakes her head. "You sound like Brianne. She's constantly asking me to go and make nice with him, but he's iced me out."

Is it wrong that I'm glad he's not talking to Em? Probably. "We don't talk much either anymore, Dustin and I."

"We've all fallen apart and I hate it. All because he couldn't keep his hands to himself over the summer." Em shakes her head ruefully, not even noticing how *my* hands start to shake. Seriously, she *would* bring that back up. It's like she enjoys rubbing my face in her and Dustin's hookups. Like she doesn't even care how she's making me feel. "It wasn't even that good."

"Em." I sound like I can barely hold it together, which is fairly accurate. This is the last thing I want to hear.

"What?" Her wide eyes meet mine and she looks like innocence personified—which I happen to know is a bunch of crap. "It wasn't! He's not really…skilled, you know what I mean? Yes, he has nice hands and he's a decent kisser, but he finishes too fast for my liking."

I can't take it anymore. I stand and pitch the nachos into the garbage can before I take a huge drink of my Coke. I need the rush of caffeine and sugar to fortify me. Fire me up. Or maybe if I keep my lips on the straw long enough, the urge to verbally tear her apart will pass.

"Hey, you threw away perfectly good nachos," Em whines.

My plans to remain quiet are shattered. "Grab them out of the garbage can and finish them off then. You should be used to that, right? Considering you're nothing but trash?" I walk away before she can say anything, before I can see her reaction. I know it'll either be fake hurt or a smug gleam in her eye because she knows she got to me.

Em knows just how to get to me. She always has.

"What the hell, Liv!" she shouts after me, but I don't turn around.

I keep walking. I can hear her come up behind me, but she doesn't try to stop me. I don't want to cause a scene yet I know she'd have no problem telling me how she felt. Em has never been one to shy away from a confrontation.

"You think what you're doing is so much better? It's like you're going after Ryan on *purpose*." Oh, Em sounds furious. Like I care. "We've all warned you about him, Liv. He's using you, you know. He'll bang you, tell everyone about it, maybe even take a photo or twenty and send them to all his friends. Once that happens, trust me, you're *really* good and screwed. And he won't give a shit either. He'll already have moved on to the next girl."

I whirl around to face her, my anger fueling me. Now I really don't care if anyone's paying us any attention. I almost want to put on a show. "Is that what he did to you?"

Em lifts her chin and I see that flash of vulnerability shadow her gaze. "Like you care."

"Did he?"

She drops her gaze and looks down, staring at her black low-top Converse. "It doesn't matter what he did. You're the one who's chasing after him when you know the two of us hooked up. You look desperate."

I glare at her, all of my angry, rude responses evaporating. I take a deep breath and turn and walk away from Em, telling myself I'm doing what's best. Fighting with her will get me nowhere. Making a scene will only end up embarrassing me.

I've had enough embarrassment. Whoever heard her call me desperate will spread that around, I'm sure. I'll become a total joke, all because I—what? Became interested in the boy she had a summer fling with? They weren't involved, not really.

It doesn't matter. Somehow she's the hurt one and I'm the bad guy. At least, that's how she made me feel.

And I hate it.

chapter twenty-five

"We need to tell them they played a good game," Amanda says as we walk toward the locker rooms. Night has completely fallen and most everyone has left the field and stands, though lots of girls are also headed toward the locker rooms. I feel lame doing this, but Amanda insists this is proper "we're just friends" behavior and it'll make Ryan feel good.

"What if he thinks I'm being clingy?" I discreetly glance over my shoulder to make sure Em isn't in the crowd, and thankfully I don't spot her.

"He won't. You're going to tell him he was great on the field with sincerity in your voice and then we're out," Amanda says firmly. "You walk away, leaving him wanting more."

"You really think that works?" I send her a doubtful look. "Have *you* tried it?"

"I read lots of *Cosmo* articles," Amanda says with a firm nod.

"Playing hard to get works. When you're beyond available, they don't care. If they have to chase after you, they want you even more."

"That sounds ridiculous," I mutter, knocking into her gently with my shoulder.

She laughs. "I know, but if *Cosmo* says it works, then it works."

"Whatever." I roll my eyes.

"Do you think Selena just gave it up immediately to the Biebs? Do you think Gigi Hadid threw herself at Zayn? That would be a no on both counts."

"Now you're busting out celebrity relationships? Please." I laugh. "Biebs and Selena are over. And Gigi and Zayn probably are too."

"It doesn't matter." She waves a dismissive hand. "What I'm saying is boys want the chase. They want to feel like they hunted and conquered."

"That is so sexist."

"It's natural," Amanda corrects as she starts to slow down. I follow her lead. "Watch and see."

A crowd has formed at the entrance of the locker room and the head coach is already standing guard, glowering at all of us adoring female fans who anxiously await the team to emerge. Amanda pushes her way to the front of the crowd and I follow after her, earning more than a few dirty looks.

"Not you too, Winters," Coach Halsey groans when he spots her.

She just grins at him. "I have no idea what you're talking about."

"You quit the band and turn into a groupie instead?" He shakes his head, the disappointment on his face clear. "Unbelievable."

Coach Halsey is in his late thirties and took over the failing team two years ago. He's slowly turned them around one season at a time, and this year everyone has high hopes. They might've lost this game, but they proved a challenge to the opposing team, with the final score ending up 21-17.

The head coach is also pretty decent-looking for an old man, and more than a few of the girls at school have a massive crush on him. He's supposedly happily married, but I've heard a few rumors of inappropriate behavior with students. Not that I can confirm or deny them, but yeah. They float around, especially during the off-season when Coach Halsey is bored and only teaching P.E.

"I'm not a groupie. I wanted to tell my friends on the team they did a good job tonight," Amanda says. "Plus, we're here on behalf of the yearbook."

"Oh yeah? And who are these player *friends* of yours?" Coach Halsey crosses his bulky arms in front of his wide chest. His voice is teasing, but he also looks concerned, and it makes me wonder...

How the hell does Amanda know the head football coach?

"Um. Tuttle and Ryan." Amanda's cheeks go bright red and I feel sorry for her. I thought *I* got embarrassed easily. This girl goes down in flames any time she thinks about, alludes to or mentions Tuttle's name. It's the craziest thing, especially since she rarely talks about him.

I've become comfortable enough to tell her all about my raging crush on Ryan, which is still raging despite my frustration with him. I told her about Dustin. I told her about my, ahem, *encounters* with Dustin, and Em's confession, and how my best friends completely failed me. Amanda's a very understanding person. But she's also very private.

Too private.

"You would become 'friends' with those two." Coach Halsey even adds the air quotes. His gaze skitters over to me and he narrows his eyes. "Who's this?"

"Olivia Hudson." Amanda smiles. "She's on the yearbook staff and she was taking photos of tonight's game."

"They played really great tonight," I say, trying to sound enthusiastic. But the look Coach Halsey shoots my way tells me he's not buying it.

"Uh huh," he says skeptically. "You two stay out of trouble, okay?" He winks and then walks away before we can answer him.

"How do you know the coach?"

Amanda sighs and looks over at me. "Years ago, he was the football coach at our middle school and my older brother played for him."

Oh, right. How could I forget Jeep Winters? Well, his real name is George, but everyone for some strange reason calls him Jeep. I don't get it, but whatever. "How much older is he than you?"

"Five years. He graduated college this last December and he's traveling all over Europe right now." She sighs. "Lucky dick."

I burst out laughing because Amanda rarely uses words like dick. She curses, but not like Em and I do. "You don't get along with your brother?"

"He's the greatest brother ever if you want me to be honest, which I also find super annoying. The guy can do no wrong," she says irritably. "It's enough to give a girl a complex."

"I'm sure." I have no idea what she's talking about. I consider myself an only child. Yeah, I have the younger brother and sister Dad has with Christine, but they don't really count in my eyes. I have to live with them six weeks out of the year, big deal. "And why does everyone call him Jeep anyway?"

"That's my fault. I couldn't say George when I was a baby, so for some weird reason I called him Jeep. Then it stuck. No one calls him George at home, though I think he ditched the nickname in college," Amanda explains.

"So you like football because of your brother."

"And my dad. And because I've been to pretty much every football game played by our school since my freshman year. It's just a part of my life. I love football." She shrugs, then her eyes light up and she nudges me in the side with her elbow. "They're coming out."

Nerves flare in my stomach and I watch the locker room entrance. A few boys exit the doorway first, guys I don't recognize but smile at anyway. Some of the girls shout their names and I watch in stunned disbelief as they run up to the boys like they're going to ask for their autographs.

"I don't even know who they are," Amanda leans in and whispers, making me smile.

One by one the guys file out, and still no Ryan or Tuttle. The longer it takes, the more anxious I get. I sense Amanda is the same way. She's bouncing on the balls of her feet, her hands wringing together, and she stares so intently at that open doorway I half expect the building might start to crumble from the force of her glare.

I'm being completely dramatic, but come on. She's acting kind of intense.

Finally, *finally* they emerge from the depths of the locker room, Tuttle and Ryan walking side by side, their hair damp from taking a shower and both of them looking painfully gorgeous.

I can admit Tuttle is very attractive, but he's not the one I have my eyes on. No, it's Ryan who I can't stop staring at. He's wearing a white T-shirt that stretches across his shoulders and chest in the most enticing way, and khaki shorts that look preppy yet somehow work on him. His white baseball cap is on backwards and my knees go weak at how cute he looks.

He spots me almost immediately and his eyes light up as he approaches, Tuttle coming along with him.

"Livvy." Ryan smiles, his green eyes sparkling. "Didn't expect to see you here."

"Glad to see the presidents of our fan club made it," Tuttle adds, his gaze glued on Amanda.

"Please," Amanda says, sounding exasperated. "We just wanted to congratulate you both on a good game. Right, Liv?"

Oh. I'm supposed to talk. I blink, trying my best to get Ryan's perfect face and adorable smile out of my head. "Um, yeah. Right. You guys played great."

Ryan turns bashful, making a cute little face. "But we didn't win."

"You came so close, though. You guys played an amazing game. I thought at one point you were going to tie it up," Amanda says.

"Our kicker isn't the best," Tuttle admits. "He's getting better, though."

"You don't have a second string you can trust?" Amanda asks.

I watch her, amazed that she sounds so sincere. And that's because she *is* sincere. She's interested too. Tuttle looks like he's about to sport wood, he's so thrilled she's talking football.

"You don't watch much football, do you?" Ryan says, his voice low. Like he's speaking only to me.

I shrug, a little embarrassed. "I don't really understand it like Amanda does. I'm just here to take photos." I point at the camera still around my neck.

"I can teach you whatever you want to know," he murmurs, his gaze never leaving mine.

Mmm, I've missed his flirtatious tone, his innuendo-laced words. "I'm sure you could," I tease.

"Well, we just wanted to tell you both you played a good game," Amanda says loudly, her hand going to my wrist and giving me a gentle tug. I step back with her, hating that she's pulling me away from Ryan. I know I'm supposed to let him chase me, but I've never liked playing games.

Not that I've played many games like this with boys. I have no idea what I'm doing. Not too sure if Amanda really knows either.

"You two should come to my house," Tuttle offers in that almost maddening unemotional tone he likes to use. Like nothing ever bothers the guy.

"What for?" Amanda asks.

Tuttle tilts his head, a mysterious smile curving his lips. "I'm having a little after game party and thought you'd like to go."

I'm about to say yes when Amanda cuts me off with a look. "I don't know, Tuttle. We're kind of tired," she tells him.

He raises a brow. "Too tired to party? Come on, Mandy. I *know* you like to party."

"Yeah, come over," Ryan adds. "It's only a few guys from the team and some girls. Nothing big."

"Very exclusive," Tuttle adds, like that's going to sway us.

He's right. He's totally swaying me. But is it working on Amanda?

I turn to her and send the most pleading look I can muster. We must go to this. We *must*.

"Come on," I whisper to her, but it's like she's not even listening to me. Her gaze goes to Tuttle, her expression ultra-serious.

"We'll leave you ladies alone so you can chat," Tuttle says as he leads Ryan away.

"We shouldn't," she says the moment they're out of earshot. "The small parties are even worse than the big ones."

"What do you mean?"

"They're like..." She looks around before lowering her voice. "Sex parties."

I giggle. "Please. We couldn't get so lucky."

"Are you telling me if Ryan wanted to do it, you'd have sex with him tonight?" Amanda asks, her brows raised.

Huh. When she puts it like that... "I don't know," I say with a shrug.

"Right. Because you're not ready to take it that far yet."

"So? I think you're overreacting. Even if they are having a sex party tonight, we just won't have sex." I feel like I just solved the world's problems.

"It's not that easy. They can be very…persuasive." She's scowling. It's almost like she's talking from personal experience.

"Then we never leave each other's side. We'll protect each other." I smile brightly. "What do you think?"

She studies me, her eyes narrowed. "You promise you won't leave me?"

"Promise," I say with all the confidence I can muster.

"Fine." She sighs, sounding completely put out. "We'll go to the party. But we're leaving by midnight."

"Seriously, Mom? Give me a break."

Amanda laughs. "I don't want to stay too late. I need my beauty sleep."

"Let me text my mom and tell her I'm spending the night at your house." I whip out my phone and start texting her.

"I thought I was spending the night at your house."

I grin at her. "See, that's the thing. Your mom will think you're at my house and mine will think I'm at yours. And we'll be at Tuttle's."

Amanda frowns. "I just said I wanted to leave by midnight."

"This way we can just crash there—it's perfect!"

"It's perfectly crazy," she mutters under her breath as the boys approach us once more.

"You girls in?" Ryan asks.

I nod, unable to contain the smile that spreads across my face. "We are so in."

The arrogant smirk Ryan sends my way promises tonight is definitely going to be interesting.

chapter twenty-six

"This is such a bad idea," Amanda says as she slowly drives down Tuttle's long gravel driveway.

Even though the moon above is nothing more than a sliver, its light still casts a silvery glow upon the acres of land the Tuttle family owns. There are no cars parked along the driveway or in the fields tonight. As we get closer to the house, I see there are only a few cars parked in the driveway directly in front of the garage. No one is really here.

And I'm so freaking excited I'm practically bouncing in my seat.

"It's a great idea," I reassure her with all the confidence I'm feeling. "You might get alone time with Tuttle."

She sends me a look. "That's what I'm afraid of."

"You don't want to be alone with him?"

"No." She takes a deep breath, then lets it out shakily. "He terrifies me."

"Why?" Oh, there is so much more going on here than she's telling me.

"I don't—I don't want to talk about it." She presses her lips together and pulls to the farthest left side of the driveway, out of the way of the other cars. Once she puts the car in park, she shuts off the engine and sits there, the engine ticking as it cools, the sounds of chirping crickets coming from the fields. "I don't know if I can do this."

"Lots of don'ts in those two sentences," I tease her. No way am I letting her back out now. We've made it this far. Now we're going all in. "We can do this and we will. Let's go."

I reach for the door handle, but Amanda doesn't even move. Unfazed, I climb out of the car and run my fingers through my hair as I go round the front and toward Amanda's door. I open it, leaning my arm on the top edge of the door as I stare at her and she stares back. "Come on."

"No." She looks away from me.

"Amanda." I wish she would tell me what's going on instead of leaving me in the dark. "You're being ridiculous."

Her shoulders sag and her lips part. It's a look of such utter defeat that for about five seconds I feel super guilty for putting her through this.

But then the guilt disappears and I'm grabbing her hand, practically dragging her out of her car. "We'll have fun," I tell her. "I promise."

Amanda mutters a few choice words under her breath as we walk to the front door, but for the most part she's agreeable. As in, she's not running back to the car screaming, so I take that as a good sign. I hit the doorbell and stand up straight, shaking my hair back before I check Amanda to make sure she's okay.

Besides the terrified glimmer shining in her eyes, she looks... great. Despite being a former band geek, she makes everything she wears look effortless. Her outfits are simple yet effective, style-wise. And I pay attention to this stuff. I follow lots of fashion and beauty bloggers on YouTube.

Tonight she's wearing an oversized white T-shirt with a wide neck that keeps slipping off her shoulder and flashing a glimpse of her pale pink bra strap. The most delicate gold chain circles her neck, a tiny pendant hanging from it; I can't make out what it is. Her cropped jeans fit her long legs to perfection and I have serious envy over her cute black sandals.

Ugh. The longer I look at her, the more she makes me feel like a total fail.

"Do I look all right?" I ask her. My outfit seems lame next to hers. I'm wearing denim shorts I got at American Eagle on clearance and a soft blue T-shirt with a white moon and stars scattered all over the front. My hair is down and my neck is sort of sweaty, which means my makeup is sort of sweaty too. I swipe a finger beneath each eye to pick up any smudged eyeliner or mascara and turn to face Amanda.

"You look great." Her smile is soft. Nervous. "Do I look okay? Not that I care. I have no one to impress."

Uh huh. Keep telling yourself that. "You look more than okay. I want your shoes."

She laughs. "I'll let you borrow them sometime."

The door swings open at that exact moment and we both turn to find Tuttle standing there shirtless, wearing only a pair of dark rinse jeans that hang so low on his hips they give us a glimpse of almost everything he has to offer.

I can't stop staring. The boy has muscles for days. I know Amanda is staring too. And Tuttle can't help but love our reactions.

"You girls looked ready to make out before I so rudely interrupted." He swings the door open wider, smirking. I notice he has a shirt clutched in his hand and I wonder when he's going to put it on. "Want to come in and put on a show for us?"

"You cannot be freaking serious right now," Amanda practically spits out, her expression enraged. Oh, Tuttle just stepped in it.

But he just laughs as he steps forward, tugging on the ends of her hair. His fingers come so close to actually touching her boob she gasps. "You know I'm just teasing." His voice is low and rather intimate. I almost feel like I'm interrupting their special moment. "Get your pretty ass in here, Mandy. You too, Olivia."

There he goes saying my full name again. Though I don't bother calling him out on it. I'm too anxious over being let into the inner sanctum. This is a big deal. Huge. Partying with the football players after a Friday night game? Hardly anyone gets to do this. Now, granted, our boys haven't played their best during the course of my high school years, but they are still considered gods at school. Even more so than our basketball team, and they've won a few regional championships and they almost won state last year.

I think it's their size. All the football players are so big. Intimidating. Handsome.

Fine. "Handsome" is a word Mom would use. They're gorgeous. Hot as hell. You get what I'm saying.

"Want something to drink?" Tuttle asks us like the polite host he is. I say yes while Amanda bites out a hostile no, and he sends her a look as he shuts the front door. One that says, *chill out*, and I really hope she does.

The house is so quiet. We walk through the living room as Tuttle leads us to the kitchen and I look around, wondering where everyone is. The last time I came here I couldn't really see the house considering there were so many people crammed inside. Now I can really take in the beautiful furniture that looks brand-new, the giant paintings hanging on the walls. The hardwood floors gleam, and thick, geometrically designed rugs are scattered throughout the rooms. A huge flat screen TV hangs above the sleek fireplace in the living room, three times as big as the one we have in my family room. His house looks straight out of a design magazine. Perfect. Beautiful.

Cold.

"Everyone's outside," Tuttle tells us as we enter the kitchen. He tugs the T-shirt he'd been holding over his head before he goes straight for the giant stainless steel fridge and pulls out two bottles of beer. "I think they want to swim."

"I didn't bring a suit," Amanda says.

He sends her a wicked grin. "You don't need one, pretty girl."

My stomach flutters with nerves. Yeah, I'm not jumping into Tuttle's pool naked. No way.

"We're not going to skinny dip in your pool, Tuttle," Amanda snaps, taking the beer from him. Guess she wanted something to drink after all. "That would be stupid."

"No, Mandy, that would be *fun*. Not that you're being much fun tonight." He grabs a beer for himself and starts toward the French doors that lead to the back yard. "Make yourself at home, ladies," he calls from over his shoulder before he slams the door so hard the glass rattles.

"What's your problem?" I ask her the moment he's gone. "He's being nice."

"He's being a perv," she mutters. She takes a long swig from her beer then sets it on the counter. "No way are we getting into that pool naked, Liv. Next thing we know, we're drunk, we don't know what we're doing and we're getting gangbanged by the football team."

I laugh, but it's not real. And the glare she sends me shuts me up quick. "They wouldn't do that," I say, my voice small.

"We don't know that for sure. Group mentality is a crazy thing. I'm not risking it." She points at me. "And neither are you."

I stand straighter and salute. "Yes, ma'am."

"This isn't a joke, Liv! Seriously, you are not leaving my side tonight. We don't know what might happen."

I know she's serious. She's making some valid points, things I don't want to think about, because come on. Who wants to dwell on the bad stuff? These guys are nice. Funny. We have an opportunity here tonight and I don't want to waste it. Meaning, I plan on spending time with Ryan—maybe even one-on-one time with Ryan. Though I promised I wouldn't leave Amanda tonight. And I'll keep that promise too.

But if Tuttle wants some alone time with her and she's down for it…

"Maybe we should leave," she says, glancing around the gorgeous kitchen nervously. "This house and everyone in it intimidates the hell out of me."

"No. No way." I grab her arm to keep her from bolting. I swear she looks that freaked out. "We're not leaving. Nothing bad is going to happen, I promise. Let's just drink our beers for liquid courage and then we'll go outside. Okay?"

"Okay." She gives a jerky nod. Blows out a harsh breath. "Fine. Okay."

We start chugging our beers in earnest when the back door opens and Ryan enters the kitchen. My heart rate picks up speed and I polish off my beer in record time, smiling at him in what I hope is an enticing way. "Ryan! Hi!"

Oh God. I sound way too excited.

He heads straight for me, his eyes on me and no one else. "Livvy." He pulls me into his arms and hugs me way too briefly. It's just a tease of a touch, a hint of warm skin and soft fabric and his intoxicating scent. I contemplate lunging for him, but that is just way too crazy. "We're so glad you made it."

"Who else is glad I'm here?" My tone is flirtatious and so is his smile.

"Everyone. Come outside. I think we're going to swim." He takes my hand and starts to drag me through the still-open door. I glance over my shoulder at Amanda and give her a head tilt, one that hopefully says come on.

Luckily enough she follows after us.

"Don't forget Amanda," I tell him as he leads me outside.

"Tuttle's already staked his claim," Ryan says, sending me a quick, warm look, one that makes my stomach tumble. "I'm just staking mine too."

Oh. Wow.

There is a cluster of beefy-looking boys sitting at the hot tub wearing just swim trunks and dunking their feet in the bubbling water. They all say hi when Ryan demands them to and I wave in response, face-checking each one of them. They're mostly seniors and I've gone to school with a few of them for what feels like forever, yet I've rarely talked to them once we started middle school.

This is what happens. You cluster off into your groups during the early teen years and it's so hard to break out of that predetermined clique. Some don't want to. Most band peeps are perfectly happy hanging with their fellow band members. They all date each other, hang out together…yet Amanda broke away from them and now she's with me.

And now we're with the football team. We're not the only girls here. I see a few cheerleaders all cuddled together on an outdoor couch, and they're watching us. Assessing us.

Probably hating on us. Not that I'm going to let it bother me.

"You want to swim?" Ryan asks when he turns to face me. He's still holding my hand and watching me with the sweetest look in his eyes. Like he's so incredibly happy that I'm here with him. My heart swells and I know my answer is going to disappoint him.

"I didn't bring a suit." I frown, hoping he thinks I'm sad, though I'm really not. Amanda's right. Swimming in our undies with the football team isn't the brightest idea.

His smile never wavers. "I don't think that will be a problem. No one's gonna protest if you swim naked, Livvy. I know I definitely won't."

I let go of his hand and give him a shove, and he stumbles back laughing. "Hate to disappoint you, but I'm not skinny dipping in Tuttle's fancy pool."

And it is so freaking fancy. It's a huge rectangle-shaped infinity pool that's lit up so the water is a vibrant turquoise and it has a sleek waterfall. I remember lots of people fell into the pool at the last party. Once that started happening, clothes went flying and it was a total free-for-all.

I didn't participate in that particular event. I was too drunk and too stressed out last time I was at Tuttle's. Not tonight, though. Tonight is filled with endless possibilities.

I'm not going to let a one of them pass me by, either.

chapter twenty-seven

"Tell me..." Ryan pushes a wayward strand of hair away from my face, then tucks it behind my ear, his finger lingering on my skin. "Did you really like watching me play tonight?"

I giggle. Only because I'm on my fourth beer and I'm not looking to stop. My entire body feels like it's buzzing with electricity and I blame the alcohol. Oh, and the boy.

Probably has more to do with the boy.

He hasn't left my side the entire night. Not even when the other girls tried to get his attention, and trust me, they tried a lot. Those cheerleaders are a persistent bunch. Yet he ignored them like they didn't exist. Any time he talked to his friends, he made sure I was with him. Like I'm his girlfriend or something...

"I've never really liked football," I admit, glancing around as if I don't want anyone else to hear my confession. Not that I care. I don't think Ryan cares either. The way he's watching me, his green eyes so intense, I don't think he believes anything I'm saying. Is he even listening to me? "I don't really understand it. I always get lost when I try to follow a game."

"I could teach you." He touches the side of my face, his fingers drifting down my cheek so lightly I shiver. "Whatever you want to know, I'm game."

"I'm sure," I drawl, hoping I sound flirtatious. We're on the same couch the cheerleaders were on when we first arrived at Tuttle's. We took over the spot as soon as the girls abandoned it and we've been cozily sitting together ever since.

Most everyone has left Tuttle's already. We've been here for hours, and while Amanda and I have stuck together most of the night along with Ryan, she up and disappeared on me about thirty minutes ago. I texted her almost immediately, and when she took way too long to answer, I started to panic.

Guess the gangbang comment really got to me, as it should've. That's serious business.

But then she sent this:

I'm okay. Didn't feel so good. Tuttle put me up in a guest bedroom

And I felt better. I also wondered if it was bullshit.

I would bet good money she's letting Tuttle touch her no-no square right about now.

"I'm serious, Livvy." Ryan's deep voice fills my head and I lift my gaze to his. I like how he always calls me Livvy. How his green eyes seem to sparkle every time he looks at me. I especially like the warmth of his touch, the way his fingers dance over my skin like he can't not touch me.

That's sort of hot. And swoony. And romantic.

He's been so attentive tonight. So...perfect. Maybe Amanda was right. He probably was tense and exhausted after the excessive practices they suffered through to get ready for tonight's game. That's why he was so horrible to me the last time we talked, why he kept ignoring me the past couple of weeks. They've been through a rough time.

And now they all seem to be letting off steam tonight. A few of them are pretty drunk. Some are hanging out in the hot tub. No one really went into the pool after all, and I'm guessing they were disappointed that none of us girls—not even the cheerleaders—jumped into the water in just our undies or even, ahem, naked.

Yeah. That so didn't happen.

"What do you think?" Ryan asks, his deep voice breaking into my wayward thoughts.

"You'll really give me football lessons?" It's the last thing I want. But if it's the only way I can spend extra time with him, I'll take it.

"Whatever you want to know, I'm here for you." He leans in and nuzzles my cheek with his nose. "I'm an excellent teacher," he murmurs.

I suck in a breath and close my eyes. His mouth moves over my cheek, his breath warm on my skin, and I tilt my head toward his. Slightly calloused fingers slip beneath my chin and lift it so I meet his gaze. His eyes are dark, his full lips part, and it's like the world just falls away. No more music, no more murmured voices and husky boy laughs. All I can see and feel and focus on is Ryan and his beautiful face, his fingers firm beneath my chin, his mouth poised just above mine.

It's finally happening. I've waited for this moment for what feels like forever. I've known Ryan for barely a month, but it's been an exhilarating ride since I first met him at Em's house.

His mouth touches mine. Soft but sure. Warm, full lips. A whisper of breath, a murmur of sound. He lets go of my chin to cup my cheek and my lips part easily beneath his. He takes the kiss deeper in an instant and chills race over my skin when he tugs me closer. When he slips his hand into my hair. When he rests his other hand at my waist, his fingers toying with the hem of my shirt...

"Get a room!"

Laughter follows and we pull away from each other quickly, my breath coming fast, my head spinning from just one kiss. Or maybe it's the alcohol too. I don't know. All I know is that one simple kiss wasn't enough.

I want more.

And from the way Ryan's staring at me, his eyes slightly glazed, his perfect lips damp, I think he's feeling the same way.

"Come on. Let's get out of here." He stands and offers his hand. I take it, his long fingers curling around mine as he pulls me to my feet. We head to the back door, a few of the guys yelling and cheering us on, and I try my hardest not to look in their direction, I'm so embarrassed.

Ryan doesn't seem bothered by any of it. We don't say a word to each other as we walk through Tuttle's house. I follow behind him, savoring the feel of my hand in his, curious over where he's taking me. We pass through the rooms so quickly they're like a blur and then we're in a bedroom, Ryan shutting the door before he's pulling me into his arms.

His lips land on mine once more, and the kiss scorches all of my brain cells. His tongue is in my mouth, sliding against mine and I moan. He slips his hands beneath my shirt, his hot fingers burning my skin, and I squirm under his touch, wanting to get closer, wanting to get more of Ryan and his mouth and his hands and his body pressed against mine.

"You drunk?" he asks after he breaks the kiss.

"Maybe." I nod, trying to catch my breath, but it's no use. I can't breathe, can't think, can't talk. I can only feel, and it all feels so incredibly *good* I don't ever want this moment to stop.

Ryan laughs and shakes his head, his gaze drifting over my face and settling on my lips. "You're hot for it, aren't you?" he whispers.

I nod, another giggle escaping me before I clamp my lips shut. He's right. I'm hot for him. I crave his touch so badly it makes my skin hot. Itchy. I try to touch his face, his shoulders, wherever I can grab him, but his strong arms wrap around me, stopping my attempts. His mouth is on mine as he walks me backwards and I go with him willingly until I'm falling, falling, falling. Onto a feather-soft bed that feels like a cloud when I finally land.

Giggling yet again, I rise up on my elbows and contemplate him. Ryan stands at the foot of the bed watching me, his gaze intense. I drink him in greedily, loving how mussed his hair is. How swollen his perfect lips are. I lick my lips in anticipation and his gaze grows darker.

What's he waiting for? I'm definitely not putting up a fight. I've been waiting too long for this moment to happen. I'd start stripping right now if I wasn't afraid I'd make a fool of myself because hello, I am a teeny bit drunk.

"You gonna pass out on me, Livvy?" He lifts a brow and I can't take my eyes off his face. As if he knows this, that dark eyebrow of his goes even higher.

He's so pretty. I shake my head but immediately stop, since the movement makes everything start to spin. "I'm fine," I reassure him, wondering if I should give him a thumbs up.

No, that's totally cheesy.

He licks his lips and heat licks up my thighs. I press them together, wishing he'd just get on with it and kiss me again. Touch me again. Maybe help me take off my clothes so we can get tangled up with each other...

"Livvy." He whispers my name and then he's right there, hovering above me, his face in mine. I can feel his breath, his body pressed close to my side. His hand is on my stomach, gently pushing my shirt up so he's touching bare skin, and I close my eyes, letting the sensation of his slightly rough fingers on my body wash over me. "Your skin is so soft."

I say nothing, too focused on the path his fingers are taking. They circle around my belly button before moving upward, skimming across my stomach, seemingly counting my ribs, exploring every inch of my torso. My T-shirt is pushed up even farther, until his fingers are tracing along my bra, over it, caressing the exposed tops of my breasts, and oh my gosh...

He leans in and presses his face against my chest, breathing deep, as if he's trying to inhale me. My hands automatically go to his head, fingers sinking into his soft, thick hair as I hold him close. His hands and mouth are doing such magical things that I start to ache. Throb. I need more. I want so much more, but I'm scared. I don't want to take this too far. Not tonight. I barely know Ryan. Yes, his kisses make my toes curl and I'm willing to do a few things, but...

Not *everything*.

Ryan lifts his body away from mine and my eyes fly open to find him watching me, his breathing ragged, his eyes glittering with lust. Just looking at him makes me catch my breath, my skin breaking out in goose bumps. When he shrugs out of his shirt I have to bite my lip to keep myself from saying something outrageous. Or moan. Or whimper.

Watching the boy I've been lusting after for weeks whip his shirt off like no problem is enough to make me weak.

He tosses the shirt on the floor before returning his gaze to mine. "Your turn," he says with a little chin flick.

I scoot into a sitting position and tug my shirt off with shaky hands, letting it fall beside me on the bed. I'm tempted to cross my arms over my bra-covered chest—it's such an automatic reaction—but I don't. Instead I sit up straight and hope he appreciates what he sees.

"Nice," he murmurs, his gaze locked on my chest.

Okay, I guess he does appreciate me, though really this isn't that big of a deal. "You've already seen me like this." I shrug, remembering the tiny bikini Em made me wear. "You've even touched them."

"I know, considering I just did it." The wicked gleam in his eyes makes me shiver.

"No, I mean at Em's party. Remember that night?" Oh God, if he forgot, that'll be embarrassing. That should tell me how much I really matter to him.

As in, I probably don't matter that much.

"I definitely remember that night." He shifts closer, his voice low and a little rough. I clench my thighs together in anticipation. "From the first moment I saw you, Livvy, I knew I had to have you."

I want to believe him. But those first encounters between us, he'd been with Em. Chasing after Em while flirting with me on the side. Now Em is forgotten and he's got me locked up in a room in Tuttle's house, our shirts off and our breaths coming fast. Something is going to happen tonight, something big, and I really don't want to stop it.

But once it happens, will he dump me for someone else, like he did to Em?

"You're so hot." He touches me, his fingers drifting down the length of one bare arm. "And so real. There's no bullshit with you."

I frown. That almost doesn't feel like a compliment. From the expression on my face, I think he can sense my uneasiness. "Is that a good thing?"

"Definitely. People can be so fake, but not you." He kisses me before

I can protest, before I can even utter a word. His kiss is all-consuming, hot and deep, and I give in easily, forgetting what he said, forgetting my earlier thoughts.

I go willingly when he pushes me back, so I'm lying on the bed. He hovers above me, his hands braced on the mattress on either side of my head, his right knee in between my legs. He leans in and presses me into the mattress, his hot, hard body covering mine, and I gasp when he breaks the kiss to trail his lips down the length of my neck. I throw my head back and close my eyes, his hot mouth burning my skin, and I clutch at him, another gasp escaping me when he lifts his knee up and pushes it between my thighs.

Oh. His knee presses against a particular spot and I shudder. I cant my hips and rub against him and there it goes again. A thousand prickly points of pleasure sweep over my skin and I blink open my eyes to find him watching me.

"You like that," he murmurs, his mouth curved in a dirty smile.

I nod, my lips parting, but he steals a kiss before I can say anything. His tongue thrusts into my mouth in time with his knee and I'm grinding down on him, essentially dry humping his leg, but ohmigod, I really don't care.

It feels too good to stop.

Ryan murmurs dark words of encouragement and I'm so caught up I can't think. Can't worry if he's dirty talking me, can't focus on the fact that I'm shamelessly riding his knee. I'm close. I don't want to stop. I don't ever, ever want to sto—

The door crashes open and Ryan springs away from me, leaping off the bed so fast I can't believe it actually happened. My heart nearly trips over itself as I scramble off the bed and then immediately duck behind it to hide, barely peeking over the edge to see who interrupted us.

Stupid Cannon stands in the doorway, a very tiny, very cute girl with long brown hair spilling over one shoulder standing next to him. I don't recognize her at all. My brain is so fuzzy with lust and confusion that I wonder what happened to the blonde from Sonic, which is stupid. Why am I thinking about that girl?

Looks like Cannon's over her, though I shouldn't be surprised. He doesn't usually stick with just one girl.

None of them do.

"Get the fuck out," Ryan says, his voice rough with anger.

Cannon grins, not bothered by Ryan's tone at all. "Dumbass. Don't you know you're supposed to *lock* the door?"

"I thought I did, asshole." Ryan grabs a pillow and tosses it at Cannon. It glances off the side of his head, making him scowl. "Now leave."

"Aw, come on. Aren't you two done in here? My girl's not down to put on a public show." Cannon wraps his beefy arm around the tiny girl's neck, giving her a squeeze before he sloppily kisses her cheek. She giggles and tries to bat his arm away, but it's pointless. He clearly overpowers her.

"We're a little busy." Ryan is so irritated it's obvious. Yet Cannon doesn't care at all. He's too intent on finding his own place to hook up.

"Looks like you're pretty much done with this one." Cannon cackles evilly, his gaze going to me. I peer over the edge of the bed, my cheeks going hot at his words.

With this one.

Well, that's sort of crude.

"I'm not," Ryan snaps. "Now get the hell out of here."

"Jeez. Whatever man," Cannon mumbles as he steers himself and the girl out of the room, pulling the door shut behind them.

"Shit," Ryan says the moment they're gone. He lands on the

mattress, his weight making it rock, and leans over the side of the bed to study me. I feel exposed in just my bra and jeans so I pull my knees up to my chest and stare back at him, unsure of what to say.

I'm also feeling really, really stupid. That entire moment was humiliating as crap.

"You okay?" he asks gently.

I nod. Look down at the floor. Anywhere but at him. I'm too embarrassed. Sobriety has hit me hard and my buzz abandoned me the moment the door slammed open. "I should go find Amanda," I murmur.

He blows out a ragged breath. "Good luck. I think she's with Tuttle."

Of course she is. She's off having some wild and mysterious affair with the most wild and mysterious boy at school, yet here I am freaking out over a minor interruption by an idiot football player. But that interruption stopped us from taking it any further. And it ruined my mood. I'm not interested anymore.

Not at all.

"I need to find her." I pull my phone out of my pocket and start texting her, ignoring how Ryan's stomping around the room, picking his T-shirt up off the floor and shoving it back on. He tosses my shirt toward me and it lands on my shoulder, startling me. I look up, surprised at the babyish way he's acting, how he won't even look in my direction.

Irritation zips through my veins as I tug my shirt back on. It's not my fault we were interrupted. He was the one who was supposed to lock the door.

I finish typing my text then hit send.

Where are you? I want to go home.

"So." Ryan's voice causes me to glance up and I find him standing directly in front of me, imposingly tall considering I'm still sitting on the floor. "Cannon ruined everything, huh?"

It's easier to blame it on Cannon. I might've frozen up eventually. I definitely wouldn't have let Ryan take it any further than messing around.

"Yeah, definitely." I offer him a tiny smile. I feel bad, but seriously. I can't get back into it. That's just…how I am. Even with Dustin. Every time we messed around, even when we only kissed, I'd get a serious case of the guilts the minute we were done and I'd end up full of regret. I don't know what it is about having to deal with boys during the aftermath, but I don't handle it very well.

Probably means I have a serious hang up and possibly even daddy issues, but I don't feel like psycho-analyzing myself at the moment.

"It was fun while it lasted, right?" He offers me a hand and I take it, letting him haul me to my feet. He tugs me closer, planting a soft, sweet kiss on my lips and the guilt slowly evaporates. He doesn't seem mad. I didn't have to turn him down so that makes the entire situation while embarrassing, also easier.

I feel like all is right in my world.

My phone buzzes and I glance down to see Amanda's response.

Me too. Meet me in the living room in five minutes.

Relief fills me and I smile up at Ryan, whose brows lower in confusion. But I don't explain myself. I just send a quick reply to Amanda before I slip out of his arms and stuff my phone back into my pocket.

It's nice having a friend I can count on.

chapter twenty-eight

The minute I walk in the door Saturday afternoon, I can tell Mom is pissed. Instead of acknowledging her, I head to my bedroom without saying a word. I don't even bother looking at her, though I can feel her watching me.

And I'm trying my best not to freak out.

My heart is racing as I open my door and walk inside, tossing my backpack on my bed. I ended up spending the night at Amanda's after all. When we met in Tuttle's living room last night, she'd looked so sad, like she'd been crying. I'd asked her if she was all right and she assured me she was fine, but I don't know. It didn't look right. And she's never one to tell me what's up with her and Tuttle. He didn't even make an appearance before we left, though Ryan was sweet and kissed me goodbye, telling me we should get together over the weekend.

My thoughts floated in the clouds the rest of the drive to Amanda's house, and she remained so quiet, her silence allowed me to bask in my head. I relived the moment with Ryan again and again, cutting out Cannon's interruption. I focused on the taste of Ryan's lips, how they felt on my skin. When he pressed me into the mattress with his big body, his knee between my legs, me rubbing against him with zero shame...

My night with Ryan was one I never wanted to forget.

We snuck back into Amanda's quiet, dark house and crawled into her bed. She crashed out almost immediately while I lay there staring at the ceiling and still thinking of Ryan. Imagining what might've happened if Cannon hadn't interrupted us. Would I have let Ryan do more? Would I have ended up doing something I'd eventually regret?

I think of his smile, his deep, rumbly voice, the way he looks at me...

"Olivia."

I squeal and turn to find Mom standing in my bedroom doorway, her arms crossed in front of her chest and a sour expression on her face.

"Hey. Uh, what's up?" I ask weakly, mildly annoyed when she walks into my room without me inviting her.

Of course if I said that, she'd give some speech about how it's her house and she owns it and blah, blah, blah. And I'd have to bite my tongue and not mention how Dad was the one who bought this house and gave it to her in the divorce, so really she can't take all the credit. It would then turn into this giant, ugly argument and I'd probably end up getting grounded, and that is the absolute last thing I want to deal with this weekend.

"You tell me." She drops her arms to her sides and shuts the door behind her. "I think we need to talk," she says.

Worst words ever. I land heavily on the edge of my bed, staring up at her as I try my best to act calm. There is a whole mess of things she could want to talk about and I have no idea which one she wants to discuss. "Okay," I say carefully. "What's going on?"

Mom sits in my desk chair, turning so she's facing me. "Where were you last night?"

What? "I told you. I went to the football game with Amanda and then I spent the night at her house."

She studies me, her gaze laser-sharp, as if she's trying to see into my brain and discover all of my dirty little secrets. When she looks at me like that, it's kind of terrifying. "I've never even heard of this Amanda girl before."

It takes everything within me not to roll my eyes. "I told you a while ago, we just started hanging out. Amanda Winters. I've gone to school with her since *kindergarten.* She's in honors classes and she plays in the band." Well. That last bit is a lie since she quit, but I'm trying to convince Mom that Amanda isn't a bad influence. *I'm* probably the bad influence in our friendship.

"So you weren't with Em?" Mom looks shocked—and confused.

I blink at her, surprised by her question. "No. I saw her at the football game, but that was it."

"You didn't leave with her?"

"No, after the game was over, I went with Amanda back to her house." *Lies.* Now it's my turn to study her carefully. "Why? What's going on?"

Mom sighs and shakes her head. "I don't know. Cindy called me last night at almost midnight, looking for Emily. She sounded very upset. And…possibly a little drunk."

Oh, shit. Yeah, sometimes Em's parents like to party, but nothing too outrageous. "Do they know where she is now? Has she still not come home?"

"I haven't talked to Cindy since she called, but I promised I would talk to you and ask you about Em and if you know what's going on. Has she been acting different lately?" Mom frowns. "I feel like you two have drifted apart since you came back from your father's."

"We sort of have," I admit, feeling bad. I don't want to tell my mom the truth. It's none of her business and besides, if I told her what happened, then I'd have to explain what's going on with me and Dustin, and that's just...too involved for my taste.

"Cindy sounded worried. She told me a lot of concerning things about Em." Mom hesitates, her expression unsure. "Are you positive you weren't with her last night? I won't be angry with you if you were. I don't care what you were doing, I just want to make sure Em's safe."

"I wasn't with her, Mom. I swear. I don't know what's going on." Worry eats at me. What if she's still gone? What if something terrible happened to her? I can't imagine losing Em for good, or even losing Em for a little while. Yeah, we're on the outs right now, but that's different.

This feels...serious.

"I'm going to call Cindy and tell her what you said. Hopefully Em's home now, but who knows? Her mom made it sound like she's gone wild lately and this was one incident among many." Mom stands and heads for the door, pausing before she opens it. "I'll let you know what I find out."

The moment she shuts the door behind her I fall backwards on my bed, staring up at the ceiling. My mind is racing at all the possibilities. What the hell is Em up to now? Where could she be? Did she run away? Is she over at some guy's house and forgot to call her parents? Where's her car? Where's her stuff? Why isn't she answering her phone? Is it off? Is the battery dead?

Reaching for my phone, I unblock her number, then send her a quick text.

Where are you???? I'm worried!!! My mom said your mom is looking for you!!! Please tell me you're all right.☹

I wait five minutes. Ten. Fifteen.

No reply.

So I decide to text someone else.

I need your help. Can I come over?

The answer comes in less than thirty seconds.

Yes.

DUSTIN IS OUTSIDE sitting on his front porch steps waiting for me when I arrive not ten minutes after I sent my last text. Normally I would've run straight over, not caring how I looked or what I was wearing. But for some weird reason I wanted to look nice. I brushed my hair and braided it. Put on a different shirt and applied mascara. It's so stupid, like I want to impress him or something, while I'm also freaking out over Em.

But I'm a bundle of mixed emotions when it comes to Dustin and Em and Ryan and…everyone. Even stupid Fitch, who eyed me appreciatively when I darted through the kitchen earlier and told Mom I was going over to Dustin's for a little bit. She seemed so pleased that I was actually going to Dustin's house she didn't even protest or stop me. Fitch told me to take my time and even winked at me, which skeeved me out.

He's being weird.

I don't like it.

"What took you so long?" Dustin asks as I draw closer.

I stop just in front of him, taking him in. The black eye is long gone but he still has that wary, distrustful attitude going on whenever I'm first around him, and I can't help but find it sort of hot. We haven't fallen back into our familiar best friends comfort zone, and maybe I don't want to.

We will never go back to that point in our lives, I've realized. We've changed. Our relationship has changed. Maybe we'll survive all of this uncertainty and maybe we won't, but right now, I need him.

"Have you talked to Em lately?" When my mom called right before I left the house, Em's mom told her she's still not home. She was crying about it too.

He scratches his chest, frowning up at me. "Is this a trick question?"

"Why would you say that?" I rest my hands on my hips. God, he really is so annoying sometimes.

"I'm afraid if I say no, you'll be pissed at me. And if I say yes, you'll be even *more* pissed at me."

I roll my eyes and plop down next to him on the step, my side brushing against his, our legs bumping. He's warm and solid and he smells good, like soapy clean boy. It's all so familiar I want to curl up into his arms and make all the bad stuff go away. "Just be honest, Dustin. Have you seen her?" I hesitate, then decide to tell him straight out. "She's…missing."

"What? Are you serious?" His mouth hangs open in shock.

"Yeah." I nod. "Her mom called mine. I almost got in trouble because Mom thought I knew what was up. Like I was out with Em all last night getting into trouble." I'm still a little miffed that she went into attack mode.

"Huh. I saw her at school yesterday." He looks off into the distance, squinting against the sun. "But that's it."

"So you really weren't with her last night?" The question leaves a bitter taste in my mouth, but I had to ask.

"Why are you asking me again? Don't you believe me?"

"Just answer the question!"

He glares at me, his dark eyes full of anger. "No, I wasn't with her." His mouth clamps shut, like he was going to say something else. Maybe mention the name of the person he *was* with last night.

My heart drops when I see the guilt in his gaze, how he suddenly won't look at me. "Who were you with?" I ask softly. I have no room to talk. I was with Ryan last night, though I don't want to tell Dustin. I don't want to make him mad.

Dustin sighs and drops his head, staring at the steps. "You'll be pissed if I tell you."

I absolutely cannot judge. "I won't be, I swear."

"Brianne." He lifts his head, his gaze meeting mine once more. "We went to the movies last night."

"How was it?" I'm proud of how calm I sound, because deep inside my stomach is a twisted knot.

"Shitty. She hated the movie and I thought it was hilarious. I guess she doesn't have my sense of humor." He gives a one-shouldered shrug. "Then she tried to attack me in the Jeep."

"Please don't give me the gory details." I shake my head.

"There aren't any gory details to give, Livvy. She doesn't do it for me. At all."

Not like you do. The unspoken words are right there, hanging between us. I'm not so egotistical to think he'd say that. More like, I *know* he wants to say that, because I know Dustin. I can see it in his eyes, read it in his body language. And if our circumstances were different, I'd want to hear him say it too.

But I don't want to hear it. I don't want to think about it either. We need to focus on Em, not us.

There is no us.

"Will you help me? Can we go looking for Em?" I ask him, desperate to change the subject. "I have a few ideas where she might be."

"Yeah, sure." He nods and stands, holding out his hand for me. I automatically take it, letting him pull me to my feet, and he doesn't let my hand go. His thumb streaks across my palm, the gentle touch making me shiver. "I'll go tell my mom what I'm doing and then we'll leave."

"Okay." I nod and he smiles, reluctantly letting go of my hand, his fingers somehow seeming to cling to mine.

I watch him walk through the front door, then turn away, my gaze going to the street. Just in time to see Ryan's white BMW come to a halt directly in front of Dustin's house.

Oh. Shit.

My heart starts to pound and icy cold dread slips over my skin, making me shiver. The passenger-side window slides down, revealing Ryan behind the wheel and Tuttle sitting in the passenger seat. I frown as they both scowl at me, and I wonder about their so-called friendship. Amanda told me Tuttle didn't like Ryan, yet I see the two of them together more often than not lately. It's strange.

"What the hell are you doing?" Ryan yells as I approach the car, sounding like a jealous, possessive boyfriend. Exactly what I've been wanting from him for the last few weeks.

Until now.

"Keep your voice down," I tell him when I reach his BMW. I'm standing by the passenger side, trying my best to ignore Tuttle and that shitty little smirk on his face, but it's difficult. I can sense he wants to say something so bad and it's taking everything within him to keep his mouth shut.

I send him a dark look before my gaze meets Ryan's. "Why are you yelling at me?"

"Why are you at Dustin's house? I thought you were through with that asshole," he practically spits out. His eyes are narrowed and his cheeks are ruddy. He looks pissed.

"We're just friends," I remind him, sending him a meaningful look. "And right now isn't the best time to have this conversation." I tilt my head in Tuttle's direction, hoping he gets it.

But Ryan clearly doesn't care. "Your so-called *friend* wants to bang you. Or maybe he already has and I'm just finding out about it now?"

Oh my God. I can't believe he's acting like this.

I round the front of the car, going to the driver's side so maybe we can keep our conversation a little more private. Though I know Tuttle is trying his best to hear every word we say. "There's nothing going on between Dustin and I. You know this. I was just with you last night," I say, my tone turning pleading. "Can we talk about this later?"

"What's there to talk about, huh? You need to make up your mind who you want to be with, Livvy. It's either me or him." He revs the BMW's engine, his expression reminding me of a pouting little boy who doesn't get his way. "You can't have us both."

"But—" I start to say, but he shifts the car into gear and pulls out, driving off so fast he creates black skid marks on the asphalt.

I swear I can hear Tuttle's laughter as they drive away, mocking me as I stand there alone in the middle of the street like an idiot.

"What are you doing?"

I turn to see Dustin standing next to his Jeep where it sits in his driveway.

"Why are you in the road?" he asks, hitting the keyless remote so the Jeep beeps and the lights flash. I hear the doors unlock and Dustin tilts his head toward his car. "Come on, let's go."

I go to his Jeep and open the passenger door, sliding into the seat.

My head is full of too many thoughts, all of them centered on what just happened between Ryan and me. I should be thrilled he's willing to stake his claim, that he's actually jealous of my relationship with Dustin. But I don't like his demand, and hate the way he yelled at me in front of stupid Tuttle. I can be friends with Dustin and *be* with Ryan. I can have both of them in my life, can't I?

Glancing over at Dustin, I catch him looking at me, his eyes full of too much emotion, his smile too soft, too sweet. My heart pangs and I smile at him in return, hating how torn I feel.

Hating worse the thought of Dustin not being in my life anymore because Ryan doesn't want him to be.

chapter twenty-nine

We drive all over town, searching for Em, but we can't find her. We visit all of her favorite haunts, the coffee shop she prefers and the bookstore that sells bongs. The pizza place close to school and even the stupid mall, though we haven't hung out there in forever. We both text people we think she could possibly be with, stop by a few of their houses, even stop by the school, but she's nowhere.

It's like she upped and disappeared.

The longer we search, the more worried I become. I forget about all of my stupid problems and can only focus on her. Our friendship. How quickly it crumbled apart, all because of the boy I'm with. The boy I can't let go of.

The boy I don't *want* to let go of.

Yet I let Em go so easily, and that fills me with guilt. What kind of friend am I? Am I partially to blame for her disappearance? I think of how she acted when I first came home from Oregon. How she always wanted to get high, always wanted to party and how clingy she became. I didn't get it then, and eventually blamed it on guilt over her messing around with Dustin when I was gone.

But maybe there was something else going on. Something more. I wish I knew what.

I wish we could find her.

"Let's get something to eat," Dustin says, sounding exhausted. It's far past dinnertime and dark, the sun having set over an hour ago. I'm starving but nothing sounds good. I feel sort of sick inside over everything that's happened the past twenty-four hours.

"I'm not hungry," I tell him, staring out the window as we drive down the busy street. We're not in the best part of town, more on the industrial side, though there are a few restaurants and a nightclub that caters to teens.

"Wait a minute," I say as a memory washes over me. "Isn't the Echo Club down here?"

Dustin makes a face. "Yeah, but that place is a shit hole."

He's right. I remember going to the teen nightclub one Saturday night last spring with Em, right before school was out. We put on our sluttiest outfits on purpose and took the city bus there, giggling and falling against each other when men blatantly stared at us. Once we got into the club, we flirted with the doorman and got in for a discount, then danced our asses off for hours, putting on a show for all the leering boys who watched us as we fulfilled their lesbian fantasies.

Boys are so simple sometimes. So stupid.

Two of them approached us, their grins huge, their breath smelling of beer. Em was feeling bold, asking them if they had more, and they took us out to their car in the parking lot, showing us the ice chest full of beer in the trunk. We oohed and ahhed over that ice chest like it was found treasure.

We'd also gotten drunk. And high. We lost ourselves in the music playing on the radio, the booze, the boys, both of us fighting them off, slapping their hands away from our legs, our chests. Our gazes would clash and we'd laugh and laugh, pissing the boys off, not like we cared.

Those boys…I hadn't sensed it then, but when I think back now, I remember how they looked at us, their gazes dark. Primal. How they discussed exactly what they were going to do with us—and what they said hadn't been very nice. Em acted like it was no big deal. She offered them both a blowjob if they just drove us home and they'd enthusiastically agreed that was a great idea.

Until Em threw up the moment the car lurched to a stop in the parking lot of a park close to our house. She vomited everywhere, all over the backseat and the guys freaking out. All I could do was laugh at her, laugh at the boys whose faces had turned red with rage.

They abandoned us in that park, the owner of the car tossing out a string of curse words at us before he peeled out of the parking lot. We walked home, Em chomping on a stick of mint gum I had in my purse, both of us laughing hysterically over how she ruined the backseat of that guy's car. She said later that was one of the best nights of her life.

I realize now how easily it could've turned into one of the worst nights of our life.

"She might be there," I say, turning to look at him. "She loves the Echo Club."

"Seriously?" Dustin sounds skeptical.

"Yes, seriously. Let's go."

He drives to the club, pulling into the parking lot and parking his Jeep. I practically run to the entrance and Dustin follows behind me, calling my name, asking me to slow down, but I don't. I'm a girl on a mission and the bouncer guarding the door watches me approach with a wary expression. There is a line of people waiting to get in, all of them shooting me dirty looks when I stop in front of the doorman and smile at him.

"Back of the line," he says, jerking his thumb in the line's direction.

"I'm looking for a friend," I start, but his ominous scowl silences me.

"You're all looking for a friend," he mutters with a quick shake of his head. "You're going to have to wait with the rest of them."

I turn to see Dustin stopping just behind me, a frown marring his face. "Do you have money?" I ask him.

He shrugs. "Yeah. Like fifty bucks."

"Fifty bucks if you let us in now," I tell the bouncer.

"Hey," Dustin protests softly, but I ignore him.

The doorman laughs. "Big deal, little girl. That leaves me, what, ten bucks after the cover charge? No thanks." He crosses his beefy arms in front of his barrel chest. "Move it."

I try my best, most imploring, sweet and innocent girl look, but his expression becomes sour. Like he's disgusted with me. Dustin tugs on my arm and I go with him, glaring at the doorman until I finally have to turn away or else I'll trip on something.

"Did you really think he'd let you in with a bribe?" Dustin asks as he escorts me to the back of the line.

"Maybe." I give a one-shoulder shrug, trying to ignore the irritation and frustration rolling through my veins. People are staring at us, their noses wrinkled in disgust, and I send them death glares right back. They turn away from us and I glance down at my clothes. I'm not dressed for a hot Saturday night at the club and neither is Dustin, so I know that's why they're passing judgment. That'll probably hurt our chances of getting inside too—they don't care if we're paying customers. Sometimes they let people in only because they look good.

"We're never going to get in," I whine as I lean against the rough brick exterior of the building. I wrap my arms around myself, shivering a little when the cool breeze suddenly washes over us. "We're never going to find her."

Dustin's not even paying attention to me. He's too busy staring at his phone, tapping at the keyboard as he sends a text or a Snapchat or whatever. I want to smack him. I want to snatch his phone out of his hand and force him to look at *me*. To listen to *me*.

He smiles a little, his gaze still glued to his phone screen, and the realization hits—whoever he's communicating with, he'd rather be with that person than me.

And that hurts.

"Maybe we should go," I tell him, my voice low, my throat raw. I'm trying to hold back the tears that threaten and I swallow hard, give a little sniff.

Dustin looks up with a frown, his brow furrowed. "You don't want to look inside?"

I shake my head. Remain silent. I'm afraid if I try to talk I'll burst into tears instead. I don't know why I'm so emotional. Maybe it's because we can't find Em. Or because I made Ryan mad and jealous when I didn't mean to. And because I'm losing Dustin and I have no one to blame but myself.

It's all of those things. Every single one of them. And I don't know which one hurts the most.

"Let's go then," Dustin says, taking my arm once more and leading me back out toward the parking lot. I say nothing, stumbling along beside him, ignoring my buzzing phone. It's probably Mom wondering where I'm at. Or Ryan, ready to chew me out for spending my Saturday night with his enemy and my friend.

I climb into the car and Dustin's behind the wheel a few moments later, starting up his Jeep before he turns to look at me. "You all right?"

"Yeah," I croak, nodding before I turn to stare out the window. My phone buzzes again, making my butt vibrate.

"You should check that," Dustin says. "What if it's Em?"

Closing my eyes, I thunk my head against the cool window, feeling like an idiot. What if it *is* Em? Why am I ignoring the phone? Fifteen minutes ago I would've jumped all over it and now I'm filled with dread over who it might be. I don't understand why I'm so reluctant.

My mind is one confused, swirling mess.

"Olivia," Dustin says, his voice deep and commanding, reminding me that yeah, I do need to check my phone, so I do.

And oh my God, it *is* Em.

I'm fine. At home. Mom wants to kill me and Dad can't stop yelling and throwing things. It's gonna be a fun Saturday night.

Relief hits me so hard I sag against the seat, exhaling loudly. I glance over at Dustin, who's watching me so very carefully, and I offer up a small nod.

Just before I burst into tears.

chapter thirty

"I want us to be honest with each other." I pause, not even waiting for an answer or a reaction. "I'm sick and tired of keeping secrets and playing games. I need someone to be real with." *Desperately*, I almost add.

Amanda steps onto the front porch, closing the door behind her. "I'm not a game player, Livvy."

Sighing, I tilt my head, contemplating her. It's a warm and sunny Sunday afternoon and I rode my bike to her house, something I haven't done in years. Ride my bike, that is. I always got a ride thanks to Em. But she's currently on lockdown and not talking, not that I'd ask her for a ride now. I couldn't go to Dustin's since that was…done. No way was I attempting to reach out to Ryan yet.

Amanda is my only option and we don't live in the same neighborhood. So I pulled my bike out of the garage, hosed it off, dried it with a kitchen towel—only to get grease on it—then left before Mom saw the mess I made.

"Neither am I," I finally say to her, noting the skeptical look she gives me. "Fine, I'm not always straightforward or whatever, but neither are you."

"What are you talking about? I don't keep secrets or play games," Amanda says.

"You so do." I pause for effect before I say, "Tell me about Tuttle."

Her lips thin. "There's nothing to tell."

"Bullshit."

With a sigh she walks over to the porch swing—yes, her house is cute and cozy and in an older part of town, a quaint, clean neighborhood with huge trees and lots of chirping birds. Where there are porch swings and rosebushes in the immaculate front yards and sweet little wooden birdhouses tucked into the trees. It's sweet and fits Amanda's personality perfectly, and I'm sort of envious of this seemingly charmed life she leads.

Though it's really not charmed. Her ex cheated on her with her best friend. She quit the band, though clearly she misses it. And she has some weird twisted relationship thing going on with Tuttle that she's not talking about with anyone.

"You gonna sit with me or just stand there and stare?" Amanda asks when I don't move.

I sit next to her on the swing and she pushes off the ground with her feet, the swing gently swaying to and fro. She's quiet and I realize she's not going to spill as easily as I hoped, so I decide to break the ice.

"I thought Dustin was still in love with me," I admit, my voice soft, my heart aching. "But I realized last night that he's probably over me."

"Why would you say that?"

I told her about us going in search of Em. How worried I was, how frantic I was feeling. How distracted Dustin had become the longer the night went on and that eventually Em texted like no big deal. I never got a thank-you, I never got an explanation on where she was either. I might never find out, and I guess I don't really have the right to ask.

Dustin dropped me off at my house with a distracted goodbye and I watched him drive away. Watched as he drove past his house and went…somewhere else.

I have no idea where or with who. I had no right to ask either. Instead, I'd lain awake in bed for half the night, unable to sleep.

"He went with you and helped you," Amanda points out when I finish my story. "He still cares."

"But it's not the same."

"So you want him sitting around waiting for you, caring about you while you're interested in someone else? That's not fair," Amanda says.

She's right. I know she's right. I tell her about Ryan seeing me at Dustin's house and how mad he'd been. I mention that Tuttle was with him, and her expression shifts. Changes. She drops her head, staring at her hands where they're curled in her lap, and I wonder what she's thinking.

"What's going on between you two?" I ask when she still won't say anything and I feel like I'm about to burst. "And don't say nothing because I won't believe you."

Amanda lifts her head, her expression pained. "I think…I think he likes me."

I frown. "Do you mean Tuttle? You think he likes you?" She nods. "And that's a bad thing….why?"

She waves a hand, her eyes a little wild. "He's Jordan Tuttle. The most popular boy in school, the richest, the smartest, the best looking…I could go on and on."

"And…" I'm still not getting the problem here.

"Why would he be interested in me? Why would he care about

me? I'm just…a nobody. I don't even have band anymore and that was my one pitiful extracurricular activity I was good at." She pushes at the ground so hard we send the swing flying, her side moving faster than mine, making the chains twist as the wooden swing jerks around.

"Come on, Amanda. You're pretty and you're smart. You're nice and you're funny," I say softly, but she just laughs and shakes her head.

"He's out of my league."

"Yet he's interested."

"We hooked up over the summer. At his house. In his room. On his bed." She slaps her hands over her face and gives a humiliated little cry. "Oh God, I can't believe I just said that out loud."

I'm in shock. That was the absolute last thing I expected Amanda to say. "Wait a minute. You *hooked up* with *Tuttle?* Over the summer?"

She nods, her hands still covering her face.

"What about at his party when you said he slipped his hand between your legs?"

"That really happened too." Her voice is muffled because of her hands. "He's very persistent."

"Have you two actually…done the deed?"

"No!" She drops her hands, staring at me. Her eyes are glassy, like she's this close to crying. "We just…messed around. Nothing serious. Well, I didn't think it was anything serious. I was drunk and upset over finding my boyfriend with my best friend and Tuttle was kind enough to take care of me that night."

In more ways than one. I come this close to saying it, but I don't want to make her mad.

"He was being so sweet. I just…I let him kiss me. And we kept kissing. Until we started doing other stuff." She covers her face once more. "This is so humiliating."

"Stop. We all do humiliating stuff. Like I have any room to

judge." I think of me and Ryan together before stupid Cannon rudely interrupted us. How I reacted afterward. What a mess that was. "He must really like you, Amanda, if he's still trying to get with you. Tuttle doesn't try to get with anyone."

"I think he likes that I resist him. I'm a challenge for him to conquer." Her hands fall back into her lap. "I don't want to be with him."

I try my best not to roll my eyes. "Come on."

"I'm serious. I don't." She turns to look at me, her expression telling me that she does *not* want to talk about this anymore. "What about you and Ryan?"

I go on the immediate defensive. "What about him?"

"What's going on with you two? Do you really like him, or do you like Dustin?" When I don't answer her right away, she continues, "I almost think you enjoy having both of them dangling on a string, fighting over you."

Her words make me flinch. "No, I don't."

Do I?

I'm not sure.

Though I can't deny the attention is…nice. I've never had two guys want to be with me before. I've never had any guy want to be with me before, except Dustin. I never planned on us hooking up. It happened almost…naturally, which sounds crazy. I knew deep in my heart I didn't necessarily want to be with Dustin, not like that, but I also didn't want to be alone either.

Frowning, I drop my head, staring at the ground. God, what's wrong with me? I'm such a selfish bitch, and it's like I never even realized it until now.

"So who do you want to be with? Dustin or Ryan?"

"Dustin and I are just friends." I look up and she sends me a pointed look. "Friends who messed around a few times. Something that probably should've never happened."

"But it meant more to him."

I nod. It meant a lot to me too. I was willing to give him a chance despite my fear.

Now that's all ruined.

"Yet you don't want to be with him like that."

I nod again. It's kind of the truth, kind of a lie.

"Then maybe you should go to Ryan and tell him how you feel," she says, her voice gentle.

"Ha. So I should hop on my bike and pedal over to his big mansion, knock on his door and ask his butler if he's in? Looking like this?" I wave a hand at myself. I'm in black cropped leggings, an oversized tank top that shows my black sports bra, and my hair is in the sloppiest ponytail ever. "I'm a mess."

"Does he really have a butler?" Amanda asks incredulously.

"I don't know! His house is huge and he's loaded, so I wouldn't doubt it." I shrug, feeling stupid.

Amanda sighs. "Well, never mind that. Go home, take a shower and text him that you want to get together tonight. Tell him how you feel."

"No way." She makes it sound so easy. Too easy.

"Then explain what happened with Em and why you were with Dustin." She elbows me in the ribs. "Go to him. He'll like it. He's been sulking for a solid twenty-four hours. He needs to get over it."

"Maybe he's already gotten over it—and me," I say sullenly.

"I doubt that."

"You shouldn't. He moved from Em to me relatively quick," I say.

Her mouth drops open. "Seriously?"

I forget that she doesn't know all the dirty details. And that's because I chose not to tell her. I don't want her to hate me. Don't want her to think I'm a boyfriend-thief either.

A change of subject needs to happen and fast.

"You should take some of your own advice and go talk to Tuttle," I suggest.

"No way," she says too quickly. "I don't like him. Remember?"

I don't bother arguing with her. She won't admit she's into him, so I'm not going to push the issue.

Besides, I'm already considering taking Amanda's advice and going to Ryan. It's not necessarily a bad idea. Better than sitting around worrying about him for the rest of my Sunday.

"Go," she says when I remain quiet. "Text him and let him know you want to talk."

"But I was hoping we could hang out." I don't want her to think I'd come over here just to ditch her for a guy. I want a friend. I need someone who's honest with me, who's *real* with me. I feel like I'm surrounded by people who are either fake or they send mixed messages. It's exhausting.

"I can't. I have to go to my grandma's house tonight for dinner. Sunday family thing, you know?" She smiles.

No, I really don't know. She's so wholesome it's unreal. "Okay. I'll see you at school tomorrow?"

"Monday is Labor Day," she reminds me.

"Oh, that's right." I totally forgot. "Okay, Tuesday then?"

"Absolutely. I'll come pick you up before school," she suggests as we both rise from the swing. "That way you won't have to walk and possibly run into someone you don't want to."

"Like Dustin?"

"Like Em." Amanda embraces me, giving me a quick hug. "I'm glad you came over," she says when she pulls away.

"Me too," I say with a little smile.

HE'S WAITING FOR me in my driveway. I see him standing there as I cruise on my bike along the sidewalk. I hit the brakes, coming to a skidding stop a few feet away from him, and he finally spots me, his familiar, warm smile not making its usual appearance. He just watches me, his expression solemn, the breeze blowing through his dark hair, ruffling it so it falls into his eyes before he brushes it away impatiently.

"What are you doing here?" My voice is scratchy and my throat feels raw again. Just like it did last night.

Dustin shoves his hands into the front pockets of his jeans and shrugs. "We should talk."

I hop off my bike and walk it up my driveway and into the garage. "What about?" I ask as I set the bike where it belongs. I don't want to turn around. I don't want to face him. I'm so nervous about him wanting to talk that I'm trembling.

"Liv." I turn around when he says my name and my gaze meets his. "I can't do this anymore. Pretend that we're just friends when I want... more. I can't go back."

"Go back to what?"

He runs his fingers through his hair, gripping it tight for a moment before he releases it. "Go back to us just hanging out, being there for each other. I thought I could. I thought I could be patient and wait you out, but...I can't do it. It's too hard."

Everything inside of me goes cold. "So you won't even be my friend."

"I'll never not be your friend, but I can't spend so much time with you, like we did last night. Being with you like that drove me fucking crazy," he admits, his gaze sliding away from mine so he can stare off into the distance. "All I wanted to do was kiss you, like, the entire time."

Would I have turned him away if he did? I was feeling weak last night and sad over Em's disappearance. "What, until you got those text messages when we were at the club? Then you couldn't wait to get rid of me."

That had hurt too. More than I wanted to admit.

He frowns, his gaze meeting mine once more. "I went and hung out with friends, okay? It was no big deal. I needed to let off some steam and we met up and played basketball. I knew we were just running around chasing our tails looking for Em. It was a waste of our time, trying to find her."

"She's our friend," I start but he cuts me off.

"Em doesn't give a shit about us. She never really has. She uses you and she uses me and we both fall into line like trained monkeys, Livvy. It's ridiculous. I'm over it. You should be over it too. You shouldn't trust her."

His harsh words hit me like physical blows and I wince. He was the one who screwed around with Em while trying to pursue me. I can't forget that. "Maybe I shouldn't trust you either."

"You probably shouldn't. You want a friend and all I can think about is ripping your clothes off," he admits, his voice ragged.

My heart does a flip. "Dustin…"

He holds up a hand, his expression pained. "Don't say it. Please. I'll leave you alone." He turns away from me, about to head back to his house, but I call his name again and he pauses, glancing over his shoulder at me.

"I'm sorry," I whisper, wishing I could say more, but…what? I'm at a loss here. He looks like he is too.

"Just be patient with me, Livvy. If I keep my distance from you for a while, let me do it, okay? Don't pressure me and don't think I hate you. I could never hate you, no matter how much I try. My problem is I need to figure out how to get over you." He smiles, and it's a cute, sweet Dustin smile. "See ya around?"

I nod, barely able to hold back the tears. He turns and walks back toward his house. Walks right out of my life.

And quietly breaks my heart.

chapter thirty-one

"Hey." Ryan opens his front door a little wider, his gaze roaming all over me, making my skin warm. "You look good."

"Thanks." I'm glad he noticed. I have on my cutest floral print dress with the too-short skirt, the one I'm not allowed to wear to school anymore since it breaks dress code. I took my time doing my makeup after I got out of the shower, watching a YouTube tutorial on my phone as I sat in front of my mirror in my room.

I'd wanted to look good for him tonight. Mom was working a night shift and that meant no one was at home waiting for me, watching the clock. Ready to bust me for breaking curfew. I could come and go as I pleased thanks to her taking that extra shift, and I was downright giddy over how *adult* it made me feel.

"Come in," he says, smiling at me as I enter the house, walking past him.

He shuts the door as I stop in the foyer and gape at his home. It's huge. Two stories, with soaring ceilings and so many huge windows, letting in the waning sunlight. The living room is massive, with blinding white couches and stark white walls, sleek silver end tables and a matching coffee table. A giant flat screen hangs on the wall and a stack of women's magazines sits in a white basket nearby. The house is very clean, a burst of sunflowers in a tall silver vase sitting on a table by the entry, a tiny silver dish filled with loose change, a pack of gum and a set of keys next to it.

Homey touches that make the room a little more comfortable, a little more real. Tuttle's house looked like something out of a magazine, and way too perfect. Em's house is big too, but I always felt comfortable there, considering we'd been friends for years. I was worried about Ryan's place, but as he leads me into the kitchen, with its cream-colored cabinets and warm-toned granite countertops, I don't feel as intimidated. Though it's obvious he's wealthy. Most everyone who goes to my school is wealthy.

My house is one of the smaller ones in the neighborhood, and when my parents divorced, Dad took all of his wealth with him. Oh, he pays child support, which Mom grumbles about all the time since she feels he doesn't pay enough, and he set up a college fund for me. But honestly, I think Mom misses being one of the ladies who lunch, who don't have to work and don't even have to clean their house, considering they have maids. They do nothing all day but get manicures and sit by the pool and gossip—according to Mom.

She kicked Dad out and eventually had to put her old nursing degree to good use by getting a job. A job she resents sometimes. I know she does. She resents living in this neighborhood too, surrounded by people she used to consider friends. But she didn't want to leave, didn't want to take me out of the school district, so she stuck around.

Torturing herself. Torturing me sometimes too.

"Want something to drink?" Ryan asks, his deep voice, pushing me out of my thoughts.

I smile, reminding myself to focus on him. Tonight is all about him. And us. "Yeah, that would be great."

He goes to the large refrigerator with doors that match the cabinets and opens them, peering inside, the light from within bathing him in a silvery glow. Gilding his perfect features—the sharp point of his nose, the strong line of his jaw, the soft curve of his lips. I stare, my insides twisting, my heart pumping, the blood rushing through my veins, making my skin tingle. He's so gorgeous, like model beautiful, and I can't believe I'm in his house. That he actually *likes* me.

It's so annoying that I still think like this. I don't have the best self-esteem and sometimes I worry too much over why he's interested in me. I tell myself I should be more confident, but it's so hard.

I texted him when I got home from Amanda's, asking if we could get together, and he readily agreed, never once mentioning yesterday's argument. I was relieved, not that I wanted to ignore what happened, but I'm not the best when it comes to dealing with confrontation. Though I'd been on a wild ride of confrontation since I came home from Oregon, that's for sure.

"Want a beer?" Ryan turns to look at me, his deep green eyes sparkling mischievously.

"Are your parents home?" Did they let him drink beer with his friends?

He slowly shakes his head, that spark in his gaze only intensifying. "My mom's working tonight. My dad and my brother went out to dinner and then to the movies."

"So we're all alone?" I should probably be nervous, but instead I'm...

Excited.

"Yeah, we are." He pulls two beers out of the fridge and shuts the door with his bent arm. I go to him and take the one he offers me, cracking it open. "Want to see my room?" he asks.

"Sure," I say softly, ignoring the nerves bubbling in my stomach. He's not wasting any time, is he? No one else around means no interruptions—just the two of us alone in this giant house.

The night is suddenly filled with endless possibilities.

He goes back to the fridge and grabs a couple more beers, and then I'm following Ryan up the sweeping staircase, admiring his broad shoulders and back, his lean torso, his butt. He's got a nice body. He's wearing black athletic shorts and a faded Nirvana T-shirt, his hair still damp, like he might've taken a shower before I came over. He smells good too, citrusy. Clean and crisp.

"You're lucky. I just cleaned my room yesterday," he says as we stop in front of a closed door. "My parents were on my ass for weeks."

"So you spent your Saturday cleaning your room?" That makes him sound so…normal. "Don't you have a housekeeper?" They all do, I swear.

"Yeah, but I'm not going to let her come in my room and go through my shit. There are things I've hidden I don't want anyone to find." He grins as he pushes open his door. "Drugs, weed, my condom stash. You know, the usual."

I laugh as he waggles his eyebrows then takes a sip of my beer, entering his bedroom, which is huge and done in typical teenage boy style, only on a grander scale. A dark blue comforter covers his king-sized bed. Awards and plaques and posters cover the sky-blue walls and a tower of folded T-shirts sit on an overstuffed chair.

The faint lemony scent is a reminder that he really did clean his room yesterday, and I glance around, see the open door that leads to a walk-in closet that's sort of a mess. Another open door that is his bathroom. His room is like a tiny studio apartment. I even spot a mini fridge in the corner. All he needs is a microwave and he'd never have to leave.

"So you have a condom stash, huh?" I ask as I walk around his room, stopping at the dresser. I run my fingers along the smooth wooden edge, checking out the framed photos sitting there. One is of him and who I assume is his younger brother—they look a lot alike. Another one is of his entire family, his parents proud and standing tall, their smiles large and showcasing perfectly straight teeth. Yet another photo of him and a bunch of people I don't recognize, most likely from his old school. Cute girls who smile up at Ryan adoringly as they surround him like he's some sort of god.

A reminder of his other life.

"Wanna see my stash?" He drains his beer and tosses the empty can in a nearby wastebasket. "It's impressive."

"Ew." I giggle and shove his shoulder because I don't know how else to react. He thinks his condom stash is impressive? What does that even mean? I almost don't want to know.

"What? I'm just saying I have the 'ridged for her pleasure' style, sized extra-large." His voice drops a couple of octaves, becoming devastatingly low. "Always thinking of you, Livvy."

I swear he's testing my mood, seeing if I'll freak out or not. "Sounds interesting. Will you share your secret stash with me?"

He looks shocked. A surge of power runs through me at the realization that yes, I *can* surprise Ryan Bennett every once in a while. "Yeah, I'll definitely share. But you'll have to promise me something first."

I smile up at him. "What?"

"Promise that you're not going to let anything ruin your mood tonight, okay?" He shifts closer to me, his hand going to my cheek, fingers drifting along my jaw. "We've been on this endless loop of misunderstandings lately."

Hmm, that's one way to put it. "I'm sorry for what happened yesterday, with you seeing me at Dustin's. It really was nothing—"

"I know," Ryan says, interrupting me. "I'm over it."

"You are? Really?" I frown, remembering how angry he'd been. How Tuttle had seemed so amused over our little fight. "You just seemed so mad and I want to explain what happened."

"You don't have to explain anything. Who am I to act like a jealous boyfriend, right? It's not like we're together or anything. We've flirted. We've kissed." He shrugs those impressively broad shoulders and I stare at him, hating how this conversation has turned.

"Okay." I take a deep breath, my brain scrambling to come up with something, anything to change the subject, but then he's right there. Standing directly in front of me, taking the beer out of my hand and setting it on the dresser. He cups my face, tilts my head back, and I meet his gaze, his eyes dark and full of intent.

His mouth is on mine before I can say another word or draw another breath. His soft lips coax and tease, keeping the kiss light at first, then taking it deeper, his tongue sweeping into my mouth, his thumbs gently brushing over my cheeks. I sigh against his lips, my hands resting on his hips, hanging on to the hem of his T-shirt. He nudges me against the dresser, the sharp edge digging into my lower back, but I don't feel the pain.

All I can focus on is the texture and taste of Ryan's lips, the hypnotic way they move against mine.

He breaks the kiss, his mouth running along the length of my neck, at the top of my shoulder, lips hot against my throbbing pulse. My heart is racing and I keep my eyes tightly closed, reveling in the sensations of his mouth on my skin, his hands at my waist, stroking slowly up and down my sides, getting closer to my chest with every sweep.

"I can't stop thinking about you," he murmurs close to my ear, his warm breath making me tremble. "Stupid Cannon ruined everything Friday night."

I smile as he pulls away to watch me, his gaze locking with mine. "He never even said he was sorry."

"The guy is a selfish asshole." Ryan studies my chest, my cleavage on display thanks to my pushup bra and the scooped neckline of my dress. He reaches out, his index finger skimming along the spot where dress meets skin, and goose bumps rise with his touch. "You like that?" His hot gaze meets mine.

I nod, breathless.

His finger dips below the fabric, tracing the lacy edge of my bra. "I really like your dress, but I'd rather see you with it off."

He doesn't give me a chance to respond. Next thing I know I'm on the bed and he's bent over me, his body caging mine in, our mouths fused, hands busy. His fingers move under my skirt, skimming up my thigh, and I spread my legs, sucking in a sharp breath when those same fingers brush the front of my panties.

I clutch at his T-shirt, the fabric gathered tightly in my hands as he strokes me there. Back and forth. Up and down. Never dipping beneath my panties, he patiently teases me, driving me out of my mind so my hips lift, seeking more. He presses harder, drawing tight circles, rubbing, rubbing, rubbing...

He withdraws his hand, making me whimper. My eyes fly open to find him lifting away from me.

"Take the dress off," he says gruffly as he whips off his shirt, tossing it onto the floor. I stare at him, drinking in his broad chest, his rippling abs. He's built perfectly, even more cut than Dustin...

God. I banish Dustin from my head, pissed that I'd even make the comparison. Focusing on Ryan, I shift so I'm kneeling in the middle of the bed. Biting my lip, my gaze never leaving his, I grab my skirt and slowly pull it up, peeling my dress off until I'm in front of him wearing only my black pushup bra and matching black panties.

Ryan's gaze bounces everywhere, like he doesn't know where to look first, and heat washes over my skin. He pounces, pressing me into the mattress, his smooth skin hot on mine, his wandering hands making me shiver as he kisses me hungrily. I touch him just as eagerly, slipping my fingers under his shorts, the elastic band of his boxer briefs. He groans against my mouth, pinning me in place so he can thrust his hips against mine, and oh God, I can feel him.

He's big. Hard. Driving me insane. We're a writhing mess, his fingers sliding between my legs, mine diving beneath his underwear, our legs entwined. I'm panting, he's panting, our kiss turns sloppy, all teeth and tongue and moans, and then I feel the heady rush sweep over me, making me shake, making me cry out.

Making me forget everything.

Ryan holds me close, one strong arm still slung around my waist, his mouth pressed against my forehead. I take deep breaths, desperate to calm my racing heart, and then he's kissing me. Touching me again. Trying to take my panties the rest of the way off as he murmurs, "I need to dip into my condom stash."

"Wait." I brace my hands against his sweat-dampened chest, stopping him. He lifts his head, his questioning gaze meeting mine. "I've—I haven't done this before."

He frowns, his brows furrowed. "What do you mean?"

"I'm a—I'm a virgin." I press my lips together, waiting for his reaction. I didn't mean to tell him this soon after...everything, but he wasn't wasting any time. I had to put a stop to him before everything got out of hand.

I'm willing to do this—mess around. But I'm not ready to make that next step yet.

When he still hasn't said anything I roll away from him, facing the wall, feeling stupid. "I'm sorry. I should've told you sooner. I just…it's not an easy thing to talk about or bring up, you know? It feels weird, talking about it."

"Hey." He touches my shoulder, gently tugging on it so I roll back around to face him. "You don't need to apologize. I'm not mad or anything."

"You're not?"

He slowly shakes his head, smiling faintly. "I'm glad you told me. I want us to be honest with each other. I—I really like you, Livvy."

My heart soars, I swear. Like it wants to fly out of my chest. "You do?"

"Yeah." He leans in and presses the softest, sweetest kiss to my lips before he murmurs, "I do. I know I've been shitty sometimes, but my feelings for you, they messed with my head."

I reach up to touch him, running my fingers through his silky soft hair. "What do you mean?"

"I didn't want to like you as much as I do." He kisses me again, his lips lingering, teeth nipping lightly on my bottom lip and making me gasp. "But it's too late. I'm totally into you."

"I'm totally into you too," I whisper just before he greedily kisses me. He reaches for my hand, placing it in front of his underwear, and I can feel him. My fingers curl, learning the shape of him, and he rests his hand on top of my head. Gently.

I know what he wants.

And I'm going to give it to him.

chapter thirty-two

"Oh my gosh, you're freaking glowing!" Amanda yells from her open window, grinning at me as I approach her car. The birds are chirping and the breeze is cool as it washes over me. For some weird reason the start of the first full week of September has ushered in cooler weather, which is unusual for California.

But it's nice. It feels like change is in the air. And *I* feel changed— thanks to Ryan.

I climb into Amanda's car and slam the door shut before I turn to look at her, smiling. "Ryan and I are official." I drop my backpack on the floorboard and lean back against the seat.

Her mouth drops open. "What do you mean?"

"We're a couple!" I'm practically bouncing with excitement and I almost clap my hands together like I'm five. "We, um, we were together Sunday night and we spent all of Monday together too." He invited me over to his house on Labor Day and we hung out with his parents and his little brother, who was sweet and clearly idolizes Ryan, though he treats Eli like shit.

"What did you guys do exactly?" Amanda's tone is sly as she puts her car into drive and pulls away from the curb.

"Well, you can only imagine what happened Sunday night. No one came home 'til around midnight." My cheeks go hot and I duck my head. I snuck out of the house just before his dad and brother came home so they wouldn't catch us together.

"Did you…" Amanda sends me a pointed look.

"Did I…" I wave my hand. "What?"

"Did you two have—*sex?*" She whispers the word, like it's extra dirty and she can't say it out loud.

I burst out laughing. Amanda's so silly. "Well, we did hook up. But we didn't do the deed." *Yet.*

"Gotcha." She nods, seeming to digest what I told her. "And what happened on Monday?"

I told her all about it. The barbecue in Ryan's backyard, hanging out with his family, swimming in his huge pool, his mother saying again and again how she was so happy Ryan had a *new* girlfriend. Though I wasn't so sure how I felt about that particular statement.

"Wow, you guys do sound like you're for real," Amanda says with wonder when I stop talking.

"That's because we *are* for real." I smile and stare out the passenger-side window. I sound smug because I *am* smug. I can't help it. Right now, I'm on top of the freaking world, and it's all because of Ryan. "He would've driven me to school but he had an early morning practice."

"Aw, that's too cute. I'm happy for you, Liv." Amanda's voice is soft, almost sad. I quickly glance over at her to see that she even looks sad. "Just when we're beginning to get close, you go and find yourself a boyfriend. I know you'll ditch me and I shouldn't say this, because it sounds selfish and I'm not selfish, I swear, but…"

"Stop. I'm not going to ditch you," I say, reaching out to briefly touch her arm. "You're part of the crew now. We'll all hang out together at lunch, after the games, whenever." I'm making assumptions. I don't even know if I'm part of the crew, whatever that means—the popular group? Do Amanda and I get to sit at their table in the quad during lunch? Will we all cruise over to Pac Out when we want to get off campus and eat giant cheeseburgers with extra salty fries?

"The crew?" Amanda laughs. "I don't think I'd fit in with that group."

"Tuttle wants you there." She goes stiff at the mention of his name. Again, I'm making assumptions, but the guy has been chasing her since school began. "Why won't you give him a chance?"

"What are you even talking about? Like I said, Tuttle isn't my type. I don't fit in with his group and I definitely don't fit with him," she says, gripping the steering wheel tight. "I'm glad you and Ryan are together, but don't try and pair me up with Tuttle. It's *never* happening." Her voice is firm and her expression is totally hostile. Guess she really means it.

"Again," I add quietly, just to be a brat. Reminding her that once upon a time, something *did* happen with her and Tuttle.

The irritated noise she makes tells me I made my point. "Whatever," she mumbles as she pulls her car into the senior parking lot.

FOR SOME MAGICAL, wonderful reason, Ryan's waiting for me at my locker before first period starts, just like I'd secretly hoped he would be. His being there is a statement, one that everyone will notice. He's staking his claim—as in he's claiming me. And I couldn't be more thrilled about it.

The moment he spots me, sending me one of those chin-nod things boys do, I smile in return, hoping I don't look too eager. It takes everything within me not to skip over to where he's standing and throw myself at him.

He drops a quick kiss on my lips when I reach him, his gaze locked on mine. "Morning."

"Good morning," I return, beaming like an idiot.

Tuttle chooses that moment to pass by, with Dustin of all people. "Gag," Tuttle mutters straight toward us, just before he and Dustin crack up.

I watch as they walk away, frowning. I knew they were sort of friends, but they'd never been what I'd call close. Who does Tuttle ever really hang out with? Guys from the football team most of the time, or any boy who's an athlete. So I guess that means Dustin counts.

"Tuttle's an asshole," Ryan says as he watches them walk away too.

"I thought you two were friends?" I glance up at him.

He shrugs, irritation written all over his face. "He mostly keeps to himself—unless he wants to cause trouble."

Unease slips down my spine at his words and I turn to my locker, entering in the combination before opening it. "What do you mean, trouble?"

"Trust me, you don't want to know." He presses a quick kiss to my cheek, making me smile. "But maybe you should tell your friend to keep away from him."

"Are you talking about Amanda?" I shove a couple of books in my locker before I slam it shut. "Why should she stay away from him?"

"Like I said, you don't want to know. Just—trust me, okay?" He wraps his arm around my shoulder and steers me so we head down the hall. "Isn't that what you're supposed to do? Trust your boyfriend?"

I gaze up at him, staring into his dreamy green eyes. "Are you calling yourself my boyfriend?"

"I thought we already established that?" He leans in for another kiss but then pulls away when he spots a scowling teacher nearby. "The anti-PDA rules suck."

Laughing, I lean into him, absorbing his warmth, his strength. Have I ever been this happy? Did I ever think things would turn out like this for Ryan and me? I might've wished for it, but I never thought this could be my reality.

I'm practically floating on a cloud a few minutes later when I enter the girls' bathroom. Ryan's class is down another hall and I want to check on my makeup anyway. My eyeliner always seems to smudge off.

The moment I enter the bathroom, one of the stall doors open and Em walks out, her expression sour, her lips a deep, rich red and her hair a mess. Her gaze meets mine and she rolls her eyes, her upper lip curling in disgust. "Where's your boyfriend?" she singsongs.

I have the worst luck. Why do I always run into her in the bathroom? "Why didn't you ever call me this weekend?"

She goes to the sink and starts washing her hands, her gaze meeting mine in the mirror. "What are you talking about?"

I go to stand next to her, running a finger under one eye, then the other. This is what I get for using cheap eyeliner. "You went missing, Em. My mom accused me of lying to her because she thought we were together. Like I was hiding you in my closet so your parents wouldn't find you."

"Oh." She shuts off the faucet and shakes her hands, little water droplets landing in the sink. "Sorry."

"That's all you can say?" I'm incredulous—and pissed. "Dustin and I went looking for you everywhere on Saturday. I texted you about a million times, left you voicemails. We searched all over town for you!"

"And I received every one of those million texts and voicemails." The bored look she sends my way irritates me even further. It's amazing how a simple look makes me want to punch her in the face. "Listen, I was going through some shit and I stayed away from home for a little while. My parents made it out into this big thing, when it totally wasn't. I was at a—friend's house. It was no big deal. I didn't mean for you or Dustin to get involved."

Her explanation means nothing to me. "You're not going to tell me what happened?"

"Are you going to tell me what's going on with you and Ryan?" She raises a brow.

I look away, taking a deep breath. I don't want to talk to her about Ryan.

"That's what I thought," she says smugly when I don't answer. "See ya around."

"Wait a second." I grab her arm before she can make her escape. I know the first bell is going to ring any minute. We're probably going to be late to class, but for once I don't give a shit. "Are you okay, Em? Really? You know you can still talk to me, if you ever need a friend."

"Please," she scoffs. Literally *scoffs*. "What, are you going to be my guidance counselor now?" She jerks her arm out of my grip and shifts away from me. "Like you'd understand my problems when you have none."

"Seriously? I have problems. You know I do. My parents are divorced, my mom focuses all of her attention on me so I can't catch a break, and we're pretty much broke while you have it made."

"Give me a break." She looks away, like she can't bear to look at me. "You think I'm a total joke while you're untouchable."

I gape at her, icy cold shock coursing through my veins. "What are you talking about? I don't think I'm better than you."

Em faces me once more. "You get everything you ever want. Your life is perfect."

Laughter escapes me, though it's not the humorous kind. "Are you serious? My life is far from perfect."

"Really? Let's recount everything you have. You're beautiful. You're smart. Dustin's madly in love with you, yet you chose Ryan over him. And somehow you worked your magic and now Ryan's totally into you too." Em counts off each item with her fingers, waggling them at me. "You two make a perfect couple." Her voice oozes with sarcasm.

"Dustin's not madly in love with me," I say, though it sounds like a lie the moment the words pass my lips. The way Em's looking at me, she knows it's a lie too. We both know how Dustin feels about me. She knew, yet she messed around with him anyway, and that freaking hurts. Though I'm not bringing that up anymore. It's fucked up our friendships enough.

"Dustin is totally in love with you. He always has been. He's so blinded by his feelings for you he can't see anyone else. Not even me," she adds morosely.

I'm shocked, yet not. I had a feeling she had a thing for Dustin. The three of us sometimes felt too close. Like I was involved in a relationship with both Dustin and Em and I wasn't sure whose role was what. It was suffocating.

I had to get out. Break free from the both of them. I just didn't mean for it to disintegrate so completely.

"Maybe you two…" My voice drifts. I can barely get the words out. I don't want her to be with Dustin. I don't want him, but I don't want her to have him either.

Yes, I'm a total bitch, but I can't help it.

"No." She smiles just as the bell rings, though she looks sad. Her eyes are glassy and her expression is pained. "He's not interested, despite the fact that we actually had sex. He's made that clear."

Her words make me flinch like she actually slapped me. It hurts all over again, hearing her say they had sex.

Em starts to leave the bathroom and I call her name, stopping her. "I'm sorry," I tell her. "For…everything." The most blanket apology I can give her, though I'm not really sure what exactly I'm sorry for. Or why I'm apologizing in the first place.

"No you're not," she says with a slight shake of her head. "Not really. But that's okay, because I forgive you." She flashes me her trademark smile, a real one this time, and I catch a glimmer of my wild best friend. "You should come over after school. We can work on our tans."

Our tans. She's funny. I don't really tan. She knows this. "Maybe I will."

"You can bring your boyfriend. Ryan and I can reminisce." She laughs and pushes open the door, exiting out into the hallway crush before I can answer her. "See ya, Livvy!"

I remain in the bathroom for a minute longer, letting the anger wash over me, through me. I can't believe she said that.

I probably deserved it.

chapter thirty-three

"I 'm having a party," Ryan murmurs in my ear just before he nibbles it. "This Saturday. For my birthday."

I shove at his shoulders, pushing him away so I can look at him. It's Tuesday night, almost ten, which is my stupid curfew during school nights, and we've been kissing in his car in my driveway for the past twenty minutes. His hair is mussed from my fingers, his lips swollen, and he looks hotter than ever. "It's your birthday this weekend?"

"Well, it's a week from today, but I'm celebrating this weekend. Eighteen, baby." He grins, leaning in for another kiss, but I push him away again, shoving at his chest. He frowns. "What gives? You have to be in your house in like five minutes. We gotta make the most of this."

Less than five minutes, more like three, but I don't correct him. "Why didn't you tell me?"

"I *did* tell you." When I don't say anything, he continues. "When I first met you at Em's house. You kept asking me all of these questions and that was one of them. My birthday is the twenty-sixth."

"Oh." How could I freaking forget? We've been going out for three weeks already. I'm officially the worst girlfriend ever. "So you're having a big birthday bash?"

"Yeah, my parents are going out of town this weekend for some business thing for my dad. I'm in charge of Eli. I told him if he breathes a word of this party to Mom and Dad, I'm going to slit his fucking throat."

I flinch at his choice of words. By the murderous glimmer in his eyes, I half believe he'd do it. "Who are you inviting?"

"Everyone. We have an away game this Friday, which sucks." He doesn't like away games. They always seem to lose those, but they've played well at home lately, winning their last two games, which is a huge deal at school. "Wanna help me decorate on Saturday?"

"What, like party decorations?" I wrinkle my nose. "Are you serious?"

"Well, yeah." He hauls me back into his arms, kissing me stupid, leaving me dizzy. "I need balloons and streamers. The housekeeper cleans on Thursday afternoons so the house should look good. But that also means we have to be careful. We can't trash it."

"If you invite everyone, then the house *will* get trashed. I guarantee it." The football players are the cliché bulls trapped in a china shop, smashing and breaking everything even when they don't mean to.

Ryan starts kissing my neck, his mouth wet and hot on my skin, making me shiver. "You'll help me clean then."

Like I really want to be part of his cleaning crew. But for my boyfriend, I'd do just about anything. "Maybe," I tease.

"Maybe? Aw, come on." He kisses me hungrily, his tongue doing a thorough search of my mouth as his hand lands on my boob, his thumb rubbing back and forth.

I break the kiss immediately, slapping his hand away. "Stop, Ryan. What if my mom catches us?" Mom catching Ryan feeling me up in his car sitting in the driveway isn't how I want to end the night.

"Give me a break, like she doesn't know what we're doing out here. Besides, she's too busy *getting* busy with her boyfriend," he says, laughing when he catches my disgusted expression.

Ew. That is the last thing I want to think about.

"I have to go." I grab my purse and lean in to give him a brief kiss that somehow turns into another tongue-tangling session. I finally pull away, breathless, my head spinning and Ryan grinning like he knows exactly what he does to me. "See you in the morning?"

"You'll have to get a ride from Amanda," he says, tapping the tip of my nose. "I have morning practice."

"Okay." I climb out of his car, leaning over to peer inside to look at him one last time before I close the door. "Miss you."

"Send me a tit pic," he says, grinning as he starts the car.

I roll my eyes. He always wants tit pics. He's such a perv. I've sent him a few, but they always make me nervous after I send them. That one-second option on Snapchat is a dream come true. I just have to hope Ryan doesn't screenshot them. "No way. Maybe I'll show them to you in person for your birthday."

"I've already seen them in person. You know what I want. I think it would make a great birthday present too." I slam the door shut, cutting off his words. He waves at me and backs out of the driveway, pulling out onto the road and turning toward the direction of his house.

I stand and watch until the lights of his car disappear before I walk into my house. I can't stop turning over his words again and again. I know what he wants, what he thinks will be the perfect birthday present.

My virginity.

I've held tight to it for the last three weeks, since we've been officially together. We've done everything but have sex. We make out until I can't see straight and my mouth is sore. He's fingered me to orgasm multiple times. Gone down on me once—but I wasn't that comfortable with it, so I made him stop. I've given him endless hand jobs and blowjobs, but we haven't done the actual deed. I just…can't. Not yet. And our last encounter, when it didn't end the way he wanted, Ryan got frustrated.

And even a little pissed.

"So you'll put my dick in your mouth but you won't let me stick it in your pussy?" he'd yelled as he paced around his room, wearing only a pair of athletic shorts and pitching a mighty big tent in the front of them.

I hadn't known how to answer his question without getting mad, so I took a deep breath. Then another. Then I'd told him I wasn't ready and he stopped protesting after that.

Of course he did. I gave him a blowjob and all was right in the world.

But I'm not bitter about the blowjobs, I swear. I sort of get off giving them to him. He loves them so much and I like having that tiny bit of power over him. The knowledge that I'm the one who makes him lose control like that is pretty heady stuff. So I keep doing it, all while my virginity remains intact.

Why I'm holding on to my virginity, I don't know. I guess I'm scared that once we actually do have sex, he'll…dump me. Which is crazy, I know it is, but I can't help feeling that way. There are so many other girls at school who would love to snatch Ryan away from me.

The possibility of losing him terrifies me. My entire life has changed since we got together. My social status has grown. I feel confident. Even…popular. I shouldn't care about that stuff, but I can't help it.

I do.

Hanging out with Amanda has helped me too. We've grown super close. She's fun—a real friend who always has my back. And I have hers as well. I'm glad we have each other.

Makes me feel like I'm more than just a girl who's become someone because of her boyfriend. I need that.

Desperately.

Entering the house, I bypass the living room, which is dark save for the flickering light of the TV, and go straight for the kitchen. I know Mom and Fitch are watching a movie or one of their favorite shows and I don't feel like talking to them. Besides, I'm pretty sure I have *made out and rubbed against each other* written all over me. I swear I can still smell Ryan's cologne and soap clinging to my skin.

I open the fridge and bend over to grab a bottled water from the very back before I shut the door and stand up straight. A little shriek escapes when I see who's standing in front of me.

"There you are." Mom smiles pleasantly, but it's false. It's what I call her phony *I've caught you* smile. "Where have you been?"

I twist off the bottle cap and take a drink. "With Ryan," I say after I swallow.

"Uh-huh." She crosses her arms in front of her, leaning against the kitchen counter. She looks weary and old and tired of my bullshit. I've seen this look before, too many times. "I don't know how I feel about you spending so much time with that boy."

"Too late, Mom. I'm spending time with him. *Dating* him. I really like Ryan and you can't stop me from seeing him," I snap, hating how she tries to control my every little move. I'm practically an adult. I can't freaking wait to get out of this house so I can be on my own.

"I can stop you, especially when you don't abide by my rules. This is my house and what I say, goes." She steps closer and points a finger in my face. I'm tempted to slap it away. "If you're late again, I'll ground you. I'll ban you from seeing him."

"Give me a break. I'm only a few minutes late, Mom."

"I don't care. I don't like that boy. I think he's a bad influence."

I actually laugh. "Please."

"Don't tempt me, Olivia. If I want to ban you from seeing him, I can make it happen," Mom threatens.

"You wouldn't dare," I breathe, my eyes going wide.

But her expression doesn't even flinch. Neither does her finger, which is still in my face. "Watch me," she says, her voice low before she drops her hand, turns on her heel and bails out of the kitchen.

I go to sit on one of the barstools that line our counter, my legs shaky, my mind spinning. Mom and I don't really fight. We bicker on occasion, especially about my friends and boys and my stupid curfew and bad grades, but I never thought she'd use keeping me away from Ryan as a threat. I'm sort of blown away.

I don't know how long I sit there at the counter, recounting every word Mom said. I can't believe she'd threaten me. I almost want to tell her to fuck off, but I'm scared she *will* take Ryan away from me.

And I can't let that happen.

"Hey, what's going on?" Fitch's soft voice makes me lift my head, my gaze meeting his. His eyes are kind, his smile encouraging as he settles into the stool next to mine. "You all right?"

"I'm fine." I smile in return, shrugging. "Thanks for asking."

Fitch I don't get. I'm not quite sure how to approach him yet. He seems like he's on my side most of the time, but he could also turn on me quick and I wouldn't be the wiser. Mom listens to everything he says. She told me recently that she *values* his opinion.

While mine is total shit. That's not what she said exactly, but it was implied.

"You and your mom arguing again?" His eyes crinkle at the corners as his smile grows. "She means well. She just doesn't want to see you toss away your opportunities."

"What opportunities? I have none to throw away."

"Your college education for one. You're going to apply to a lot of colleges soon, right? Isn't the plan for you to get a scholarship to a good school? She doesn't want you to throw it away, all for a boy."

"I would never do that. I'm not stupid," I mutter, glancing down at the counter again. "Does everyone have such little faith in me or what?"

"Not me." When I look up, I find he's grinning at me. Like, full on grinning, as if it's the happiest day on earth. "You're smart and beautiful and you've got the world by its tail. Don't ever let it go, baby."

I wrinkle my nose. "Did you really just call me baby?"

"Figure of speech." The smile fades and he waves a nonchalant hand, as if he calls every female he talks to baby. "I'm just trying to say don't give up on your dreams. Or else you'll be stuck in some shitty house, married to some shitty guy and taking care of his shitty kids while you're barely making it and stretching out that pittance of a paycheck you earn, so you can pay the mortgage," he says, his gaze getting that far-away look that happens with Fitch sometimes.

What he just described, it sounds…fucking awful.

I wonder if he's talking about himself, about his life. Mom mentioned a while ago he's divorced, and that he has a couple of kids he has partial custody of, but I don't know the particulars.

"And if I sound like a bitter old man, maybe I am," Fitch continues. "But at least I'm with a woman I care about now, instead of that hateful bitch I was married to." He practically spits out the words "hateful bitch." She sounds lovely.

"I have zero plans on getting married, especially after high school or college or whatever." I seriously don't want to talk about my future plans with Fitch. I don't know if he'll still be around when I graduate in June.

"Life never happens like you believe it will. You think you have it all together, that you'll never deviate from your plan, but it'll happen. Forces beyond your control will come along and bam, everything changes," he says with a little shrug. "Sometimes it'll be a good change, sometimes it's a bad one. You just gotta roll with the punches."

He leans in closer and punches me lightly on the shoulder, as if emphasizing his point. I stare into his eyes, smell the beer on his breath, and I recoil from him a little, hoping he doesn't notice.

Shit. The sneer curling his lips indicates he does.

"Think you're better than me, don't you?" His voice is quiet. Chilling. "Think you can tell your mom that I'm no good for her and she'll dump me? Well, she won't. She's in love with me and there's not a damn thing you can do about it."

Weird. His entire demeanor has changed so fast. I blink rapidly, willing myself to get up, get the hell out of there, but it's like I'm paralyzed. He grabs hold of my wrist, fingers clamping tight, and my entire body goes stiff. "Let me go," I whisper.

"No. You listen to me first. We can come to an agreement, don't you think? Stay out of my business and I'll stay out of yours. Quit trying to convince your mom I'm not good enough."

I have no idea what he's referring to. I don't talk about Fitch to Mom. She knows I'm not thrilled with their relationship, but it's not like we sit around trading stories about our boyfriends.

Gross.

"You can go ahead and spend all your time with your little boyfriend," he murmurs, his gaze turning steely. I never noticed before how gray his eyes are, or how cold. "Just leave me alone."

Jerking out of his hold, I leap to my feet, the stool knocking to the ground with a clatter. I grab my bottle of water and get out of there, ignoring my mom when she calls out, "Is everything okay? Olivia? What's going on?"

I run down the hall, straight into my room, locking my door behind me. I flip the light switch on and glance around, my breath coming fast. Why does my room look…different? I swear to God someone's rifling through my shit, looking for something.

But what? Maybe I'm just being paranoid.

A sharp knock sounds on my door, making me jump. "Who is it?" I ask shakily.

"Who do you think it is?" Mom. She rattles the door handle. "Open the damn door right now."

Reluctantly, I unlock the door and she barges in just as I back up a few steps. "What's wrong?" I ask her. God, if Fitch said something to her about our weird little talk…

"What happened in the kitchen?" She shuts the door behind her before she turns to face me once more. "With Fitch? Were you two actually talking?"

Oh God. This is my moment to tell her the truth—that her boyfriend is kind of a creeper who might or might not have a minor thing for me—or I can remain quiet and act like nothing is wrong.

"Yeah." I try to smile, but it's like my lips won't cooperate. "Um, he was offering me advice."

A skeptical brow shoots straight up. "What sort of advice?" Mom asks.

"About life." I shrug. "How things can change no matter how much I try to plan." Well, that isn't a total lie.

"Huh." She studies me, her gaze penetrating. I try not to squirm, since that's a dead giveaway I'm uncomfortable. Instead I square my shoulders and stand up straight, pretend that nothing is bothering me. "You two are acting weird lately. If I didn't know any better, I'd wonder if you were both planning a birthday surprise for me."

Oh. That's right. Her birthday is October 2nd, right after Ryan's birthday. I couldn't remember my own boyfriend's birthday and I sure as hell wasn't thinking about Mom's either. "Why would you say that?" I ask innocently.

She smiles. Out and out beams, really. "Okay. I can play along with this. But please, I have one request."

"What's that?" I ask weakly.

"No surprise parties. They're the worst. And I don't want an over the hill themed party either. I'm turning forty—that's not a death sentence."

"Whatever you say," I call after her as she exits my bedroom.

Mom flashes me a sly look before she shuts my door. I go to it, quietly turn the lock and then collapse on my bed, staring up at the ceiling.

What a weird night.

chapter thirty-four

"Thank you so much for coming over and helping me," I say in greeting as I answer Ryan's front door.

Amanda sends me a begrudging look as she enters the house, stopping in the grand foyer. "I'm only doing this for you," she mumbles, her head shooting back so she can take in the impressive soaring ceiling. "Wow."

"I know." I shut the door and turn the lock. It's early Saturday afternoon and the party doesn't start until eight, but I'm not taking any chances. I don't want someone busting into the house unannounced. "This place is ridiculous."

I follow Amanda deeper into the house, and she collapses on one of the giant white couches, smoothing her hand over the surface. "Love the couch. His mom has good taste."

"Could be his dad who came up with this." I sit on the loveseat opposite Amanda.

"Come on. His dad is some techy nerd who lives for video games. He wouldn't care what the house looked like as long as he has the latest game systems and a giant screen TV." She points to the flat screen hanging on the wall. "And he's got that, so life is good."

"You know what's weird? Ryan doesn't play video games. At all." I asked him if he did, and while he didn't come out and actually say it, I do think he resents how much his father loves video games. It's to the point where he doesn't spend much time with his family. He's always working. His little brother Eli loves them and plays with their dad every chance he can get, which isn't often.

"Typical. The boy who has every game at his fingertips isn't interested. We always want what we can't have." She glances around the living room, taking in every perfect detail, no doubt. "Why am I here so early again? You wanted me to help you clean? This place is immaculate."

I roll my eyes. "We need to go shopping first, for party supplies."

Amanda makes a little face but remains quiet.

"And then we're coming back here and we're going to decorate!" I clap my hands together excitedly, but her lackluster response tells me she's not feeling the same way. I drop my hands and mock pout instead. "Come on, Amanda. It'll be fun."

"Fun helping you put up cheesy decorations so your boyfriend will think it's true love and I won't get any credit? No thanks," she mutters, crossing her arms in front of her chest.

Ouch. Negative much? "I promise I'll give you equal credit."

"Right, and that'll make all the difference to Ryan." She leans her head back on the sofa, sinking into the plush cushion. "I can think of a lot better ways to spend my Saturday."

"Why are you being such a jerk?" I rise to my feet so I can quickly slap her thigh before I fall back into the loveseat. She glowers at me, rubbing her bare leg. That's what she gets for wearing short shorts. Another heat wave has come through the Valley and it sucks. "You're usually up for anything!"

"Sorry." She shakes her head, still absently stroking her thigh. My smack left a red mark on her skin and I feel bad. "It's been a shitty week."

And I've been a shitty friend because I haven't noticed. "Why? What's going on?"

Sighing, she starts plucking at a thread on the couch. "Since I quit band my parents have been on my back, especially my mom. She truly believed it would be my ticket to college."

"Playing in the band?" I don't get how, but whatever.

"Getting a music scholarship. My family isn't like everyone else around here. They can't afford to send me to the college of my choice. And though I've always been in honors classes, I'm not what you would call a well-rounded student. The only activity I ever participated in was band."

"I don't think that's necessarily a bad thing…"

"The problem is it was the *only* thing. Now I'm not in band and it's our senior year. My parents think I ruined my chances." Her face crumples and I'm scared she's going to cry. "They said since I have all of this free time now, I need to go find a job to help pay for my college expenses."

The tears start to flow down her face and I move so I'm sitting next to her, wrapping her up in an awkward hug, trying to pat her back, offer up some comfort. Mom won't let me to get a part-time job. She says high school is my job and she wants me to focus on my schoolwork. I'm a decent student, though not in all honors classes like Amanda. While I would never get into an Ivy League university, I bet Amanda could. She's super smart and ambitious.

"What if you joined some clubs?" I suggest, still patting her shoulder.

Amanda sniffs and lifts her head, our gazes meeting. "What sort of clubs? The Chess Club? Math Club? Space Club? Those are all for nerds."

I can't believe she'd bash her own kind—and I mean that in the nicest way. I've always been middle of the road at school. Not totally unpopular, but not quite popular either. Amanda strays toward the nerd side and she'd never deny it. Quiet, studious, in band—she fit all the particulars. And she liked it there, had admitted to me recently that she felt comfortable there. Safe.

Moving out of her regular social circle scared her. It scared me too.

"There's a Space Club?" I ask, wrinkling my nose. I know there's one, but I'm trying to make her laugh. It doesn't work.

She makes a noise of frustration and pulls away from me, swiping at her tear -stained cheeks. "There's all sorts of clubs on campus, but they don't count for shit when it comes to getting into a quality school. Unless maybe I can get on the yearbook staff—that would look good." Another sniffle, but at least there's no more tears. "Maybe you could help me with that?"

"I can and I will. I already told you I would. Consider it done," I say firmly. "Maybe you could talk to one of the guys on the football team too. See if they can help you."

"With what? How can they help me?" Amanda asks incredulously.

"You never know. Maybe you could assist with games or whatever. Take stats. Everyone knows how much you love football." I shrug, feeling dumb.

"Hmm. Maybe I should do that for the basketball team. They have assistants who take stats for every game." She taps a finger against her pursed lips. "That's a good idea."

Basketball makes me think of Dustin and I immediately feel…I don't know. Sad? Conflicted? I miss him. He's kept his distance just like he said he would. He doesn't talk to me, not really, but he's not out and out rude either. We say hi in the one class we share and that's about it.

He's spending lots of time with Tuttle lately, which is weird. Tuttle seems to have turned his back on pretty much everyone on the football team. It's odd. But no one ever said Tuttle made much sense. The guy does whatever he wants and if anyone questions him, they can go fuck themselves.

I know this is true because I witnessed him saying exactly that to Ryan once.

"I still need to find a job, though," Amanda says, interrupting my thoughts. "I'm going to start searching on Monday. I have a few prospects lined up."

"That sucks." I feel bad for her and wish I had a solution. "Want me to help you?"

"Only if you want to." She shrugs. "I know there are financial aid options and student loans for college. I really don't want to take on loans, though. Debt scares me. I don't even know if I can get into the university of my choice. I mean, my SAT scores are good, but still." Her mouth curves downward. " I don't want to be stuck going to the local community college for a couple of years."

Her face starts to crumple again, but I won't let her cry. No way. This is a day for celebrating, not being sad.

I leap to my feet and take her hands, dragging her along with me. "Come on. Let's go eat lunch—my treat—and then we'll go to Party City and pick out the silliest decorations we can find, okay? It'll be awesome."

"Okay." Amanda offers a watery smile and nods. "Okay."

IT'S MUCH LATER in the afternoon and we're stringing black and white streamers all over the living room, careful to only use tape for fear of putting holes in the wall with pushpins when Ryan enters the living room, accompanied by...Tuttle.

For real.

Amanda scowls from her perch on top of the step stool, the black and white streamers twisted around each other slipping from her hand and unraveling on the ground. "What the hell are you doing here?" Her question is clearly directed at Tuttle.

We talked about him over lunch and she admitted how glad she was that Ryan and Tuttle weren't really hanging out anymore. It meant she didn't have to deal with him as much, and while I still didn't quite understand what was going on with those two, I did get that she wanted nothing to do with Tuttle. He must've really hurt her feelings or did something stupid to make her act like this. Because I can admit this—though I would never say it in front of Ryan—Tuttle is smoking hot. But his intensity scares me, so I'm not tempted.

Maybe all that intensity freaks Amanda out too. I'm not sure.

"Love of my life." Tuttle's gaze is locked on Amanda as he rests his hand on his chest, just like always. "You wound me with your cruel and wicked tone."

"What's the deal? Have you turned into Shakespeare?" I ask him, smiling as Ryan approaches me. I tilt my head back for his kiss and he doesn't disappoint, his mouth moving lazily over mine, a quick swipe of tongue before he pulls away.

"You have to admit she treats me like shit," Tuttle says to me, pointing at Amanda. "When I've done nothing wrong."

Amanda snorts in response.

"It's true." He turns to her. "You know how I feel. You're the one who keeps pushing me away."

My ears perk up. Ah, now the conversation becomes super interesting. I've only ever heard Amanda's side of the story...

"Come with me," Ryan murmurs close to my ear, his lips touching my skin and making me shiver. "I want to show you something."

Damn it. I want to eavesdrop, but I can't say no to Ryan. So I follow after him, clutching his fingers tightly as he leads me through the house and outside where there are two giant kegs set up on the lawn near the pool. "Whatcha think?" He points at the kegs.

I thought he was going to show me something romantic. Or say something romantic. Anything romantic. But he's too excited by the prospect of all that beer for tonight. "Um, they're awesome?"

"Hell yeah, they are. Tuttle's birthday present to me," he says proudly.

"How...thoughtful." I make a little face, but it's like he doesn't even notice. He's too enthralled with the kegs. In fact, he's standing beside one now, running his hand over the top of it almost lovingly.

"I have good friends." He lifts his head, his gaze meeting mine. "And a great girlfriend."

He comes to me then, wrapping me up in his arms and lifting me off my feet. I squeal, my arms shooting around his neck and holding on tight. He's laughing, and I'm laughing and I remember when I first met him, how intimidating he'd been, yet sexy. So incredibly sexy and a little edgy, a little intense...

Ryan isn't really like that now. He's my boyfriend. We flirt and we have fun and he's the best kisser and the best everything else, though I have to admit, he's a little selfish. Where Dustin always wanted to make sure I was satisfied too, Ryan wasn't as conscious of that.

And I shouldn't be thinking of Dustin right now. That's totally wrong and unfair. Everyone's different. Ryan is the *perfect* guy for me.

His mouth finds mine once more, and I'm lost. Dizzy. His damp lips and hot tongue, his roaming hands and whispered words of promise for later. What would happen later.

I plan on giving him everything he wanted tonight. I'm not even nervous. This night belongs to him.

It will be perfect.

chapter thirty-five

"You're staying the night with me, right?"

I glance to my right to find Ryan standing beside me, a red cup clutched in his hand, a loopy grin on his face. He's drunk, but so am I, so I guess we make an excellent match.

The party has been raging for a couple of hours. At one point there were so many people spilling out into the backyard, I was afraid the neighbors would report us and the cops would come break the party up. But I'm guessing Ryan has easygoing neighbors because we haven't seen the police yet.

"You want me to stay, right?" I bat my eyelashes, trying my best to give him a suggestive smile and his gaze heats, his brows shooting up. He taps his cup against the one I'm clutching in a silent toast and we both drink.

I nearly choke when Amanda's elbow digs into my side, reminding me that she's standing right next to me. I was gossiping with her not one second before my boyfriend approached and asked me that silly question.

My boyfriend. I loved thinking that. Saying it out loud.

"You two are so disgustingly into each other, it's gross," Amanda mutters, shaking her head.

Ryan glares while I swallow the rest of my beer. For some reason, he's not digging Amanda tonight. It's like he wants all of my attention and I've been giving it to him, but I finally needed a break. There's only so much I can tolerate, listening to him drone on about football and stats and workouts and practices with his circle of friends. Amanda is better at listening to that stuff, but she's staying away from Tuttle like he has a disease so I can't count on her hanging out with us.

Lots of people have brought Ryan gifts for his birthday, especially the jealous, pretty girls who act like they want to take him away from me. I've stood next to him for most of the night, clutching his arm and glaring at any female who dares cross his path. He doesn't seem bothered by my possessiveness, though a few times he did tell me to lighten up after I gave the death stare to yet another group of giggling girls who wanted to wish him a happy birthday.

"I'm going to hang out with Amanda for a little bit longer, okay?" I grab his hand and stand on tiptoe, kissing his cheek. He smells good, spicy and warm with a hint of beer. I run my lips along his strong jaw before they find his mouth. "Meet me in your room in an hour?"

His hand settles on my butt, giving it a squeeze and making me yelp. "Midnight," he whispers. "You better be waiting."

Anticipation races through my veins as he sends me one last, meaningful look before he slips away. The crowd seems to embrace him, Cannon patting him on the back as Tuttle hands him yet another beer.

"I saw Cannon kissing Emily earlier," Amanda says after Ryan left.

I nearly drop my beer. "Wait a second—*my* Em?"

"Yep, *your* Em." She nods, her lips quirking into a smirk. "I needed to use the bathroom and they must've forgot to lock the door. She was sitting on the counter and he was standing between her legs, and let me tell you, they were going at it like they were starved for each other."

"Em and Cannon?" I couldn't imagine her with the big, muscular, blond, irritating Cannon. He was the complete opposite of the dark and moody Em. He was loud and obnoxious, and a total and complete player. "I don't believe it."

"Believe it. I saw it with my own eyes." Amanda giggles. "It was kind of disgusting. I saw Cannon's tongue in her mouth."

We collapse against each other, giggling uncontrollably. We're acting stupid, like we're little kids but I've had way too many beers to worry about it. I'm trying to have fun and loosen up, not stress about giving my virginity to the one and only Ryan Bennett.

"You're nervous, aren't you?" Amanda asks.

My giggles disappear. "Yeah."

She reaches out and clasps my hand in hers. "You'll be fine. Don't worry about it."

"Are you talking from all of your wild past sexual experiences?" I tease, and her expression turns serious.

"I've had my moments," she says mysteriously, her gaze not meeting mine.

I almost don't believe her, but she can be pretty mysterious when she wants, so…

"What if I mess it up? What if I do or say something stupid?" Those are the least of my fears. I lower my voice, not wanting anyone else to hear me. "What if it…hurts? Like, really bad?"

"You've done everything else right?"

"Pretty much."

"Well, just make sure you're good and—*prepared* before you actually do it." She widens her eyes, reminding me of an owl. "You know what I mean?"

"I guess." I shrug. I mean, yeah, I'm not stupid, but it's probably going to hurt no matter how much we prepare.

"This is a night you'll never forget," Amanda says, gazing out at everyone milling about the backyard. The temperature is dropping and I'd rather go inside or find one of Ryan's hoodies to keep me warm. But that would ruin my outfit and no way am I covering it up. I'm wearing a cropped floral long-sleeved shirt and a short black skirt I picked out especially for tonight. Even with the long sleeves, I'm showing lots of skin and I know Ryan likes my outfit, what with the appreciative looks he'd been sending my way all night.

"I know. I'm trying to make it perfect," I tell her.

"Forget perfect. Just try to focus on the good stuff. You care about him and he cares about you, right? You two are in looooove." She draws out the word and starts giggling again, and I giggle too, though it's really halfhearted.

Am I in love with Ryan? I just…I can't say it. Can't even think it. I like him. I like him a lot. He makes me laugh and he makes me burn inside every time he touches me or kisses me. I like how I feel when I'm seen with him. When I walk down the hall at school, his arm around my shoulders. Running up to him after a football game when he looks so cute yet manly in his uniform.

I probably could fall in love with him.

Eventually.

"Hey Amanda."

We both look over to see Tuttle approaching, his expression bland, though his eyes are only for Amanda, and they're greedily eating her up.

"Tuttle. Fancy seeing you here," I tell him, my tone teasing.

He doesn't flinch, smile, nothing. "Can we talk?" he asks Amanda.

She shrugs. "What about?" She's just as bland, just as emotionless.

His gaze slides to me for the briefest moment before he returns his attention to her. "Privately?"

"I'll leave you two alone," I tell her, our gazes meeting. She looks a little freaked out. "Unless you don't want me to leave?"

"No, it's okay." She smiles weakly, a noticeable shiver running through her when Tuttle rests his hand at the small of her back. "Go ahead. We'll catch up later?"

"You have a way to get home?"

"I'll drive her home," Tuttle says firmly, sending her a look when she opens her mouth to protest. "I will," he tells her. "Don't bother arguing."

I leave them be, heading into the house in the hopes I can warm up. A few people linger in the kitchen at the small table in the breakfast nook, and there is a group of guys sitting in the living room, all crowded around the big screen as they play video games. Thank God no one has made a huge mess. Ryan said if we directed everyone outside they would mostly stay outside. Guess he was right.

"Livvy! Oh my God, there you are!"

I turn to see Em running toward me, her mouth stretched wide in a grin, her arms thrown open as she tackle-hugs me. I grip her tight, afraid she might knock me over, and she laughs before giving me a sloppy kiss on the cheek.

This feels very familiar. Almost comfortable...yet not.

"I heard you were here," I tell her, pulling away so I can take her in. She's wearing skin-tight jeans that show off her long legs, along with a flowy white shirt with embroidered multi-colored flowers decorating the neckline. She looks great.

"Who told you I was here?" She wraps her arm around my shoulders and guides me through the house, away from the living room and all the yelling boys. I swear I saw Cannon in there, but I can't be too sure.

"Amanda. She said she ran into you in the bathroom." I send her a sly look, but she doesn't even flinch.

"Oh really?" She sounds bored.

I poke her in the ribs. "Come on, Em. Fess up. You're hooking up with Cannon."

"Shh!" She tugs on my arm and the next thing I know I'm in a bathroom. Probably the very same bathroom she was hooking up with Cannon in. "Why did you say that so loud?"

"No one was listening to us," I defend myself, but she keeps talking over me in that typical way of hers.

"And we're not really hooking up. Well, we have, but only once. Okay, a few times. But it was nothing. *Nothing.* He's just…a scratch for my itch." She lifts her chin, appearing perfectly content with that explanation.

"A scratch to your itch?" That sounds awful.

She sighs, her shoulders sagging. "Listen, it's happened, but the moment is always accidental. He's very—persistent."

"Uh huh." I cross my arms in front of my chest.

"Stop giving me that judgmental tone. You're the one who's messing around with Ryan," she points out.

"Yeah, because he's my *boyfriend*," I remind her.

I'm also reminded of the fact that Ryan supposedly took Em's virginity too. Or did he? No one has ever really confirmed it and I know Em lies about all sorts of stuff. But if I think about the two of them together too hard, it's kind of creepy.

Okay, fine. It's *really* creepy. So I shove it out of my brain, forcing it to the very darkest corner.

"What's wrong?" Em asks after no doubt seeing the dawning horror on my face. "You look like you just saw a ghost."

"It's nothing." I shake my head, trying to smile, but it's shaky at best. "Just—I'm glad you're here. And I'm glad you were honest with me about Cannon."

"Yeah, well don't spread it around," she mumbles.

"I won't." But I can't promise Amanda won't say anything. "You look good."

"Thanks," she says softly. "You do too. I like the shirt." She touches my side, her fingers streaking across the exposed skin above my skirt so lightly I shiver. "Lookin' sexy, Liv. All for the birthday boy?"

I remain quiet. What can I say? With a few words, this situation has turned all sorts of awkward.

"You guys make a great couple," she continues, her smile never fading as her gaze returns to mine once more. "I know you're totally into Ryan, and that's great. Just—keep tabs on your man."

I frown. Here we go again with the Ryan warnings. "What do you mean?"

"He has wandering eyes." She pauses, her eyes sparkling, like she's enjoying this. "And wandering hands."

My stomach sinks to my toes and my mouth goes dry. "You're just saying that."

"I'm trying to watch out for a *friend*," she practically sneers.

"Right, more like trying to ruin my relationship by telling me a bunch of lies." I shove at her shoulders, so pissed I can barely see straight. She falls back against the counter, her eyes wide, her mouth dropped open in shock.

Good. I'm glad I can surprise her. She loves setting off these little verbal bombs just before she runs away, and I'm sick of them. Sick of her.

I don't know why I put up with her shit for this long.

"They're not lies, at least not what I'm telling you. I can't help it if you're a stupid, naïve bitch who believes everything your lying boyfriend says," Em taunts, straightening to her full height, which is about equal to mine. We stare each other down, neither of us looking away and I clench my fingers into tight fists. I've never been in a physical fight before.

But I'm angry. Like, *violently* angry. I've never felt this mad in my life and I'm ready to throw down on her if I have to. Right here in the middle of Ryan's guest bathroom during his birthday party—my timing isn't the best, but screw it. I'm so sick of Em's crap.

"We keep doing this," I tell her. "We're friends, we're not, we're sort of friends, we're sort of not. Which is it, Em?"

"We definitely can't go back to the old us," she says, her gaze wavering. She looks down, looks to the side. She looks anywhere but at me. "Too much has happened."

"Like you messing around with Dustin."

"Like *you* messing around with Dustin," she yells back, shockingly loud in the tiny bathroom. "Though that wasn't enough for you, so you stole Ryan away from me. I had him first!"

"He wasn't interested in you, not like that." *Not like he's interested in me.*

"Oh, is that what he told you? So I'm okay to mess around with all summer, but once you come along, forget it? He's over me?" She thrusts a finger into the air, pointing it straight at me. "You came home from Oregon and both Ryan and Dustin didn't care about me anymore. All they cared about is you."

I've already heard this. I don't need to go over it again. "We keep having this same stupid conversation," I remind her. "It's getting really old."

"No shit. So forget it. I'm done." Em pushes past me, hitting my shoulder hard. She yanks open the bathroom door before she glances over her shoulder to glare at me. "You can have him. You can have *both* of them. I hope they make you miserable for the rest of your pitiful life."

"Fuck you!" I yell, but she slams the door before I can get the words out, effectively cutting me off. I pound my fist on the closed door once. Twice. I'm so angry I'm shaking, my teeth chattering, and I turn to the sink, flipping on the faucet so I can splash water on my flushed face and wash my hands.

I stare at my reflection the entire time, Em's words running on repeat in my head. "God, she's such a bitch," I mutter under my breath, turning off the water and grabbing a towel. I dry my hands, run my fingers through my hair, tell myself to calm down, but it's no use.

I'm jittery as hell.

Slowly I open the bathroom door and make my exit, relieved to see there's no one else around. I glance at the decorative clock hanging nearby and see it's almost midnight. When I'm supposed to be waiting for Ryan in his room.

Anger and other swirling, confusing emotions driving me, I run up the stairs and go to his room, searching through the overnight bag I brought with me. My phone is nestled deep inside and I check it, though luckily I have no messages. I dig some more until I find the sexy bra and panties I bought a few days ago. Hurriedly I change out of my clothes and shove them into the bag, before I slip on the lace thong and then the bra.

I go to the mirror hanging above his dresser and take a few steps back, staring at my reflection. My cheeks are still flushed with anger and my boobs for some miraculous reason look pretty good. The bra and thong are lacy and white and I can see through both. Like...see *everything.*

Whoa.

Deciding the hell with it, I grab my phone and curl up in the middle of Ryan's bed, tossing my hair over one shoulder as I work out a provocative pose. I do a couple of practice runs, holding my camera up high so my cleavage and everything else I've got is on prominent display.

I'm already in the Snapchat app so I take a photo, a little smile curling my lips. I study the photo, surprised at the outcome. I look sexy. Like, really sexy. Smiling to myself, I type out one sentence before hitting send.

Come and get it birthday boy.

chapter thirty-six

The bedroom door crashes open so loudly I jump, a gasp escaping me. Ryan is standing in the doorway, his green eyes seeming to eat me up as he takes me in, poised in the middle of his bed in the skimpiest underwear I've ever worn. "Damn," he breathes.

I sit up straighter and thrust my shoulders back, giving him a good look. I don't think even five minutes have passed since I sent that Snapchat. "Like your birthday present?"

"I fucking love it," he practically growls as he shuts and locks the door.

He's stalking toward the bed, tearing off his shirt, kicking off his shoes, tugging at the fly of his jeans. I'm breathless, weightless as I watch him, anticipation racing hot through my veins as he reaches me. Reaches *for* me, his hands curling around my face and tilting my head back. He stares into my eyes, lowering his head until his mouth hovers above mine.

"Happy birthday," I whisper.

Ryan crushes my lips with his, the kiss hungry. Hot. Devouring. I rise up on my knees, reaching for him, my arms sliding around his neck, my hands diving into his hair as he slips one hand between us to touch my chest. His fingers claw at the lace, brush across my nipples, and I moan against his mouth, shocked at the heat that washes over me.

God, I think that argument with Em somehow fueled me and... turned me on? I don't know, I can't explain it, but I was so mad earlier, I swear I'm running on pure adrenaline now.

"You're so hot, Livvy," Ryan whispers against my neck as he kisses and licks me there. He reaches around my back and undoes the bra clasp, tearing the delicate fabric off until I'm completely bare, the scrap of lace fluttering to the floor. He cups my breasts in his hands before he pushes me backward. I'm lying on the bed and he's above me, kneeling between my legs.

I watch him, drinking in those smooth muscles as they flex, his biceps bulging as he reaches for the thin straps curved around my waist. He tugs off my panties, his mouth burning a path down my legs, his hands shoving them open just before he puts his mouth *there*, between my thighs.

"Oh God," I say on a gasp, panting as I tug his hair, desperate to push him away. But he persists, ignoring my protests, and soon I'm not complaining. I'm pulling him closer, spreading my legs wider, crying out when he thrusts his fingers inside me, and then I'm freaking lost.

Wave after wave crashes over me, my entire body trembling. Consumed. Overwhelmed. Lost to the sensation of this boy and his magical mouth, his magical tongue and fingers and everything else he's using on me.

"Damn, that was fast," he murmurs, sounding surprised as he lifts away from me. I lay in the middle of his bed a trembling, shaky mess, watching as he reaches for the bedside table drawer. I lift up and reach for the fly of his jeans, pulling on the zipper and spreading the denim open. He strains against the black cotton of his boxer briefs and it doesn't matter that I just came a few seconds ago.

I want him. I want him right freaking *now.*

"Slow down, baby," he says as he leaps to his feet and shucks his jeans and underwear all in one tug. Until he's gloriously naked in front of me and while we usually fumble around in the dark or I don't look at him for too long before closing my eyes, this time around, I'm staring. Taking in every inch of him.

And he's got a lot of inches.

He grins as he tears open the wrapper and rolls the condom on. I watch, my breathing so fast my chest hurts. Everything tingles and I fall back against the mattress as he moves over me, his mouth finding mine, his kiss lazy as his tongue tangles with mine.

"So fucking sexy," he murmurs after breaking the kiss, his mouth on my neck. "And all mine."

Yes, I want to say. *All yours.* But I don't. I keep quiet and close my eyes, savoring the sensation of his hands igniting sparks as they slide all over my skin. I touch him in return, my fingers exploring, my breath coming in short little gasps, his ragged and labored.

"You want this?" he asks as I feel him slowly thrust between my legs. "Livvy? Do you want me?"

I hear the doubt in his voice. The vulnerability. He's as raw and unsure about this moment as I am, and for some reason, that makes me feel more secure, more sure in my decision.

"Yes." I open my eyes to find he's watching me and I smile faintly, touching his cheek with my fingers. "I want you, Ryan."

He turns his head, his mouth on my palm in a wet, open-mouthed kiss. Then he's gathering me up in his arms, holding me close, kissing me again, and again as he slowly enters me.

I wince, my entire body going tense, and he stops, breathing hard against my ear. "I'll go slow."

His words, his voice, are a promise and I nod, pressing my lips together tight. He takes his time, whispering how I should relax, and I try yet it's so difficult. But he's also patient and after a few minutes of kissing and coaxing and touching, he's finally inside me. Filling me up.

And oh God, then it all happens so fast, so incredibly freaking *fast*, his hips pumping, pressing me into the mattress. He groans, his body shaking, and the next thing I know, he's already coming. I'm laying there a gasping, shivery mess, still keyed up and anxious and needing *more*, so much more. While he's slumped over me, a giant smile on his face, a satisfied rumble deep within his chest as he nuzzles my neck.

"Happy birthday to me," he murmurs with a chuckle, his lips warm against my skin.

I shiver and wrap my arms around him, holding him close, trying not to let the disappointment wash over me. He feels good surrounding me, his skin damp with sweat, his mouth still on my neck, one big hand sprawled across my breast. Like he owns it. Owns me.

"Shouldn't you, uh, get rid of the condom?" This is awkward, but...

"Yeah." He pulls away from me and drops a kiss on the tip of my nose. "I just wanted to hold you first."

I melt at his words. They make up for the disappointment I'm feeling over my first experience with actual sex. It wasn't bad, not at all. I actually let him go down on me and that was pretty freaking amazing. I felt like a wild animal for those first frantic moments and I can admit, that was hot, letting go, not caring, just being a person with basic needs.

But it happened so fast. He finished so *fast*. I thought he'd have more stamina than that.

He drops another kiss on my lips before he crawls out of bed and saunters into the connecting bathroom. I hear the toilet flush, the faucet run. Then he's back, scratching his chest and watching me as I tug the sheets and comforter up until they're covering me just under my chin.

"You're cute when you're modest," he teases as he rejoins me in bed, hauling me into his arms.

I nestle close, my cheek pressed against his chest. "Is the party still going on?"

"There are a few people downstairs, but mostly just guys from the team. Eli is supervising," he explains.

"You're trusting your brother to supervise your friends?" I'm shocked.

"He can handle it." Ryan tilts his chin down to smile at me. "Anyway, I'd rather be with you."

"Aw." I lean up and kiss him, losing myself all over again in the taste of his lips, his persuasive tongue. "Did you like your birthday present?"

"It was the best present I've ever had." Another kiss, this one soft. Sweet. "Thank you, Livvy."

Before I can manage to answer, he kisses me long and deep. And just like that, we start all over again.

Thank goodness Ryan has an entire pack of condoms in that bedside table.

chapter thirty-seven

I'm in the kitchen just after seven in the morning when a door opens from down the hall. I go stiff, unsure of who else could be in the house except for Ryan and me and Eli. Eli's bedroom is upstairs, right next to Ryan's. I know he's in there because I heard him snoring as I crept by his door earlier.

My body is sore from last night's extracurricular activities and I'm sipping on a glass of orange juice, wearing one of Ryan's old T-shirts and nothing else. My hair is a mess and my makeup is smeared all over my face, but I don't care. I lost my virginity last night. I don't necessarily feel different yet…somehow, I do. I can't explain it, but it's like I'm more mature.

Crazy, I know.

I nearly drop my glass of orange juice when I see who shuffles into the kitchen.

"Oh my God, this is so embarrassing." Amanda covers her face when she spots me.

My mouth drops open. "What are you doing here?"

She shakes her head, her hands still over her face. Her hair is a dark, riotous mess and she's wearing a boy's white T-shirt and nothing else too. I shuffle closer, sniffing the air, and I'd know that expensive cologne still lingering on the fabric anywhere.

"You were with Tuttle last night, weren't you?" I whisper-hiss at her.

Amanda drops her hands, her expression pleading. "Please don't say anything. I don't think I can handle your judgment this early in the morning."

"Like I'm going to judge you. Look at me." I wave a hand at myself. "Where did you guys sleep? Or was there any sleeping involved?"

"In the downstairs guest room. It's right next to the bathroom." She stares at my orange juice glass. "Got any more of that?"

"Yeah. I'll get some for you." I go about the kitchen and grab her a glass from the cabinet while she settles herself on the barstool at the counter. She runs a hand over her hair again and again, trying to tame the beast, and whispers "thank you" when I hand her the juice.

"I want deets," I say.

She shakes her head, sipping on her juice. "I'm not giving them."

"Come on."

"No way. Unless you want to give me details."

I make a face. "Not yet."

"Okay, right back at ya then."

We sit in companionable silence, sipping on our juices, checking our phones. There are Instagram photos from Ryan's party last night and I appear in a few of them. I told Mom I was going to Ryan's party and then spending the night at Amanda's. She'll never check up on me. She worked yesterday and was going out with Fitch last night.

I'm covered.

There are a bunch of Snapchat stories about the party too. Lots of them. Em posted all over both sites, even Twitter, and that irritates me. She makes it look like she's the life of the party when I barely saw her last night. She was too busy getting busy with Cannon.

Eventually I spot a photo of us. We're not posing together, but she took a selfie and captured me in the background, her index finger pointing right at me with a sly expression on her face.

I frown, staring at the photo. There's hidden meaning here, but I can't figure it out. What's she trying to pull?

Tuttle joins us in the kitchen minutes later, wearing jeans and nothing else, running a hand through his messy dark hair and making his abs ripple with the movement. I glance over at Amanda and she practically has to shove her tongue back in her mouth, her cheeks going up in flames.

By the looks of it, she's got it bad for him.

"Aren't you two adorable first thing in the morning?" Tuttle says with a sexy smile.

I stick my tongue out at him and Amanda ducks her head. Poor girl. She seems embarrassed, not that I can blame her. She just spent the night with Jordan Tuttle and he's strutting around the kitchen looking like a god.

Life is weird sometimes.

"Are we back to not talking?" Tuttle asks, stopping by Amanda's side.

She can barely look at him. "No, of course not."

"You act like you can't look at me."

"Tuttle..."

"Jordan," he corrects.

"Stop." She shoves at his chest, but he grabs her wrist, keeping her hand there. The expression on his face is serious. Intense, as usual, and I slide off my stool, ready to get the hell out of the kitchen, when there's a knock on the door.

"Who can this be?" I mumble under my breath as I escape the rife with sexual tension kitchen and go to the door. Rising up on tiptoe, I check the peephole, icy cold shock coursing through me when I see who's standing on the doorstep.

"I know you're in there, Olivia! Open the damn door!"

Oh. God.

It's Mom.

I unlock the door and throw it open. "Uh, hey. What are you doing here?" I sound casual, but inside I'm a trembling wreck. Why is she here? How did she figure out that I was at Ryan's house?

"I should be asking you the same question." She looks furious. Her hair is a mess, her face pale with dark circles under her eyes. I'm fairly certain she's wearing the same clothes from yesterday.

Meaning she's stayed up all night…worried about me?

"It's not what it looks like," I start but she doesn't give me a chance to finish.

"Go collect your things. We're leaving." Her voice is low. Firm. "Now."

Turning away from her, I don't protest. I just do as she says, running into the kitchen to see Amanda and Tuttle still sitting at the counter, their barstools pulled close together. He's tucking a strand of hair behind her ear and she's looking up at him as if he just created the moon, the stars and the entire sky.

"I have to go. My mom is here," I tell them, my voice surprisingly normal despite how shaky I am.

Amanda jerks away from Tuttle, her wide gaze meeting mine. "*What?*"

I nod, glancing around, looking for a trace of my stuff before I remember it's upstairs in Ryan's room. God, Mom saw me in his T-shirt and nothing else. I'm sure she can figure out exactly what I was doing. It's pretty obvious.

"Does she know I'm here?" Amanda asks.

"I told her I was with you, so…yeah. I assume so."

"Oh God. What if she called my parents?" She slaps her hands on her face, covering her eyes and yeah, I feel bad, but I've got more pressing things to take care of.

"Hurry up before I come in there!" Mom yells, reminding me I need to get it together.

I race up the stairs and barge into Ryan's room. He sits up straight in bed, the sheet falling to pool into his lap. Pausing, I watch as he rubs his face, his hair a mess, his bare chest on tempting display.

"What's going on?" he mumbles, sounding sleepy.

Damn it, I can't be swayed by his morning adorableness. Tearing my gaze from him, I spot my clothes on the floor, the tiny backpack I brought right next to the pile. I hurriedly put on a pair of black leggings I was smart enough to pack before I search through the bag, finally spotting my phone.

Whatever else I might leave here is no big deal. I need to look presentable and have my phone. That's all that matters.

"I have to leave." I go to him and kiss his cheek. "My mom is here."

Ryan jerks away from me. "Are you serious right now?"

"Yeah." I look around the room one more time before I give him another quick kiss. "Don't come downstairs. I'm fine. I'll text you later."

"Bye baby," he says softly, his words making me want to melt.

But I don't have time to melt. Mom is waiting on the Bennett doorstep quietly seething.

I hurry downstairs and go to the front door, which is still cracked open, Mom waiting on the front porch. I shut the door behind me, barely able to meet her gaze.

"Ready?" she asks.

Nodding, I fall into place beside her as we walk toward her car where it's parked in the driveway.

"I'm not going to talk to you about this right now," she says, her voice deadly quiet. "I'm too angry. I'm afraid I might say something I don't mean."

I remain silent too. No way am I going to protest.

"You're in a lot of trouble, Olivia. I can't believe you would do this."

Again, I say nothing. My mind is racing. The same thing keeps repeating in my brain again and again.

Who told my mom I was here? Who ratted me out?

THE MOMENT WE walk through the front door of my house, Mom is on me like a fly on shit, in all her hovering, finger-wagging glory. I step away from her and do as she tells me, sitting in an old recliner that we keep in the living room since Mom doesn't like to throw things away.

The first thing she says is, "I saw the photos."

I frown. "What photos?"

"From Ryan's party. I saw them. You were hanging all over him and he had his hands all over you."

People take photos all the time. I'm so used to it half the time I don't even notice. "How did you see these photos?"

Her lips go thin. "Emily showed them to me."

What? That *bitch*. Why? How? I part my lips, ready to ask all of those questions but Mom beats me to the punch.

"Why didn't you tell me what was really going on?" she asks, standing above me like a giant, though really we're the same height. "I called Amanda's mom and she said Amanda was supposed to be spending the night at *our* house. Tell me why you were lying, young lady, right now!"

I tilt my head back and lean against the chair, hoping for calm. I'm furious about the photos but I can't focus on that right now. "I can explain everything." So she talked to Amanda's mom too? Great. Amanda is most likely getting in trouble as well. Wish we could've talked first and got our stories straight.

"You better start explaining now. Though I don't think anything you say is going to sway my punishment plans," she says menacingly.

My heart sinks, but I forge on. "Ryan had his party last night, right? So one of the guys on his team gave him beer kegs as a birthday present."

"Who?" Mom asks, interrupting me.

"I don't know," I lie. "Anyway, I—we drank. Amanda and I drank, okay? I'm sorry. But we were at a party in the neighborhood and I didn't think you'd be too upset. We got a little drunk, though, and Amanda didn't feel capable enough to drive. So we decided to stay there for a while and sober up."

"Okay." Mom draws the word out, sounding skeptical, but not completely pissed off.

Progress.

"Right, so we hung out, drank a lot of water, ate some snacks. But eventually we fell asleep together and didn't wake up until this morning! I don't know how that happened, but we freaked out! And my phone was in my purse upstairs and I couldn't find it at first, and Amanda couldn't find hers and shit, Mom. It was a total mess and I'm so sorry we worried you. We never meant to worry anyone, I swear." I start crying, semi-fake tears because I really will cry if she grounds me forever.

She crosses her arms in front of her, that narrowed gaze still focused on me. "What's the deal with you supposedly spending the night at her house and Amanda spending the night at ours?"

I sniff, wipe at my eyes like I really have tears. "I honestly don't know. Some sort of mix-up? The plan was always to come to here. Since we live in the same neighborhood as Ryan and all."

"Okay, so why didn't you just walk home? Our neighborhood is perfectly safe."

"In the middle of the night? By myself, or with Amanda? Isn't that too risky? You always tell me it's better to be safe than sorry." I chew on my lower lip, hoping I didn't blow it.

She's quiet for a moment. So quiet I can hear the ticking on the clock hanging on the wall, the hum of the fridge in the kitchen. Otherwise, it's silent in this house and I'm going to freak out if she doesn't say something soon.

This is not how I planned for this weekend to end.

"I guess you do have a point," she says reluctantly, and it takes everything I've got not to gloat.

I sit on my hands instead and tell myself to remain calm.

"While I don't approve of you not having your phone on you at all times—" I open my mouth to protest, but she shuts me down with a look. "And I'm definitely not thrilled with the idea of you drinking when you're only seventeen, which is illegal, I might add."

I say nothing, just duck my head and act sad. I'm sadder that I got caught, which is the last thing Mom wants to hear. I wisely keep my mouth shut.

"But I guess I can look at your and Amanda's choice to stay at Ryan's house versus driving as—the right decision," Mom admits.

Relief courses through me, leaving me weak.

"But that doesn't mean you're off the hook. You're grounded."

"Mom—"

"Hush. For a week, you can't go out, can't use your phone, nothing. You go to school and you come straight home. No football games, no hanging out with Amanda or Em or Dustin, no going on dates with Ryan."

"It's Ryan's actual birthday on Tuesday." Okay, now I really am on the verge of tears. "His family is taking him out to dinner and he wanted me to go with them and I promised I would, Mom. Come on, please."

"I'm afraid you're not going to be able to make it," she says softly, holding out her hand. "Give me the phone, Olivia."

Pulling the phone out of my bag, I rise to my feet and hand it over to her, knowing full well I can read all of my text messages on my dad's old Mac Air laptop he gave me to use for school.

But Mom doesn't know that.

The smile on her face is smug as she closes her fingers around my iPhone. "Next time something happens, maybe you'll use your phone to text me, okay?"

I want to yell at her that she's ruining my life, but I'm scared if I say it, she'll ground me for longer. Instead I go to my room, slamming the door behind me, wincing when I shut it harder than I meant. I hear her yell my name and I call out "sorry" before I drop my bag on the bed, looking around.

Again I have that sense someone's been in here recently—someone that's not me. I search through my closet, run my hands along the top shelf, digging into the secret spot I have in the back against the wall and behind my shoes, where I smuggled a couple of Coronas a few weeks ago. They're still there, untouched and nestled in an old tote bag. I go to my dresser, searching each drawer, pulling open my underwear drawer last.

Wrinkling my nose, I push past my panties to the very back of the drawer where I keep an envelope of joints. Well, there's only two. Dustin gave them to me when I first came home from Dad's. I haven't smoked them yet, hadn't needed to, but I might need them to get through my week of imprisonment.

But the joints aren't there. The envelope is empty, save for a folded note.

That's weird.

With shaky hands I open it, staring at the unfamiliar handwriting scrawled across the paper.

Thanks for the pick-me-up. I owe you two joints, cupcake.

xo,

Fitch

"Cupcake"? Seriously? That he had the nerve to paw through my underwear—*ew.*

"That asshole," I mutter under my breath, disbelief and shock making me burst out laughing. I crumple the note in my hands and toss it into the nearby wastebasket, pleased when the balled up note lands inside.

Seriously. My life couldn't get any more surreal than this.

chapter thirty-eight

om is leaving me alone at the house to go out to dinner with Fitch. "I shouldn't go," she tells me as she paces the living room. I'm sitting on the couch watching a stupid Lifetime movie on TV, praying she won't realize I still have my laptop and access to pretty much all social media, with the exception of Snapchat.

"Not like I can make my escape," I remind her, never taking my eyes off the TV. It's a crazy story about a senior who impregnates two girls at the same time—his girlfriend and some random hookup from the summer. Talk about a nightmare. "I don't have my phone so I can't contact anyone. We don't even have a house phone."

"Oh, but I'm sure you have your ways. All of your friends live in the neighborhood," Mom points out as she goes to the mirror that hangs near the front door. I sneak a glance at her, watching as she applies copper-colored lipstick. I hate the shade but no way am I telling her that. "You'll probably sneak out and go to Em's the minute I leave."

"No way," I say emphatically. "We're on the outs."

So on the outs I'm unsure if we'll ever get back in.

"What about Dustin?"

"He hates me." That's an exaggeration, but I'm still mad at him. Plus, I can't call up my old best friend, my former hookup, the day after I have sex for the first time with the guy he got in a fight with.

That's all kinds of messed up.

Mom turns to face me, clutching the lipstick in her fist. "Fitch told me I should trust you. That you wouldn't dare do something to make me mad this soon."

"He's right." I don't understand Fitch or his motives. I'm still puzzled by his sneaking into my room—and letting me *know* he snooped around by leaving that note. That he stole my weed isn't even the point.

He pawed through my things. Who knows what else he found? Looked at? I have old diaries in my desk. What if he read them? So embarrassing. And he went through my underwear, which is just... gross.

I think I might do laundry tonight. Wash everything he might've touched.

Mom blows out a harsh breath, her gaze meeting mine. "Fine. I'll leave you here. But I'll be back by ten. I need to go to bed early."

"Great," I say weakly, calculating how much time I might have to see someone—*Ryan*—before Mom comes home.

"Be good." She points a finger at me. "Don't step foot out of this house."

"I won't. I promise."

The minute she's gone I run to my room and grab my laptop, bringing it out to the couch with me. I open up iMessage and immediately send a text to Ryan.

OMG I miss you! My mom is such a tyrant.

I wait for him to reply, chewing on my lip. He takes way too long. What if he's with someone else? All I can think about, focus on, is Ryan, but he's still free. He can do whatever he wants, with whoever he wants.

That terrifies me.

The familiar ding sounds, pushing me out of my head.

Hey babe. Can you come over?

I wish.

No. I'm grounded for one week. ☹

You're going to miss my birthday dinner?

My heart cracks. I feel so bad.

Sorry. Maybe I can convince my mom to let me go?

You should try. I really want you there.

I will. I promise.

I hesitate, then decide to go for it.

Can't stop thinking about last night.

His reply is immediate.

Best birthday present I ever got. ☺

I smile in return. He's so sweet. I hate that I'm grounded, but last night was definitely worth getting in trouble for.

What are you doing right now?

Hanging out with Eli. It sucks. I should come over. Reenact last night.

You can't. My mom will kill me.

What she doesn't know won't hurt her.

We can't take the chance. I don't want to get in more trouble.

Or give Mom more reason to hate Ryan.

See you at school tomorrow then? ☺

Yeah. Miss you. <3

Miss you too babe. xoxo

Aw, he sent me kisses and hugs. I love it.

What I don't love is knowing Em sent those photos to my mom. How messed up is that? Why would she sabotage me? Does she hate me that much?

I'm starting to think she seriously hates my guts.

A knock sounds, startling me. For a moment I wonder if it could be Em. Or maybe even Ryan. Standing, I quietly walk over to the front door and look through the peephole, then open the door.

"Amanda!" I grab her hand and pull her inside, slamming and locking the door behind her. "What are you doing here?"

"Thanks for the enthusiastic greeting." She smiles at me and goes to the couch, her gaze zeroing in on the TV. "Oh, I've seen this movie before! It's a juicy one."

"Almost as juicy as our lives," I tell her as I sit next to her on the couch. It feels like I haven't seen her in forever, even though it's only been a few hours. "What's going on? Why are you here? Didn't you get in trouble with your parents?"

"For some reason, they totally believed the story I gave them. I said we were too drunk and I didn't want to drive so we stayed the night at Ryan's house." Amanda's expression is solemn. "It was the right thing to do."

Her good girl act is perfection. "Wow, our stories were pretty similar." I'm impressed. "I tried that and my mom was still pissed."

"Yeah well, you're her only child. My parents have already been through this sort of thing with my brother. I look like a saint compared to him. I think they're just relieved I made it home and didn't land in jail." She sends me a look. "How bad is your punishment? I figured your mom took away your phone since you never replied to my texts."

"She took it away, but I have iMessage on this." I tap the laptop that's sitting on the couch. "I never got your messages though. Sometimes it glitches."

Amanda shrugs. "It's no big deal. I was just checking on you."

I fill Amanda in on everything that happened, including how Fitch stole the joints.

"You had joints in your underwear drawer?" Amanda asks incredulously.

"That's not the point." I shake my head. "He went through my panties. He actually *touched* them." I shivered.

"That's freaky." Amanda makes a face.

"*He's* freaky!"

Yeah. No denying that. I don't know what to do about him.

Then I tell her about my text conversation with Ryan.

"Do you think he'll wait for me while I'm grounded for a week?" I ask her, nibbling on my thumbnail. The boy has turned me into a self-conscious idiot, I swear.

Amanda sends me a look. "He'll live. It's only seven days. Plus you'll see each other at school. If he ditches you for someone else, then he's a total douche and you're better off without him."

I almost want to tell her to stop insulting my boyfriend but I keep my mouth shut. "I just hate that she grounded me. I don't worry so much about Ryan. I worry more about the bitches who'll try to steal Ryan from me."

"If he's truly into you, he won't notice those other girls. I promise." She smiles, leaning over to slap the top of my thigh. She hits me so hard it stings. "That's for smacking me yesterday."

"Ouch." I rub my leg, glaring at her before we start laughing. It's time for me to ask the real question. "So. What's going on with you and Tuttle?"

Her laughter dies, and she gets that dreamy look in her eyes. The one I recognize from before when she thought about Jordan Tuttle. "I think he really likes me."

"Well, duh," I start but she shakes her head.

"No, I mean he *seriously* likes me. At first, I was just a game for him, but now I think he's sincere. He said he's liked me for a long time. That we could make this work if I would just give him a chance." Her voice is soft, her eyes a little glazed over.

"So did you give him a chance by getting naked with him last night?" I ask innocently.

She grabs a throw pillow and smacks me on the head with it. "Of course not! I'm not that easy. It's not like he's my boyfriend."

"You two have been dancing around each other for a while. I would never hold it against you if you let him slip it in." I can barely hold back my laughter at the horrified expression on her face. "But remember, just the tip."

"Stop." Her cheeks are bright red. Poor girl. "You're being so incredibly gross." A giggle slips past her lips, and I'm guessing she doesn't think it's so gross, getting naked with Tuttle.

"Sorry." I'm not that sorry though. I love giving Amanda a hard time. She makes it so easy. Besides, anything to cheer me up, you know? "I'm excited for you two."

One of her trademark dazzling smiles appears on her face. "I'm excited too. I just hope he means it."

I frown. "Why wouldn't he?"

She shrugs. "I don't know. He's Jordan Tuttle and I'm…me. We're from totally different worlds. I still don't really get why he wants to be with me."

"Because he *likes* you." I reach over and touch her knee, giving it a squeeze. "You're sweet, cute, smart and fun. Why wouldn't he want to be with you?"

Amanda smiles in return. "Thanks, friend. I guess…he just makes me nervous."

"He makes everyone nervous." I squeeze her knee one more time before I let go. "I hate to be a jerk but you should go. I only pulled you into my house because I was afraid Mom has neighborhood spies."

"If she does, you look bad *because* you pulled me into the house." Amanda stands. "But I get it. I should go anyway. I told my parents I was going for a bike ride. They probably expect me home soon."

I have Amanda go out the backdoor because I'm paranoid. Even though her bike is leaning against the front of the house and anyone who passes by could see it. Whatever. If Mom somehow found out, I'd tell her Amanda came by to check on me, which is the truth.

Better to tell the truth than a lie, right?

I go back inside and settle on the couch, picking up my laptop. I should prep for the SAT test coming up next weekend but that sounds boring as hell. My score was decent last year, though I should take it again and try to bring it up. Or I could finish watching the cheesy movie even if it is pretty awful.

Instead, I bring up Ryan's Instagram feed on the laptop.

Boring. The boy hardly ever posts, like most boys.

Next I check out Dustin's. He hasn't posted since the end of summer. Sheesh.

I look at Amanda's, which is mostly full of photos of kids from band since she hasn't posted much lately. There are a few cute photos of her with that ex-boyfriend of hers, Thad. He's not a bad looking dude. I can't believe he cheated on her.

Jerk.

Bracing myself, knowing this was the feed I wanted to check when I started this search, I go to Em's next.

And it feels like my jaw hits the floor.

There they are. The photo is in black and white. I can't tell when it was taken. She posted it twenty minutes ago. It could've happened twenty minutes ago for all I know.

It's a selfie. Em is sitting on—Ryan's lap. He's laughing, his eyes practically closed, his hands spread wide across her bare midriff as he clutches her close. Tuttle is next to them, his arm slung around a girl's shoulders, half of his face buried in the crook of her neck.

I recognize the girl. She was in the kitchen, when Amanda and I went to Tuttle's party for the first time together. The girl who said she gave him a blowjob yet he couldn't remember her name.

Oh. My. God.

I read the caption below the photo and it reminds me of the first time I saw Ryan in Em's Instagram feed.

Bored with love. Need more lust. Wallow in hate. #justfriends #relationships #lies #heartbreak #bullshit #TuttleSucks #SoDoesRyan #SoDoIAllNightLong

The words blur from my tears. My stomach is in knots. Not only is Ryan a total douche, so is Tuttle. I guess I shouldn't be surprised. The minute we're not around, they're finding our replacements.

Pushing the laptop away, I run into the bathroom.

And promptly puke my guts out.

I'M LYING IN bed with my ear buds in, listening to depressing music through my laptop. I never ate dinner. Mom came home around nine-thirty and asked me a bunch of questions I gave monotone answers to. When she asked me what was wrong I said I was feeling sick. She muttered I was probably hung over but mostly let it go and left me alone.

Whatever.

My bedside lamp is still on, casting the room in a weird glow. I should go to bed for real but I know I won't be able to sleep. All I can think about is Ryan with Em. I screenshot that stupid photo just in case she deleted it from her feed and now I have it forever so I can look at it whenever I want.

I don't think I can possibly stomach looking at that photo again.

Tearing the ear buds out, I toss them on my bedside table, then close my laptop and lean it against the wall near my bed. I miss my phone. I miss my friends. I miss Ryan.

Stupid, disloyal, can't-keep-his-dick-in-his-pants Ryan.

A little ping sounds against my window and I go still. Then it happens again. And again. I quietly crawl out of bed and make my way to the window, peeling back the blinds to see a familiar lone figure standing out in my yard, throwing tiny pebbles at my window.

Dustin.

I tug the blinds up before I open the window and wave him closer. "What are you doing here?"

He stops in front of my window, concern written all over his face. "I wanted to check on you."

We got rid of the window screen a long time ago, after he or Em tore it from sneaking in and out of my room. We used to do that sort of thing all the time when we were younger, when life was simpler.

Now it's just a screwed up mess.

"Can I come in?" he asks when I don't say anything and I nod in answer, taking a step back so he can crawl through my window. Once he's in my room, it's like his presence fills the entire space. I can smell him. Reach out and touch him. I'm tempted. So tempted.

But that would be me taking my revenge out on Ryan by using Dustin. And that's not fair to either of them.

"Why are you checking on me anyway?" I ask as I go sit down on the edge of my bed.

He sits down next to me, though keeping a respectable distance. "I heard what Em did to you."

"How?" I ask incredulously.

"She sent the photos from Ryan's party to me and said she showed your mom. Like she thought I'd be proud of her getting you in trouble or something," Dustin explains, glancing over at me so our eyes meet. "But I'm not. I told her what she did was wrong."

"But she doesn't care." It takes everything within me not to mention her latest photo. I refuse to bring it up. Refuse to give Dustin a reason to say, "*I told you so,*" about Ryan. "Why is she so determined to screw me over?"

"She's mad about…us. That I like you more." Dustin sighs and runs both hands through his hair, nearly making it stand straight up. "I hate what I did, Livvy. I should've never let it happen."

"Between us?" I ask, confused.

"No." He drops his hands so they land on his thighs. "Between me

and Em. I don't like her like that. I never really have. She was just…
there. And by me getting with her, I ruined everything between us. It
sucks." He looks over at me, his gaze imploring. "I fucking miss you,
Liv. I miss *us*."

My heart is breaking. It would be so easy to fall into his arms and
tell him I miss him too. To let him kiss my pain away so I can forget
what Ryan did. But that's not right. I can't be like the rest of them. I
should rise above the mess. Maybe the photo could be explained.

I don't know.

"I miss you too." I pick up his hand and interlace our fingers. His
touch is comforting. Just what I need after the disaster that was today.
"I want us to be friends, Dustin. But you told me that wouldn't work
for you."

"I was wrong. It's hard…not being able to spend time with you.
Seeing you with Ryan." He blows out a harsh breath. "You'll still be my
friend, even after what I did?" When I nod, he squeezes my hand. "I
don't deserve you, Livvy."

I say nothing. Just smile faintly and continue to hold his hand.

"Are you happy with him?" he asks after we're silent for a few
minutes.

Not right now. The words are stuck in my throat and I drop my
head, staring at my lap. "I don't know," I mumble. I can't get that photo
out of my mind. Ryan's hands all over Em. The smug look on her face.
The way she's sitting in his lap, like they belong together.

God, the ache deep inside me keeps growing, spreading throughout
my body. I need…I need something.

I need Dustin.

"Just know that if you were mine, I would do everything possible
to make you happy, Livvy," he murmurs, his fingers tightening around
mine. "He doesn't deserve you either."

Slowly I turn to face him, our hands still linked, my knee brushing against his thigh. He's wearing a faded blue T-shirt and a pair of baggy basketball shorts. He looks so familiar, so much like my beloved Dustin...

I launch myself toward him, my mouth somehow finding his with ease, my hands going to his nape, fingers diving into his soft hair. He holds me close, his arms wrapped around my waist, his hands sliding up and down my back before they slip beneath my shirt. I'm not wearing a bra and I don't stop him when his hands wander everywhere. Along my sides, across my stomach, counting my ribs until he's actually touching my breasts—

"You feel so good," he whispers against my neck just before he kisses it. Licks it. His hands are still on my chest. "You need to know I didn't come only for this. I just wanted to make sure you're okay."

"Stop talking," I tell him, not caring if I sound rude. I tug on his hair, bring his mouth back to mine and then I'm falling backward onto my bed, Dustin on top of me, our mouths locked, his tongue tangling with mine. I'm shoving at his shirt just like he's shoving at mine, and our legs are wrapped around each other, my foot driving up his hairy calf, my hand diving past the waistband of his shorts.

And then he's gone. He pulls away from me and is standing next to the bed, his breath coming in short pants, his eyes wild as he watches me. I sit up, tugging my shirt down, smoothing out my hair. My body still aches but for different reasons now.

"Is this how it's going to be?" he asks between harsh breaths. "You hit a rough patch with Ryan and you use me to make yourself feel better? To remind yourself that I'm always going to be there for you?"

"You *told* me you were always going to be there for me," I point out, confused by this entire mess. I'm an idiot. I shouldn't have kissed him. I'm a total tease and I don't even mean to be.

Which means I'm an awful, terrible person.

"You need to make up your mind who you want, Olivia." I watch him warily as he moves about my room so casually it's like he belongs here. "You can't have us both."

With that final statement, he goes to the window and opens it up, crawling through it. I hear his feet hit the ground, hear the slide of the window as he pulls it shut.

He's gone.

I flop backwards on the bed, pissed at myself. Dustin is right. I totally used him because I'm angry with Ryan. I can't deny that I have feelings for Dustin, but my feelings are stronger for Ryan.

I need to focus on him—no one else but him.

If Ryan hasn't already moved on from me.

about the author

Monica Murphy is the New York Times, USA Today and #1 international bestselling author of the One Week Girlfriend series, the Billionaire Bachelors and The Rules series. Her books have been translated in almost a dozen languages and has sold over one million copies worldwide. She is a traditionally published author with Bantam/Random House and Harper Collins/Avon, as well as an independently published author. She writes new adult, young adult and contemporary romance. She is also USA Today bestselling romance author Karen Erickson.

Want to know what happens next?
The second book in the **Friends** series,
MORE THAN FRIENDS is coming soon!
Check out the next page for an unedited sneak peek!

Prologue

Amanda

I'm cruising on my bike, contemplating everything Livvy just told me. She's going to lose her mind being grounded that long, unable to see Ryan unless we're at school. At least I'm not in trouble like she is. Guess it pays off to have a trouble-making older brother.

Liv's going to stress out over Ryan though. She worries about him all the time. I get it—sort of. He seems to play games, and that must get exhausting.

Truthfully, I wouldn't put up with that crap. But I'm not Livvy.

Thank goodness.

The wind blows through my hair as I make a right into my neighborhood, turning the wild strands into a tangled mess. Not that I care. There's no one I'm hoping to impress. It'll just be Sunday night dinner with the family, as usual. I'm not even sure if they're home yet. Dad mentioned something about going to Home Depot to pick out fall flowers for the yard.

Bleh. I'm glad I made my escape when I did.

My house slowly comes into view and I smile to myself. I might not live in a giant mansion in a fancy neighborhood like my new so-called friends, but our house is nice. Small and on the older side, but it's cute, with a pretty front yard and a cute porch with a white swing…

Oh. Crap. There's someone sitting on the swing. His arms are spread out along the back of the wooden frame, his gaze locked directly on me, like he knew I was going to appear at any second.

It's Jordan Tuttle.

My heart is racing as I press gently on the brakes. It's like I want to slow down the moment, revel in the anticipation of finding *him* waiting for *me*. He rises to his feet, runs a hand over his hair almost nervously and a shuddery breath leaves me.

I remember what it felt like, having those hands on me just last night. His mouth on mine, the words he whispered in my ear. It wasn't a dream. It wasn't something I made up inside my head, because seriously. I was starting to wonder if I really was losing my mind when it came to Jordan Tuttle.

But no. Jordan is real. He's in my life because he *wants* to be here for some crazy reason. And now he's waiting for me, his hands on his hips, the faintest smile on his face as he continues to watch me.

"What are you doing here?" I ask as I make my approach, hopping off my bike so I can roll it up the front walkway.

We meet in the middle, Jordan stopping just in front of me. "Nice way to greet me."

I frown. "How should I greet you?"

"Like this." His hand is suddenly on my nape when he pulls me in for a too quick yet somehow lingering kiss. My lips tingle when he pulls away and by the smug expression on his face, I know *he* knows the affect he has on me.

"Jordan," I chastise, stepping away from him and nearly tripping over my stupid bike. Luckily enough, he catches me by the elbow, steadying me before I fall over like an idiot. "What if my parents are inside?"

"They're not." He grabs the bike from me, nudges the kickstand down and sets it in place on the sidewalk a few feet away from us. "Where've you been?"

His confidence makes me crazy. He's so sure of himself and I wish I had even an ounce of his self-assuredness.

I don't. Not even close. He lives in another realm. I'm just a lowly peon compared to His Majesty, Lord Jordan Tuttle.

"I went over to Livvy's," I tell him when I realize he's waiting for my answer. As usual, my mind wanders when I'm in his presence. "I wanted to make sure she's okay."

Jordan frowns. "She is, right?"

"Oh yeah, her mom just grounded her for life." When he sends me a *come on* face, I readjust. "Fine, she's grounded for a couple weeks. No phone. No Ryan."

"It might do her some good, the no Ryan thing," he mutters.

I say nothing. I don't understand the relationship he has with Ryan. They're friends. Then they're not. They're teammates always, and that's something Jordan has to deal with no matter what.

"What are you up to right now?" I ask, hoping to change the subject.

He smiles. Reaches out to tuck a wayward strand of hair behind my ear. I feel that innocent touch all the way down to my toes, which are currently curling in my battered white Converse. "I want to take you out."

My mouth drops open. "In public?"

The frown is back. It's not fair, how attractive he still is despite the scowl he's currently wearing. "Of course, in public. What the hell, Mandy."

I shrug, my cheeks burning with embarrassment. "We haven't actually been seen together."

He grabs my hand and pulls me in close. My body immediately goes hot and I wonder if he has some sort of powerful force field I can't resist. "I want to change that."

My gaze meets his and I can't look away. He's so sincere. So serious. "What happened between us last night was…"

"Real." He kisses me again. Another brief brush of lips on lips yet I'm decimated. Shaky all over when he pulls away. When my ex Thad kissed me, I never felt like this. Ever.

Never.

Ever.

Never.

"Maybe we were just caught up in a moment?" I ask tentatively. It's like I'm always waiting for the bomb to drop. For the joke to be on me. No one in a million years would ever match me with Jordan Tuttle. Not even me. So what's his deal? Why is he so persistent? I don't get it.

I like it, but he also scares me. I don't want to get hurt.

I don't want my heart to be broken.

"Every time I'm near you, I get caught up in a moment." One side of his perfect mouth tips up in this semi-smile that is absolutely adorable. I wish I had my phone out so I could snap a pic of him. "Maybe we need to give this a try and see if all we ever experience together is one giant moment."

"That's impossible." The words are out before I can stop them and I slap my hand over my mouth, my eyes wide as I stare up at him.

Jordan actually laughs, shaking his head. It's a rare sound, but wow, is it amazing. "Nothing's impossible if you want it bad enough."

I drop my hand, gaping up at him. "So are you saying that you want—*me*?"

"Yes." He dips his head, his mouth hovering above mine. "I do."